P9-DJV-182

SKELETON PLOT

Recent Titles by J.M. Gregson from Severn House

Lambert and Hook Mysteries

AN ACADEMIC DEATH
CLOSE CALL
DARKNESS VISIBLE
DEATH ON THE ELEVENTH HOLE
DIE HAPPY
GIRL GONE MISSING
A GOOD WALK SPOILED
IN VINO VERITAS
JUST DESSERTS
MORE THAN MEETS THE EYE
MORTAL TASTE
SOMETHING IS ROTTEN
TOO MUCH OF WATER
AN UNSUITABLE DEATH
MORE THAN MEETS THE EYE
CRY OF THE CHILDREN
REST ASSURED
SKELETON PLOT

Detective Inspector Peach Mysteries

DUSTY DEATH
TO KILL A WIFE
THE LANCASHIRE LEOPARD
A LITTLE LEARNING
LEAST OF EVILS
MERELY PLAYERS
MISSING, PRESUMED DEAD
MURDER AT THE LODGE
ONLY A GAME
PASTURES NEW
REMAINS TO BE SEEN
A TURBULENT PRIEST
THE WAGES OF SIN
WHO SAW HIM DIE?
WITCH'S SABBATH
WILD JUSTICE
LEAST OF EVILS
BROTHERS' TEARS
A NECESSARY END

SKELETON PLOT

A Lambert & Hook Police Procedural

J.M. Gregson

This first world edition published 2015
in Great Britain and the USA by
SEVERN HOUSE PUBLISHERS LTD of
19 Cedar Road, Sutton, Surrey, England, SM2 5DA.
Trade paperback edition first published
in Great Britain and the USA 2015 by
SEVERN HOUSE PUBLISHERS LTD.

To George and Harry, who read much and will go far in the years to come.

British Library Cataloguing in Publication Data

Gregson, J. M. author.
  Skeleton plot. – (A Lambert and Hook mystery)
  1. Lambert, John (Fictitious character)–Fiction. 2. Hook,
  Bert (Fictitious character)–Fiction. 3. Police–
  England–Gloucestershire–Fiction. 4. Murder–
  Investigation–Fiction. 5. Detective and mystery stories.
  I. Title II. Series
  823.9'14-dc23

ISBN-13: 978-0-7278-8510-4 (cased)
ISBN-13: 978-1-84751-613-8 (trade paper)
ISBN-13: 978-1-78010-664-9 (e-book)

All Severn House titles are printed on acid-free paper.

Severn House Publishers support the Forest Stewardship Council™ [FSC™],
the leading international forest certification organisation. All our titles that
are printed on FSC certified paper carry the FSC logo.

MIX
Paper from
responsible sources
FSC
www.fsc.org   FSC® C013056

Typeset by Palimpsest Book Production Ltd.,
Falkirk, Stirlingshire, Scotland.
Printed and bound in Great Britain by
TJ International, Padstow, Cornwall.

ONE

D amon Jackson had read that there was a bond between grandparents and grandchildren. It cut across the generations, made the years irrelevant. But you read a lot of things when you were sixteen, and you were told a lot of others. You didn't yet know what was significant and what was trivial.

Damon thought that this one might be true. He'd always got on well with Nana Pat and Grandpa Joe. Better than with his dad, sometimes. A lot of times, really. He knew that it was because his dad had to discipline him and give him standards, because Dad had told him that. And Mum too – but she always said it as though it was an afterthought, some sort of apology. Grannies can afford to spoil you, Mum said, because they don't have to live with you all the time, don't have to bring you up.

Sometimes Damon thought he wouldn't have minded being brought up by Nana Pat and Grandpa Joe. They seemed to know quite a lot about life. They seemed to be able to put things into perspective better than Mum and Dad. Especially things which happened at school. They knew all about bullying and what you should do about it. Damon had been twelve when he'd dealt out his first bloody nose. Alan Harrison, it had been, and he'd asked for it. Damon had got into trouble over the fight, but he'd sensed at the time that the teacher who'd put him into detention had secretly understood and approved what he'd done. And Harrison's bloody nose had stood him in good stead ever since.

Down to Granddad, that was. It was Granddad Joe who'd told him he must stand up for himself. Mum would have told him not to fight, and Dad would have shied away from anything which might make the school want to talk to him as a responsible parent.

Damon enjoyed going round to his grandparents' new bungalow

at weekends and holidays. They lived four miles away, but he could be round there quite quickly on his bike. He liked it better when he was there on his own than when he went with his parents. Everyone seemed to be watching what they said carefully then, and that meant that nothing of any consequence was said at all.

But Damon rode more slowly today. He wasn't anxious to get there as quickly as possible, the way he usually was. He wasn't timing himself and trying to beat his record today, even though the streets were quiet. Nana Pat and Grandpa Joe would have heard his news by now. He was wondering how they'd react.

This would be the first time they'd know that they were talking to a gay grandson.

The older generation took these things differently. He knew that from what they'd been told at school; it was one of the few things he'd accepted without question. Apparently being homosexual had been against the law when the grandparents had been his age. That sounded incredible, but it was absolutely true. He'd checked it.

Billy Johnston, who was in the class above Damon, said that his grandfather had refused to speak to him when he found out he was gay. But Billy's granddad was really ancient, about ninety, he thought. He'd fought in the war against Hitler and the Nazis. He said they'd landed in France on D-day and fought their way across Europe to make a land fit for heroes, not for queers and poofters. And he hadn't spoken to Billy since, which made it over two months now. They'd made a joke of it at school, their group, but Damon knew that Billy was sad about it.

Damon rather liked that word 'poofter', even though he knew that it was only offered to him as an insult. It rolled off the tongue nicely and had a real ring to it, unlike 'queer' and 'bumboy' and the other assorted epithets. They were merely vulgar and easy, but 'poofter' had a certain impact and distinction.

But he knew he was only distracting himself with that thought. As he pedalled nearer to his grandparents' bungalow, he was increasingly nervous about how they would react to his new sexual status. They were nothing like as old as Billy's granddad, who was more like a great-granddad really. Pat and Joe – it was the first time he had ever thought about them without their titles – were about seventy, he thought, though that seemed quite antique to Damon. Joe hadn't fought in the war, hadn't even done that National Service thing which Damon had seen in a programme on the telly, where apparently all young men had had to suffer two years of being yelled at by manic sergeants and corporals.

Would the fact that Gramps had never been a soldier moderate his attitude to poofters? Damon wheeled his bike up the path more slowly than he'd ever done before and leaned it carefully against the side of the house, studying the bricks and the cement between them for several seconds. His legs moved more unwillingly than ever before to the familiar back door; he was sure his knock was far too tentative. He opened the door six inches and called in a deliberately loud and confident voice, 'It's me, Nana Pat. All right to come in?'

'Of course it's all right, lad. Come in and sit down.' It was Grandpa Joe, being as hale and confident and as determinedly normal as Damon had tried to be himself. 'Kettle's on. Sit yourself down and we'll have coffee. I think your nan's made some of those ginger flapjacks we both like.'

Grandpa Joe was as brisk and friendly and welcoming as he'd ever been. A little too much so, possibly. He chuckled nervously and busied himself with plates and beakers and the flapjack tin. He didn't look at Damon.

The flush of the lavatory down the hall sounded louder than usual to both of them. They were both glad when Nana Pat came in. Unlike her husband, she did look directly into her grandson's face as she said, 'How nice to see you, Damon. And what a grand day you've brought with you!'

They sat round and enjoyed the coffee and her flapjacks. They tasted as good as ever; both Damon and Grandpa Joe said that in turn. Nana Pat was good at making conversation; women were usually better at that than men, in Damon's so far limited experience. But she talked about what she'd been doing during the week, instead of asking Damon about the latest happenings at school, as she usually did. And there was something artificially bright and brittle about their exchanges, as though they were all on their best behaviour.

Damon realized that his gayness was not going to be discussed. He thought that he should perhaps take that as a slur. But he found that he was actually immensely relieved about it.

He had a second flapjack, wondering how this taut and edgy conversation was going to end. 'You're a good baker, Nana. There aren't many as good as you.'

'I learned when I was young. There weren't so many bought cakes then, and they were expensive.'

Damon glanced out of the window and found a little inspiration. 'I see the fencing's finished, Granddad. That paddock's going to look good, after you've given it a couple more mowings.' He knew nothing about gardening and he was just repeating what Joe had said to him a couple of weeks earlier. But that was one of the things about old people: they didn't always remember exactly what they'd said to you. You could feed their ideas back to them and they believed they were your own and thought what admirably good sense you were showing.

That happened now. Like most modern bungalows, this one had a pitifully small and cramped garden. But five months ago Granddad Joe had bought a patch of ground from the farmer whose field came up to his boundary. It was almost a quarter of an acre and it made the plot around the detached bungalow suddenly very spacious. Joe was a keen gardener; he was looking forward to creating a vegetable plot and an orchard on this new ground. His enthusiasm took over and he became more natural as soon as horticulture was mentioned. 'The man's done a good job on the fence. And I've already marked out where I'm going to put our vegetable patch.' He gestured towards the far side of the newly acquired ground, where his grandson could see sticks and string delineating the bounds of the area which was going to be cultivated.

Damon said eagerly, 'I could do some of the digging for you. Double dig it, like you showed me, if that's what it needs.'

'That's what it needs all right. Virgin ground, you see.' With the mention of that daring adjective, Joe glanced full into his grandson's face for the first time since he had arrived. 'Damned hard work, but rewarding, in the end.'

Pat came in promptly then. 'I wish you would help your granddad, Damon. He'll overdo himself and put himself on his back for days, if I don't watch him. Just won't accept he's not as young as he used to be, silly old beggar!'

They'd have said 'bugger' or something worse at school, Damon thought. But Nana Pat never swore, and neither did Granddad Joe, at least when he was around. He rather liked that. 'Why don't you get your spade out and we'll get started, Granddad? Soonest started, soonest finished, I always say.' It was one of Nana Pat's sayings which he was repeating, but both of the old people seemed to be delighted when they heard it.

Joe trundled out wheelbarrow and spade and instructed him again about the technique of double digging, even as Damon waited impatiently to begin. He was stocky and strong and dark-haired, just as Granddad Joe must have been in his youth. The old man insisted on cutting out the first neat row of turf himself and piling the sods in his wheelbarrow. Damon wheeled them to the other end of the plot and stacked them carefully there, ready to be turned upside down and buried beneath the last trench they would dig at the end of the plot, over by the new fence.

'Once you've removed the turf, you need to go a full spit down in the soil. That's what double digging is,' said Joe. He did the first trench himself and Damon trundled the soil away to dump beside the turf at the other end of the plot. It was heavy work, as Joe had said it would be. But satisfying work, the old man kept insisting, more and more breathlessly. Damon insisted on taking over for the second trench and Joe was in no state to resist. They were perfectly natural with each other now. Joe had forgotten all about the thoughts which had troubled him with Damon's arrival, and Damon had lost all his embarrassment in the release of physical activity. Gardening diverted them and engrossed them, working its therapy in this as in a host of other anxious situations.

Joe had exhausted himself by working too quickly on that first trench, wanting as usual to show the youngster how fit and able he still was at seventy. He had to confine himself to advice, which became increasingly irritating to a sixteen-year-old who thought he already had the measure of the task. Perhaps Nana had been watching the pair through the window, because she now appeared, bringing relief when Damon's patience was wearing thin. 'You're staying here for lunch, Damon,' she called from the doorway. 'I've rung your mum and she says that's fine with her. And Joe, you come inside and slump in your armchair. Give the lad a chance to get on with the job without you standing over him and watching his every move!'

The old man and the young man grinned at each other. Then Joe said, 'I'd best do what she says, Damon. You sure you'll be all right on your own?'

'I'm sure, Granddad. I've got the hang of it now. Take the turfs off the top, then one spit down.'

'That's it, lad. The grass rots down and makes the soil above it more fertile, you see. Gives you what they call a deep tilth. The veggies will like that, once we get them going.' He looked up at the high white clouds in the Spring sky. 'We'll be able to plant by the end of the month. You'll be able to take cauli-flowers home for your mum, in August.' He retreated reluctantly towards the kitchen and his watchful wife. When halfway there he turned to look at his grandson, who had resumed his work, anxious to show the old man how thoroughly fit and capable he was. 'You're a good lad, Damon!' he called. 'Anyone who says different will have to answer to me!'

They both knew what he meant. That was good, thought Damon, as he waved his thanks and bent again to his task. That was a proper relationship, when you both understood things of which you never spoke. Things like love, which men like Granddad Joe never mentioned and wouldn't know how to discuss. Nana Pat would give him a long hug which said everything, but men like Granddad Joe didn't do hugs, much less kisses. Perhaps that was something to do with the laws being different when they were young.

Despite his determination to show how strong and vigorous he was, he was glad when it was time for lunch. Granddad Joe was right: double digging was damned hard work, though his grandson was never going to admit it. There were sausages and mash and broccoli. He was so hungry that he ate every bit of his greens, which he usually pushed around his plate. And apple pie and custard to follow. 'The labourer is worthy of his hire,' said Granddad portentously, as if he and not Nana had prepared the spread.

But they got on well, the old folk; Damon could see that as he caught them glancing across the table at each other. He watched some of the lunchtime football on the telly with Joe, then said with a sigh which recalled his dad, 'Well, I must get back to work now. The garden won't dig itself, will it?'

Granddad Joe came out with him to supervise, but Nana called him off after ten minutes on the pretext of having some job for him in the house. Damon worked on alone, slowly and methodically. He never worked in the garden at home; his dad would be amazed when he heard what he had accomplished at Granddad's home today. Not really gardening though, this, was it? This was more a few hours of honest toil. Any man could be proud of that.

He bent to his task again, enjoying the steady, effective rhythm of hard manual work. The part he enjoyed best was when he'd removed the turf and put it upside down in the welcoming trench. You could then sink your spade to its full depth into the soil, turning it methodically on top of the grass you were burying, watching the great clods break down into the beginning of what Granddad Joe called a good tilth.

He looked up and waved to the two fond, aged faces at the window, then resumed his work like a conscientious employee. He was panting steadily now, but he wasn't going to stop until the whole plot was double dug and ready for old Joe to work on. He'd be tired when he was finished, but it would be that pleasant fatigue he had felt after a long walk by the Wye or a day climbing in the Brecon Beacons. Exhaustion was good when it carried a sense of achievement with it.

Nana Pat came out and said he should stop for a cup of tea, but he said he'd have one when he was finished. Half an hour, three quarters at the most, he said; it had become a matter of personal pride to finish the whole plot and leave it brown and welcoming and ready for Granddad's efforts. Virgin land, old

Joe had said. Well, Damon wasn't defiling it. He was merely presenting it at its best for the expert gardener to have his way with it.

He was almost at the last trench now, the one Granddad had said at lunchtime that he would never reach. He'd be able to put the sods and the soil he'd dumped ready all those hours earlier into the last trench, and bring the old man out to see it. Joe would be full of approval and gratitude. 'Job's a good 'un!' he'd say. Granddad always said that when some task had been completed.

There were very few stones in this excellent soil. That was why Damon was surprised when he felt his spade grate on one. Quite a big one, it felt. But it was at the bottom of his spade, at the base of the full spit which Joe had told him to dig. He'd get it out, though, set it on the grass beside the plot to show Granddad what he'd extracted and how diligent he'd been in his work on the new vegetable plot.

It was at that moment that he saw it.

The skull lay at the bottom of the trench, staring up at him with sightless eyes as though it was startled to see him, as if it was questioning why its rest had been disturbed.

Damon went to the back door and called softly inside for Granddad Joe. He didn't want Nana Pat: this was a sight which was not fitting for a woman, even an old, experienced woman who had always seemed unshockable. He was surprised how light and uncertain his voice sounded as he called for his grandfather. It was almost as if the voice didn't belong to him, as if this sudden horror in the bright sunlight had affected his power of speech.

Damon found that he couldn't tell Joe what he'd discovered. Instead, he led him slowly across the grass of the new paddock to where he'd been digging, scarcely hearing the old man's compliments on how well he had done. He had half-expected the skull to be gone, vanished back into the ground whence it had come. But it lay exactly where he had left it, at the bottom of his final trench.

Granddad Joe hadn't seen it; he was still congratulating his grandson fulsomely on the work he had done. Damon could think of no words which were not banal. He said, 'I found this.'

Old Joe looked at the skull without speaking, as if he could not credit the presence of such a thing in his ground. It seemed a long time before he said, 'You'd best not dig any more, lad. The police will need to know about this.'

It was confirmation to Damon that it was real, that this awful thing which had thrust itself into the climax of his day was what he'd known it was as soon as he'd seen it. As he gazed down at it, a worm slid out silently through what had once been an eye, then back in through what had once been a mouth. Damon watched as if under hypnosis. Then he turned and vomited up Nana's lunch into the other end of the trench.

He stumbled back across the grass with the old man's arm around his shoulders, their strengths suddenly reversed. Damon felt a compelling need to speak, to say something, anything, to break the silence as they approached the door of the bungalow. 'You must think I'm a wimp, Granddad Joe!'

'Nay, lad, you're never a wimp! You're sixteen, that's all.'

Less than half an hour later, two police cars drove into the quiet close.

TWO

By the time Detective Chief Superintendent Lambert and Detective Sergeant Hook arrived from Oldford police station, the bones had already been accorded a status they had not enjoyed since their interment.

The end section of Joe Jackson's recently erected fence, which had separated his newly acquired paddock from the farmland beyond it, had been carefully removed. The trench where the skull had been found and the area beyond it were being examined with the minute attention required in a case of unexplained death. However old these bones might prove to be, they would be accorded the status of a suspicious death until the full facts of the demise could be ascertained.

Whether those facts would ever be established was a matter of speculation in these first hours of the investigation. The remains were human, but nothing was yet established beyond that. No one knew how old the skull was or whether the rest of a body was here as well. No one knew whether the victim – it would be treated as a victim until any more innocent explanation could be provided – was male or female. No one knew how long the skull had been here. It hadn't even got a nickname yet. Policemen who deal with death in all its harshness and finality usually give nicknames; they bring levity and relief to things which can make life very grim. This head had been the operating centre of a human being, the body part which distinguishes a person from the rest of the animal kingdom, but it was too anonymous as yet to prompt even the grim humour of the practised CID officer.

John Lambert sent DS Hook in to deal with the elderly owners of the bungalow whilst he went down to the area which had already been screened off as a scene of crime. Bert was good with people, adept at calming the shocked and the bewildered. Far better than Lambert was himself; eleven years of working with Hook had taught him that.

The Jacksons were certainly bewildered. After ten minutes
with Bert Hook's village-bobby persona, they relaxed a little.
Hook was far more intelligent than the public face he presented.
The criminal fraternity with whom he dealt for much of his
time often underestimated him, which brought him and his
chief many advantages. Bert decided in his first sixty seconds
with the Jacksons that they were entirely innocent of whatever
had happened at the edge of their property. And the Jacksons
decided that this burly figure with the weather-beaten features
was entirely trustworthy and reliable.

'My grandson was double digging a new vegetable plot for
me. Going down to almost eighteen inches. He'd almost
finished it. He was on the very last trench when he found that
– that thing. He's a good lad, Damon,' Joe Jackson concluded
irrelevantly.

The grey-haired woman beside him put her hand on his
without looking at him. 'I suppose there's no doubt that what
Damon found out there was human?' she asked Hook.

'None at all, I'm afraid. That's one of the very few things
we can be sure of at the moment. Had you any reason at all
to suspect that there might be anything like that out there?'

'No!' They chorused the negative in horrified unison.

'I know that seems a silly question, but it's one we have to
ask. You haven't heard any rumours of mysterious deaths or
disappearances in the area?'

'No. We've only been here for three years. Our bungalow
is the only one in the close. It was the last home to be built;
I think the planning permission for the houses said that they
had to include one detached bungalow. A gesture to pensioners,
I suppose.' Joe managed the first smile he had produced since
he had seen that grim thing at the boundary of his newly
extended garden.

'And the ground where you were digging your vegetable
plot was not originally part of your property.'

'No. I bought it from the farmer. The purchase wasn't
completed until last week. I wanted to get on with digging
the vegetable plot, so that we could have some crops this year.
I was going to plant maincrop spuds in most of it. That breaks
up the ground, you see; makes it more suitable for brassicas

later.' The facts, relevant and irrelevant, tumbled out of him, as if he needed to divest himself of all of them to prove that he had no involvement in this awful thing.

Pat Jackson broke in as if it was important to stop her husband talking, to cut the strings on his involvement with what was going on in their garden. 'Have you found other things? Have you found other bones to go with what our grandson turned up in that trench?'

'The scene of crime team are working on it now, Mrs Jackson. They have to go carefully, you see. It seems slow to us, but they know what they're about. They will search the earth very carefully. They want to find everything they can, but they can't rush things because they don't want to risk destroying evidence.'

'Destroying evidence'. It was that word 'evidence', with its legal connotations, which made her appreciate for the first time what was involved here. 'What they're turning up out there is evidence, isn't it? There's a crime involved, isn't there, and the people out there are looking for the evidence to find out who put that thing into our land?'

'There might be a crime, yes. We don't know yet. If there is a crime, it may well be a very serious one.'

'Someone might have killed him, mightn't they?' said Joe Jackson. He looked suddenly older, his scant hair thinner and more untidy as he ran a gnarled hand quickly through it.

Bert Hook noted that Joe had assumed that the skull was male, just as policemen always assumed that a killer was male, until they knew otherwise. The facts supported them: four out of five killers were male. He didn't know how many skulls found in the ground were male, though. He thought of these two suddenly frailer people holding on to each other in bed, trying to sleep through the night, which was now not far away. 'There might be a perfectly innocent explanation for this, you know.' Bert couldn't think of one at the moment.

Joe Jackson said defiantly, almost aggressively, 'It wasn't our ground. Not when that thing was put there, it wasn't.'

Pat Jackson seized on that thought. 'No. And we've no idea how long it's been there, have we? It could be quite old, couldn't it? It must date from before these houses were built.'

Bert hadn't yet seen the skull. There'd been no hair on it, apparently. He nodded at the two anxious pensioners. 'That's almost certainly so.'

Pat nodded. 'Could that thing be really old? There were battles fought round here, weren't there?'

DS Hook smiled. 'Yes. Most of them were fought near rivers like the Wye and the Severn. There was a big battle at Tewkesbury, near where I live.'

'Do you think this could be left over from one of those battles?'

'I think that's very unlikely.'

'They found a multiple grave a few years ago, didn't they? From the Wars of the Roses, I think. They found skeletons of lots of soldiers who'd been killed in a battle. Do you think this could be something like that?' She was torn between horror at the thought of there being others out there, multiple deaths near her quiet modern home, and her original idea that distancing this death would make it less sinister and less threatening than something more recent. Pat was seventy now. She didn't want this to be anything which had occurred in her lifetime.

Bert Hook said gently, 'I doubt that this would be a multiple grave, Mrs Jackson. There's no record of any major engagement in this area. But we shall know more very quickly, I'm sure. Once the experts get to look at whatever is unearthed out there.'

He looked out through the window at the screen around the plot, wondering exactly what his chief and the scene of crime team were discovering behind it. 'You won't be planting vegetables for a little while, Mr Jackson.'

Hook had been trying to lower the tension. But old Joe said dolefully, 'I don't know whether I'll ever plant vegetables out there now, after that thing Damon turned up. I don't think Pat would fancy anything I grew in that plot. She'd be thinking of what had been buried there.'

'I expect you'll feel differently in a few weeks. I'm a vegetable man myself. It looks to me as though you've got good ground there. Be a shame not to use it, now you've put the work in.'

'Our Damon put the work in. He's a good lad, our grandson.' Joe Jackson was clinging to that thought, amidst a welter of much darker ones.

Hook said, 'We'll give you back your ground as soon as we can. I expect in a year's time this will seem no more than a bad dream to you.'

He had no real belief that that would be so. This was a new experience to him as well as to them. He left the Jacksons to talk with each other in their living room and walked across their newly acquired paddock to the square in the corner which was now hidden from public view. John Lambert greeted him with a curt nod. Bert said, 'I've never been involved in a death like this before. I don't suppose you have.'

Lambert said tersely, 'Once, when I was a young copper – before I was even CID. They found remains on a Second World War bomb site in Bristol. They went down deep because they were building a tower block. Those bones had been there for forty years. Natural causes, they decided, in the end. If you can call death from one of Hitler's bombs natural causes. Actually, I think they included something about enemy action.'

They looked automatically to the other end of the scene of crime area, where someone had set the skull which had prompted all this activity on top of a wooden box. It was only five yards away and it reminded Bert Hook of a scene in *Lord of the Flies* which had frightened him as a child. The head looked as if it had been set up there as a bizarre object of veneration. He wished someone would put it inside the box and out of his sight.

The pathologist was totally unconscious of Hook's reaction. He was all brisk professionalism, as if buried skeletons were something he dealt with every day of his working life. 'He's drying off nicely. Not that we want to lose all of the soil around him: it might help us to establish how long he's been there, the soil. Possibly even give us a clue as to how he got there. We'll be able to tell you more when we have a few more bones to add to the head.'

He gestured to where two of his acolytes were on all fours with trowels in hand, sifting the soil in and beyond Damon Jackson's final trench with infinite care. They looked like archaeologists discovering buried treasure. Hook supposed that within this context they were doing exactly that. The earth they were treating with such respect might reveal more of this mysterious person, might give him or her some sort of identity. It might even reveal how he or she had died, the key question for CID men and for everyone else on the site at this moment.

There was a plastic sheet beside the two who were working with trowels. It already had bones upon it. Hook recognized a femur, a collar bone, ribs and what looked like fragments of a pelvis. The strange jigsaw of what had once been a living thing, a person who had spoken and moved, who had loved and hated, was being put together after being hidden from human sight for many years.

It was Chief Superintendent Lambert who voiced the question which was dominating the thoughts of the seven people here at this moment. 'Any thoughts yet on how long chummy's been here?'

The pathologist gave him the supercilious smile of the professional dealing patiently with the amateur. He was a balding man with rimless glasses; neither Lambert nor Hook had seen him before. He had a patronizing air, treating experienced policemen as novices in death, feeling that in this case his presumption was wholly justified. He was used to dealing with corpses who had been killed the hour before or the night before, not a decade or even a century ago. Bert Hook looked at the bones being assembled so meticulously upon the plastic sheet and tried to think of this incomplete assembly as a living, breathing human being, with emotions like love and hate – and fear, perhaps, in the final passage of life which had led to its presence here.

He sensed that this rather pompous expert wanted to be prompted with questions which would enable him to display his knowledge, so he repeated his chief's query. 'How old do you think this is?'

Dr Patterson smiled at such naivety. 'We shall know more when we have more complete evidence. The nearer we get to a full skeleton, the more I shall be able to tell you. I shall, of course, need the equipment of my laboratory to furnish you with any degree of accuracy.'

Lambert said, with a touch of acid, 'What we really need for a start is some idea of how long he's been lying undetected in a shallow grave. We can't even formulate questions until we have some idea of that.'

Patterson looked at the soiled collection on the plastic sheet, watching the woman who knelt beside it depositing a slender bit of bone which might once have been a finger. 'Not centuries.'

It was a start. Bert wasn't sure whether he was pleased or disturbed by the thought. A recent interment would need investigation, might lead to the complex operations involved in a murder hunt. The zest for the chase, for the probing of a mystery, stirred within him; such curiosity and excitement are necessities for all successful CID officers. On the other hand, the investigation of a death which had happened many years earlier and been undetected at the time would almost certainly be complex and prolonged, and quite possibly ultimately unsuccessful.

The awful crimes of Fred and Rose West some thirty years earlier were still vividly present in the minds of all Gloucestershire police officers. Hook was immediately disturbed by the thought of the corpses interred by West which had never been found, despite intensive digging in the areas thought to be relevant. That was ridiculous, he told himself firmly: there had never been any suggestion that the Wests had operated in this area. And these bones might be centuries old. They might even, as Mrs Jackson had suggested, be remains from some much older, long-forgotten conflict.

But Patterson had said the skull wasn't centuries old, hadn't he? Bert looked at the thing on its temporary pedestal. It seemed for a moment to be grinning mockingly at him. He glanced at the impassive Lambert, then repeated to the pathologist, 'How old is this, do you think? What are your first impressions?'

'Oh, I can't possibly give you anything definite standing here on the edge of this field. I'm a scientist. I need my laboratory and my instruments around me to provide you with scientific findings. You shall have them, in due course. But in the meantime—'

'In the meantime we need to speculate!' said John Lambert abruptly. 'I shouldn't need to remind you that you're employed here as a forensic pathologist: speculation is part of the deal. Until we know otherwise, this is a suspicious death. There may be a serious crime involved, perhaps the most serious of all. You're not in a court of law here. No one is going to hold you to account if you have to revise your opinions after a full laboratory investigation. We need your thoughts right now.'

The pathologist was around forty, bearded, bespectacled and entirely unused to being spoken to in this manner. He looked for a moment as if he would protest, but then tightened his lips and looked at the accumulating bones on the sheet. Perhaps it was the fact that he was being taken to task by an older man which made him cooperate, or perhaps it was his awareness of the local and national stature of the detective who was pressing him.

'There is an almost complete absence of soft tissue. That is a limiting factor in establishing the date of death.'

'I understand that. We need your thoughts at this moment.' Whilst remaining coolly polite, Lambert managed to convey the fact that his patience was growing thin.

'There is no hair adhering to this skull. That suggests to me that chummy has been in the ground for at least twenty years, though different soils have different effects.' He moved carefully across the designated scene of the crime path to stand beside the skull, which was dominating the scene as if at the centre of some ancient pagan ritual. He looked down at it and said almost reluctantly, 'There are some teeth left. That suggests to me a date within the last century, probably within the last fifty years. For teeth formed after 1965, carbon dating of tooth enamel can enable us to predict a year of birth which should be accurate to between one and five years. One of my first laboratory tasks will be to establish how much if any enamel is left on these teeth.'

Lambert resisted the temptation to point out sarcastically that this revelation hadn't caused any great pain, even to an anally retentive pathologist. 'What else? You will understand that it is important to us to have even an approximate date for this death as soon as possible.'

The pathologist nodded his pedantic head and glanced again towards the plastic sheet and the work going on beside it to unearth this forensic treasure trove. 'We haven't found any nails yet. We may still do so: they survive quite well in most soils. Radio carbon dating based on nails is accurate to within three years.' He looked at the two detectives, then decided upon what he regarded as a confession of weakness. 'It may surprise you to know that this is new territory to me as well as to you. I've investigated bones before, but they've been centuries old, without the urgency of serious crime surrounding them. I will genuinely be able to speak with more authority in a few days. Apart from laboratory testing, there are experts I would like to consult on this.'

Lambert recognized the concession, the unspoken acknowledgement that they were working together here, rather than pursuing their own interests. 'Thank you, Dr Patterson. You would say then that death was relatively recent but not very recent.'

'I'd say between eighteen and twenty-five years ago. I reserve the right to revise that after more scientific analysis in my laboratory.'

'Thank you. That is a starting point for us. DS Hook and I will go back to Oldford and set detective wheels in motion.'

They walked slowly across the paddock towards the back door of the bright modern bungalow and the couple who were more shaken than anyone by what had lain undiscovered on the edge of their land.

They were almost at the door when Patterson appeared breathlessly at their heels. 'By the way, there's one thing I didn't mention but which I'm now quite sure about. These remains are female.'

THREE

'**O**ldford CID section here, sir. We need to speak to you. It's in connection with your development at Brenton Park.'

Jason Fowler was immediately defensive. 'It's around twenty years since we began the development there. The guarantee extends for ten years only and it excludes—'

'No one is threatening to sue you. At least no one that we know about. We need to speak to you about a much more serious matter.'

'And what is that?' Jason was playing for time now. You couldn't deny the police. You had to speak to them when they demanded it. But if he could get some notice of what they wanted from him, he might at least be able to cover his tracks.

'I'm not at liberty to disclose that. You will find out soon enough. Detective Chief Superintendent Lambert and Detective Sergeant Hook need to speak with you urgently. You will find out what this is about from them.'

The woman rolled the ranks out as if she was assembling the heavy artillery, he thought. What could this possibly be about? That latest consignment of bricks had come suspiciously cheap, but he was pretty sure they'd been genuinely bankrupt stock. The bank had been selling as receivers, on behalf of a twat who'd overreached himself hopelessly in Birmingham and been downed by the Inland Revenue. And they surely didn't set Chief Superintendents chasing dodgy deals on bricks, did they? He said roughly, 'This is Sunday. Day of rest they used to call it, when I was at school. You work hard all week and now you can't even rest on the sabbath. Can't this wait until tomorrow?'

'I'm afraid it can't, sir. Crime doesn't recognize weekends. Our officers are losing their Sundays too. They are quite prepared to come to your home to speak to you, so as to minimize the inconvenience.'

'No. There's no need for them to do that. I wanted to go down to the Wye View site this morning anyway.' It was contradicting what he'd said about looking forward to his Sunday rest, but he didn't want the police coming here. Things were dodgy enough with Jane as it was. If the neighbours saw senior cops coming into his house on Sunday morning they'd ask questions, and Jane wouldn't like that. She'd give him hell, stroppy cow, and his conjugals would be contested again. 'Tell them I'll see them in the office at the Wye Vale site at ten o'clock. They'll know where it is?'

'Oh, they'll know where it is, sir. Thank you. You can expect them at ten o'clock.' She spoke briskly and managed to make it sound like a threat.

Ten miles away, John Lambert was having his own marital difficulties. Christine saw him in his working suit and anticipated the worst. 'We're going across to Caroline's for tea this afternoon. It's your grandson's birthday.'

'I know that. Murder doesn't choose its moments.'

'And I know that too. I've had thirty years to learn to live with it. This is murder?'

He smiled grimly. He'd flung the big word which was the best excuse at her, hoping she wouldn't query it: everything and everyone deferred to murder. 'We don't know yet. But it's very possible. We should know within a couple of days.'

'A skull, you said last night.'

'Yes. Found where you'd least expect it, on the edge of—'

'It's an old death then, this. Twenty years or more.'

'Very probably, yes.' He knew what was coming next.

'Not urgent, then. It can await the attention of the Great Detective for a few more hours. Super-sleuth can afford to have tea with his wife and his daughter and his grandchildren.'

She was throwing in the newspaper phrases that she knew he hated. She must be really irritated with him. Christine was amazingly tolerant of his work really, until it affected family. Then she was like the mother tiger with her children – not that John Lambert knew whether tigers were more or less maternal than other animals. He said, 'This is a suspicious death: a new murder, as far as we and everyone else are concerned. There will be a press release this morning. As soon as the guilty people know that a body has been discovered, they'll start covering their tracks.'

'They've had around twenty years to do that. There won't be any tracks left for you to follow.'

'You'd think so, wouldn't you? But whoever is responsible will be surprised by this. They probably thought they were safe for life. They might reveal things by their reactions to this discovery.' He wondered if he was deceiving himself. Was he seeking arguments to justify his presence at the heart of the investigation, which was at this moment stirring into life like an animal crawling out of hibernation? 'This is a new situation for almost all of us at Oldford, Christine. And everyone remembers Fred and Rose West. Every copper round here has nightmares about that. I'm sure this had no connection with those crimes, but I don't want any melodramatic conjecture; you know how the media would seize on that.'

His wife knew now that she was going to lose the battle, as she always did. Work would come first, as ever. That had almost destroyed their marriage once, when she was at home with two young children and he was chasing villains at what had seemed like every hour of the day. At least he told her a little about what he was up to now, whereas he had shut her out completely in those days. She sighed. 'I suppose Caroline will make allowances for you. She's grown up with it and known nothing else. You can't expect a grandson of eight to understand. George is bound to be disappointed.'

'He'll have his presents and his Nana Christine to amuse him. He won't miss the old man who tries to play football with him.'

'You know that that is exactly what he will miss. He loves telling the rest of us how many goals he's put past you.'

'I'll do my best. I'll be there for the meal if I possibly can.'

'You'd better mean that, John Lambert.' She reached up, threw her arms round his neck and gave the troubled face a kiss which surprised both of them.

What Jason Fowler had called an office was little more than a shed with a table and a computer in it. It was normally occupied by a secretary who doubled as a guide to the site for those putative purchasers who were anxious to get in early and secure the best plots in this extensive development.

There were three rather uncomfortable upright chairs in the shed. Fowler took the one behind the desk and seated his unwelcome visitors upon the other two. He appeared to Bert Hook to be a successful builder trying hard to look the part of the industrial entrepreneur he had now chosen to become. His hair was so determinedly black that it had certainly received help from a bottle. His heels were substantial, designed to add the height he desired to his stature. His grey-blue eyes were narrow and watchful. They said that he did not trust the police and did not expect to be trusted himself. The thin moustache gave him the air of a wartime spiv rather than the sophisticated executive he was aiming at. Bert Hook wasn't sure whether or not he built good houses. He didn't think you would get many bargains from this man, and he would want to check any which were offered very carefully indeed.

Fowler leaned back behind his desk and said, 'I trust this won't take very long.'

'As long as it needs to,' said Lambert briskly. 'Your full cooperation is the factor most likely to speed the process.'

'You have that, of course. You will find everything is perfectly in order here. If you want the paper work to prove that, you will need to come back when—'

'It isn't this site we are concerned with. I'm sure Mr Caffrey will be pleased to know that,' said Lambert.

Fowler glanced at him sharply. Caffrey was the local councillor who had been forced to resign amidst accusations of corruption and back-handers from Fowler to secure planning consent for the extent of the building on this site, where over one hundred residences were planned in four phases of building. 'Nothing was ever proved over that. There has been no court case and there will never be one.'

'No. You and I know the truth of the matter, Mr Fowler, but there will be no court case, because of the lack of sufficient evidence. I am sure that Mr Caffrey feels well compensated for his loss of office.'

'I shall offer you no further comment. I have nothing at all to feel guilty about in that business.'

'Really? Well, let us hope that the same is true of the issue which DS Hook and I need to discuss with you today.'

'And what would that be?'

'You heard the announcement on radio and television this morning?'

'No. I was otherwise engaged.' He leered his suggestion of the connubial bliss which had in fact been emphatically denied to him.

Lambert didn't believe for a moment that Fowler had heard nothing of the dramatic find at Brenton Park. Even if he hadn't listened to the bulletins, someone would have rung him by now. He wondered what texts had been recorded on the mobile phone which Fowler had been fingering when they arrived here. He'd terminated a call very abruptly when he'd seen them approaching. 'A body was found yesterday at one of your former building sites. Brenton Park.'

'It's twenty years since we began work there. Just over that, probably.'

'That's interesting. The remains we found appear to be just about twenty years old.' That was pushing it a little: the pathologist had said he'd be able to be more precise in a day or two. But he didn't mind stretching things, if it would discomfort this irritating man. It wasn't personal prejudice, he told himself. The man could well be a suspect. That did rather bypass the thought that almost anyone who'd been near the Brenton Park development at that time could be a suspect. Still, a man who bribed councillors to secure planning permissions might well be capable of darker crimes as well.

'I know nothing about any bodies.'

'Of course you don't. But you will understand that a lot of people will need to convince us of just that, in the next few days. We're starting with you.'

'Right. I'm telling you formally that I know nothing about any bodies you've found up there and that I have no connection with how they came to be there. Any suggestion that I have might harm my reputation as an honest businessman, which I have worked assiduously to acquire.' He struggled a little over the adverb, as if it were a word in a foreign tongue.

'You were in the early years of your career when you were building at Brenton Park.'

Fowler nodded. 'It was the first major development I undertook as an independent contractor. It helped to establish the reputation for sound work and excellent value which has stood me in good stead in the years since then.'

'Yes. I seem to recall some of those phrases in your publicity literature.' Lambert glanced down at the glossy pamphlet advertising the latest Fowler development, with its artist's impressions of the properties at present under construction at Wye Vale. 'I also recall that in your early days, including the ones at Brenton Park, you employed some dodgy characters.'

Jason Fowler swallowed hard. He didn't want any detailed investigation of the practices he had favoured in his early days. 'I did my bit for the community, if that's what you mean. I gave people who'd been in prison a second chance – helped them back into society.'

Bert Hook smiled grimly. 'Very public-spirited you were in those days. You employed them to carry hods and paid them less than the minimum wage, if I remember rightly. I was a fresh-faced young copper in uniform at the time and I remember being sent to check on your activities.'

'That's the thanks you get for trying to be the good citizen and help unfortunates back into the community,' said Fowler sententiously.

'You employed labour on the "lump". Almost ended up in court over it, if I remember rightly,' said Hook evenly.

The 'lump' was a method unscrupulous employers in the building trade used to avoid tax and National Insurance contributions for workers whom they classed as self-employed. Jason Fowler said defensively, 'Everyone did it then. You had to cut costs wherever you could.'

Lambert ignored this defence and said thoughtfully, 'I suppose that will make it difficult to trace some of the people you employed for short periods. Some of the people who might have been among your more violent employees. Some of the people who might have killed a woman and buried the body at the edge of the Brenton Park site.'

They weren't interested in chasing him for these far-off offences, and probably all three of the men in the hut on this Sunday morning knew that. This was part of the softening-up process, the kind of reminder which would make Fowler more amenable and more ready to reveal whatever he knew about any ancillary events which had accompanied his construction work at Brenton Park. Lambert said, 'We'll need the details of whoever was working for you then. We won't be interested in your sins of omission, as long as you cooperate fully with us in the investigation of a major crime.'

Lambert noticed that he was already assuming there was murder or manslaughter here, even though that was still to be established. Perhaps it was just that men like Jason Fowler brought out the aggressor in him and made him wish to give them as uncomfortable a passage as possible. He didn't think it was just that. From the moment he had seen that skull grinning helplessly at him, he had suspected foul play. And the pathologist's parting information that the remains were those of a woman had only reinforced that feeling. Women and children were more natural victims than men. The weak usually suffered, in the world of violent crime in which he spent so many of his days.

Fowler said nervously, 'I didn't have much capital in those days. The Brenton Park site was developed in stages. I used the money from the sales of the first houses to finance the next stage of development. There was a rambling old house and a plant nursery on the site when we purchased it. I had to clear all that away before we could start building.'

Lambert made a mental note to contact the owners of the plant nursery, if they were still alive. Perhaps this body had been buried in the field beside the plant nursery before Fowler and his dubious employment practices and the dubious employees that came with them had ever appeared on the scene. But would the owner of the plant nursery or anyone else who lived in his house have considered burying a corpse so near to their home, particularly if they knew it was about to be sold as building land? He wondered how precise a date of death and interment they would ever establish for that jigsaw of bones he had seen accumulating on the plastic sheet beside the vegetable plot.

He said gruffly, 'We'll need details of the people working for you throughout those phases of development at Brenton Park.'

'No can do. My records are long gone. Even the tax people allow you to throw things away after five years.'

'You've not even got the names and addresses of your work force?'

'Ships that pass in the night, Superintendent.' He was becoming more truculent as he felt himself on safer ground. 'My secretary from those days is no longer around. Went down to be nearer her daughter in Dorset. Be dead now, I should think.' He nodded as if he thought that a consummation devoutly to be wished. 'I've got a PA now, of course. But she wouldn't know anything about those days.'

'Then it seems we're going to be almost totally dependent on you. We'll need you to cudgel your memory and come up with whatever you can in the way of names and significant incidents from the several years you spent on building the houses and bungalow at Brenton Park.'

'Bloody nuisance it was, that bungalow. The council made us put one bungalow in, as part of the planning permission.'

'You didn't have Councillor Caffrey in your camp then, of course.'

Fowler glowered, but didn't rise to the bait. 'Last property on the site, that bungalow was. Right up against the farmer's field. He got quite shirty when I tried to pinch a bit of his land. But farmers are like that, aren't they? You never get owt for nowt from a farmer, do you?' He shook his head, possibly in recognition of his deplorable attempt at a Yorkshire accent.

'Difficult was he, the farmer?'

'Just bloody awkward, most of the time. Resented that there was no money in it for him, I expect, after what we'd paid for the nursery. But I wasn't interested in his land – green belt you see, not building land.'

'He did all right in the end, though, didn't he? Sold bits of agricultural land to the residents on that side of the site, to supplement the meagre gardens they'd been allotted by the builder.'

'Aye. Sold ground that was just pasture land for him for quite handsome sums, the crafty sod. I'm not sure that was him, though. I think he'd sold the farm and moved out by then. He were a rum bugger, old Burrell. A right rum bugger.'

FOUR

D
r Patterson, the pathologist, had been a little too self-important and a little too protective of his status on the site when the skeleton had been discovered. In the subsequent investigation his professionalism was exemplary and he produced the rapid results John Lambert had requested.

He conducted the detailed laboratory tests he had outlined to the CID men on site, he consulted colleagues who had more experience of bone analysis than he had and he swiftly produced a detailed report. This was immensely useful in pinning down the time of this death and eventually in the identification of the victim. As Lambert said, it was all very well for Hamlet to reminisce over Yorick, but modern police officers had to be certain of the identity of a skull before they could indulge in any philosophy.

Patterson's tests on carbon and teeth revealed that the remains were those of a female of between twenty and twenty-two years. She had died around twenty years ago, after the house and greenhouses of the nursery had been cleared from the neighbouring site and the first phase of the building development had begun. Largely because there was no soft tissue to investigate, it was impossible to be certain about a cause of death.

There was a severe blow to the side of the head which might in itself have been terminal but could equally well have been a posthumous injury. It could even have been caused by a spade or stone in the course of the burial: the shallowness of the grave and the face-down position of the body indicated that the interment had probably been hasty and rapid. Strands of hair had been found in the ground which were detached from the head but had certainly belonged to this corpse. Hair retains its evidence for a long period, and this hair indicated that its owner had taken illegal drugs in some quantity in the months before death.

Lambert digested these findings in his office with Bert Hook and Detective Inspector Chris Rushton, who was anxious to file any information which would narrow and concentrate their search for whoever had ended this young life and whoever had consigned her body to the earth. They were not necessarily the same person or persons, as Rushton had already reminded the young constables who were being assigned to the team which it had now been accepted was necessary.

DI Rushton, who always organized the welter of information which accrued quickly around a murder hunt, was edgy because so far he had almost nothing to file on this one. Ignorance distressed Chris; so long as there were findings to record from house-to-house enquiries and the standard procedures which went into operation around a 'normal' killing, he was content. Even though he knew that in the end most of what he filed would eventually prove to be irrelevant, he was happy in the knowledge that nothing must be missed, because apparently random facts often provided the keys to solving serious crimes.

The strange hiatus surrounding this older death distressed Chris. Until they knew precisely when an unknown woman had died and been thrust hastily into the ground, most of the normal procedures were suspended. He now reported what he could to prove to the two older men, and perhaps to himself, that he had not been idle. 'There's no record of anyone in the immediate area being reported missing at around that time. It could be a missing person from somewhere else in the country, of course, but until we have a more definite date, there's no point in opening that can of worms.'

Mispers. That vast, anonymous army of people who choose to disappear from families to seek anonymity elsewhere in the country, for a huge variety of reasons, most of which involve fear or panic. A feature of British life in the twenty-first century which is both depressing and dangerous to the rest of society. Some of these people become criminals in order to survive. Many more of them become prey for the vicious predators who need both a market for drugs and a host of junior dealers to sell them.

When minors disappear, the police do their best to locate them before they are absorbed into the murky underworlds of drugs or prostitution. With adults, they take the details of mispers and, unless there are criminal acts to be investigated and criminals to pursue, do very little more. The details of the person who has disappeared are recorded on the Police National Computer and are available for officers anywhere in the country to pursue; this usually only happens when they become either criminals or victims. There are simply too many mispers for the police service to pursue. When the police find mispers, they cannot compel them to return whence they have come unless there are criminal charges and arrests. Apart from these cases, it would be foolish and uneconomical for officers to dissipate their energies for very meagre returns. Their favourite and justified reaction is 'We are officers of the law, not social workers.'

Lambert said with a conviction he could not really justify at this moment, 'We'll get a definite date for this. And when we get a definite date, we'll soon find a definite person. And when we find a definite person, that person will also be a victim.'

Daniel Burrell was the farmer who had owned the land where the bones had been interred around twenty years earlier. He did not at first sight justify Jason Fowler's description of him as 'a right rum bugger'.

He looked, in fact, quite benign. He had thinning white hair which was tidily parted and a broad face in which the red veins were only visible at close quarters because of the permanent tan which comes from many years of outdoor life. He had a broad nose and blue eyes which narrowed as he was approached by these two formidable men. The young woman who had brought them to him said rather too loudly, 'These are two important policemen who want to talk to you, Daniel. Mr Lambert is very important indeed and Detective Sergeant Hook used to play cricket for Herefordshire. You might remember him doing that.'

'There's no need to bloody shout, woman! I'm not deaf, like most of the poor sods in here. And it's Mr Burrell to you, not Daniel. And why the hell should I remember some sod playing cricket?'

'He's like this,' the attendant said to the CID men with a shake of her head. 'Got out on the wrong side of the bed today did we, Mr Burrell?'

'No, I bloody didn't. And you can piss off now, young woman. This is private business, between men.'

She bathed the three of them in her benign, understanding smile and then departed with a measured, upright dignity. Burrell watched her go; an unexpected smile flashed briefly across his face as he studied her curvaceous and mobile rear. Then he turned not to Lambert but to Hook. 'I do remember you playing cricket, but I wasn't going to let on to her about it. Bloody good bowler, you were. You should still be playing.'

Hook smiled. 'Age catches up with all of us, Mr Burrell.' He glanced down sympathetically at the wheelchair. 'My boss here has introduced me to golf. I play that now, but I don't find it an easy game.'

'GOLF!' Burrell delivered his outrage in capitals and invested the monosyllable with a massive contempt. He looked as though he would like to spit but had no receptacle available. Then he said unexpectedly, 'You're the rozzer who got yourself a degree, aren't you?'

'I am, yes. But—'

'You must find a degree no bloody use at all when you're trying to knock sense into young toughs, I should think.'

'It's not of much use in the job, no. But I never thought it would be. And we don't use any physical violence nowadays, except in self-defence and—'

'I'd be using a lot of self-defence, if I were a copper. Wouldn't stand for the lip some of these young yobbos think they can dish out.'

'I see. Well, much as we'd like to discuss methods of modern policing on this pleasant Sunday morning, we have more important questions to ask you.'

'Sunday, is it? You hardly know one day from another, in places like this. Oh, they're kind enough, most of the staff, but they think we're all as daft as some of the old biddies who've completely lost it, poor devils.'

Lambert took his chance to intervene in a conversation which had so far bypassed him completely. 'I'm glad to see

and hear that you still have all your considerable wits about
you, Mr Burrell, because we have a few questions to ask you.
We need your help rather desperately, as a matter of fact.'

Daniel Burrell turned his wheelchair a fraction to give the
senior man the full benefit of the glower he now produced.
'And what if I choose not to answer your bloody impertinent
questions?'

'Then we could take you down to Oldford police station
with us and charge you with obstructing the police in the
pursuit of their duties. But we won't need to do that, because
you're a highly respectable citizen and you will wish to demon-
strate that, by offering us every assistance you possibly can.'

Burrell glared at him for a moment before shifting his attention back to Hook. 'Gobby bastard, isn't he, your gaffer? Treat
you badly does he?'

Bert Hook smiled, recognizing the fun the man in the wheelchair was having. No doubt he found life in the care home
trying: it seemed to be an environment which looked after him
physically but denied him much fun. 'He's not a bad gaffer,
for most of the time. He did introduce me to golf, but I can't
think of anything else he's done that's really cruel.'

'Aye. Well, he's top brass, isn't he? But at least he's not
sitting on his arse behind a desk and ordering others about.
At least he's out here wasting his time on old sods like me,
instead of letting others do it.'

Hook grinned, studiously avoiding any eye contact with
Lambert. 'I bet you didn't do much sitting about on your arse
when you were running the farm, did you, Mr Burrell?'

The old man leaned forward, grinned briefly at Bert. 'You
can call me Daniel, if you want to. Or even Dan. Not Danny,
mind – I never liked Danny. But you're right: I didn't sit on
my bottom and expect others to do all the work. Never asked
any bugger to do what I wouldn't do myself. Mind you, we
have machines for almost everything, nowadays. Young 'uns
don't know they're born.'

Bert nodded. 'I should think you knew every bit of your
land.'

Burrell nodded. His eyes looked out through the window
at the sky and his mind slid back forty years. 'I knew every

foot of it. I knew where it was stony and where it was boggy
– that was only in the lowest bits. I had my cattle and my
hens. I knew what grew hay and what grew wheat and what
was only good for pasture. They said mixed farms were
finished, but I ran one and made it pay. That was when I was
young. It's all gone now.'

He didn't sigh or express any regret in words, but there was
a huge sadness in his face as he looked resolutely at the sky
and away from his present surroundings. He looked in that
moment like a figure from a Hardy novel, or a detail from a
Victorian painting on the theme of rural decline. Hook waited
until his attention came reluctantly back to his visitors before
he said, 'When did you sell the farm, Daniel?'

Burrell took his time over his answer. It seemed like
yesterday to him, but he knew that it was a long time ago, in
this world of younger men. And it was important to him that
he got the answer not just correct but precisely correct. That
was the way you showed in this place that you were still a
person who could think, not an old fossil waiting to be buried
and forgotten. 'Be eighteen years come September. Fourteenth
of September. That's when I signed the farm away. I gave Jim
Simmons time to pay, but I gave up control then. I was sixty-
six then, and they all said pensioners shouldn't be farming.
I'm eighty-four now and I could still teach 'em a thing or two,
if they'd only listen.'

They could check that easily enough, but Hook had no doubt
that the old man would be right. It meant that Burrell had
been at the farm when this still unidentified young woman
had died and been buried at the edge of his ground. Bert said
gently, 'You were still there when the building work began
next to your land, then?'

'Where the old nursery was, yes. Jumped-up little sod he
was, that builder. But I put one across on 'im, didn't I?'

'Did you, Daniel? Tell us how.'

'I 'ad a piggery quite near to the edge of that plant nursery
he'd bought. He thought the stink would stop people buying
his posh new houses, didn't he? You get 'ell of a pong from
pig shit, as you two probably know. So he paid me five thou-
sand to close it down.' He looked from side to side, as if he

feared other geriatrics might hear this and peach on him, even at this stage. Then he leaned forward towards Hook and said, 'Daft bugger didn't know I'd already shut the sties down and got rid of the pigs, did he?'

The cackle of Burrell's ancient laughter rang loud around the big room, causing white heads to turn in consternation towards him. Bert Hook grinned conspiratorially at him. 'I can see no one would put one across on you, Daniel. Your memory's obviously as sharp as it ever was.'

''Tis for those days. Can't always tell you what we had for dinner yesterday, though.' He stared out at the sky again. 'Every day's the same in 'ere, see. Rain or shine. Even snow doesn't make much difference when you're in here.'

'No. You're warm and dry and well fed here. Not out in all weathers and wondering where the next meal's coming from.'

Burrell stared at him for a moment, then reluctantly accepted the logic of this. 'I suppose so. But I still miss being out in the open and feeling the sun and the wind on my face. Even the rain and the hail and the snow, if it comes to that.' He glanced down sadly at his thinning legs in the wheelchair.

What he really missed was being thirty or forty and full of energy rather than eighty-four and physically failing, thought Hook. Just as he himself missed marking out his run, running up to the wicket rhythmically and making the best minor counties batsmen hop about a bit. At least you could play golf for as long as you could walk round the course; people had told him that, but he didn't find it much of a consolation when he was searching among the bluebells for his ball. He smiled at Daniel Burrell and said, 'This is from your farming days, Dan. And it might be rather important, so we'd like you to think carefully about it. Did you employ any women when you were running the farm?'

'No. I remember Land Army girls when I was a kid. One of them had a nice tight bum which I can still remember.' A dreamy smile infused his lined features, then was swiftly dismissed in favour of sterner thoughts. 'But they disappeared after the war. And we didn't have no girls there, not in my time. More and more machinery, but no girls. Well, there was my Emily, of course: she kept us fed and did the washing.

She didn't work on the land. She could tell you a tale or two, if she was still here.' His eyes were misty with remembrance of things past. But after a moment he said gruffly, 'She died three years ago. Not long before I came in here.' He glanced up resentfully at the stuccoed ceiling, as if the two events were connected, as no doubt they were.

'I see. And were there any young women who came regularly to the farm – perhaps as visitors, rather than workers? Girl friends, perhaps, or daughters of people who worked with you? We're thinking of someone quite young, perhaps about twenty.'

He considered the question for quite a long time. 'No. Not regularly. There were my sister Barbara's two girls. They'd have been around that age when I sold the farm. They're both married with kids now.' He leaned forward again, glanced at the watchful Lambert, but swiftly transferred his attention back to the man whom he had now decided was a kindred spirit. 'This is about that skull you dug up near the edge of that building site, isn't it?'

Hook gave him a conspiratorial smile. 'It is, yes. You don't miss much, do you, Daniel?'

Burrell grinned back at him. 'I try not to. I heard the girls here talking about it. The nurses – that's what they are, most of the time. They call themselves carers, but most of it's nursing, with this lot.' He looked round disapprovingly, obviously not counting himself among the denizens who needed nursing. 'I've got my own telly in my room. I caught it on the Central South news, after I'd heard the girls talking. Was this thing found on my land?'

It hadn't been his land for years now, of course, but he still thought of it as such, which was entirely understandable. When you tended land throughout your working life, it remained yours for ever, in a sense. It bore the results of your labour and your aspirations long after you had left it, sometimes long after you had left this world. Hook nodded. 'It was found at the very edge of your land, yes, Daniel. A complete skeleton, not just the skull. Can you tell us anything about it?'

'No!' He looked suitably aghast at the thought. 'I'd no idea it was there until I heard the news broadcast. I knew it was in my area, but I didn't know it was on my land – not until you two turned up with your questions.' He looked accusingly at Lambert, as if the Chief Superintendent and not he was a suspect here. 'I know bugger all about it. Been there for centuries, I expect.'

'I'm afraid it hadn't, Daniel. The experts are still working on the bones, but we already know that they were put there – buried in a shallow grave, in fact – when you still owned the land.'

Burrell paused for a moment to digest what was clearly highly unwelcome news. 'Well, I had bugger all to do with it. I know nothing about it.'

'You've no idea who this girl might have been? It would be much better to tell us now, if you have. Even if the people who worked with you on the farm prove to have nothing to do with these bones, it would be useful to have your ideas on what might have happened. We think there was a serious crime here, but we know practically nothing, as yet. We're not sure exactly when this woman died. We don't even know her identity yet, but we're pretty sure she was a victim.'

Burrell nodded slowly, staring at his feet. 'I know nothing about this.'

'You had a son, didn't you, Dan?'

'Aye. He had nothing to do with this either.'

Hook let it pass. Had he been questioning more aggressively, he would have pointed out that Burrell had just denied all knowledge of the matter, and that in those circumstances he couldn't rule out anyone who'd been around at the time. But he had decided from the outset that persuasion was going to bring more than confrontation from the spiky old man in the wheelchair. 'How old was your son twenty years ago, Daniel?'

Burrell glared at him, resenting the question but perhaps realizing that it had to be asked. 'He'd be nearly twenty-four then.'

'Married, is he?'

A pause. Then Burrell spoke as if he was surrendering a tooth to them. 'Married and divorced. Living and working in Cheltenham. Having bugger all to do with the farm.'

'I see. But he grew up with you on the farm. Worked

there, I suppose, as a boy and a young man. I expect he knew the ground almost as thoroughly as you did.'

Burrell's lips set sullenly. 'Andrew wasn't interested in the farm. He worked hard at his books and his mother encouraged him. I thought he'd go to agricultural college and then come back with some new ideas for the farm. But he went off and studied history. Started teaching it. That's what he's doing now. Andrew has no interest in farming and the land. I don't see much of him now. He comes and visits me every couple of months, but we don't seem to have much to talk about, since his mother went.'

It compressed a long relationship and a small domestic tragedy into a few words, but it didn't deny Hook's original point, that this son would have known the terrain of the farm well – an important fact if he had needed to dispose of a corpse. Burrell watched the DS make a note in his notebook in his round, unhurried hand, but was not drawn into any further comment. Bert looked up at him, gave him a sympathetic smile and said, 'Not easy, this, is it? But suspicious deaths bring trouble with them. It's inevitable that we have to upset people with our questions, even though most of them prove to be entirely innocent. You must have employed other men at the farm?'

'Not as many as when I started. Tractors took over from horses even before I was around, but we used to have more casuals then. Hedgers and ditchers. And Irishmen who turned up out of nowhere when we cut the hay.' He stared misty-eyed for a moment at the greenery he could see through the window, nostalgic not so much for a vanished agricultural world as for his lost youth and vigour. 'I had one or two who passed through, didn't stay more than a year or two.'

'We'll need the names of any of them who were around at the time when these bones were buried on your land.'

Daniel Burrell nodded. He'd remember those names; he hadn't lost his marbles like so many of the folk in here, had he? He said slowly, 'And then there was Jim Simmons, of course. I trusted him.'

They took the details, which Burrell delivered precisely and without effort. It was as they drove between the carefully cut lawns to the exit of the care home that Lambert said thoughtfully, 'I wonder why he left the most obvious man until the last – it was almost as though he was reluctant to mention him.'

FIVE

In her office at Severn Trent Water in Coventry, Katherine Clark, MBE, glanced at her watch and decided that she had time to make the phone call before her next appointment.

She preferred phone calls to e-mails whenever the matter was important. The personal touch still counted, even when you were delivering admonitions rather than praise. And when you had questions to ask, you put people on the spot when you spoke to them without notice on the phone. They'd no time to think up excuses or fob you off with inadequate explanations, as they often tried to do when answering e-mails.

'Have you found the fault yet?'

'Yes. It was pinpointed an hour ago. We've got the team on it.'

'And when will they complete the repair?'

A pause. The person on the line didn't know, hadn't pressed for that piece of information, hadn't expected to have this harridan on the other end of the phone on a Sunday. 'It's difficult to give a time in the case of repairs like this.'

'Of course it is. But you're speaking now to a senior officer of the company, not some punter who can be fobbed off with pious hopes. How many people are on this so-called team?'

'I'm not quite sure. Four, I think. It's difficult to get hold of the right people and assemble a team, on a Sunday.'

'Of course it is. That's why we pay people good money to be on standby. So that a company of our size and with our reputation solves problems like this one quickly and efficiently.'

The woman on the receiving end of Kate Clark's thoughts was resentful – probably even more so than if it had been a man who was pressing her. 'I've got the men out. They're working on it now. I haven't the technical knowledge to know exactly what they should be doing.'

'And meanwhile three hundred households in Cinderford have no water and have no idea when they'll be able to use their loos or bath their children. Tell your team to get their fingers out and get this thing solved. They work on until the system is fully restored, whenever that is. On into the night, if necessary. They're paid good money for this. Let them know that the good money won't continue without swift and efficient action from them in emergencies like this. What's your name?'

A pause. Kate pictured the woman wondering whether she could refuse, then heard her deep breath as she decided that she couldn't. 'It's Jones. Mrs Jane Jones. And I'm only here because—'

'Thank you. I've made a note of that. I'd like to be able to commend you to others for your prompt action and your diligence in seeing this job carried through, in due course. I trust that I will be able to do that. Goodbye for the present, Mrs Jones.'

Kate Clark put down the phone and smiled at it. She did these things easily now, whereas once she'd had to steel herself to do them. She'd gone through the glass ceiling which was supposed to keep women contained a few years ago: she didn't consider issues of gender any more, except when she was planning her next move up the ladder. The strident calls for more women in the higher echelons of management had come at the right time for her. Big companies like Severn Trent were looking to promote women because they knew that they were under scrutiny and needed to have a certain number of women in top jobs. As a utility plc providing services which had once been publicly owned, they were under closer scrutiny than most.

The time and public sentiment had been right for a woman like her; Kate acknowledged that. But you still had to take advantage of what was offered to you. You might have society pressures working in your favour; you might have the advantage over men of similar abilities; the situation might be the reverse of what it had been for centuries. But you still had to harness these things. You still had to work the system, even though the system was now geared to give you greater rewards. She must be working it well, because she was an MBE already, with a suggestion from those faceless people who controlled the honours system that there was a damehood in prospect if she kept her nose clean and maintained her present rate of progress. Not bad for a woman of forty-three who had come from the background she had.

Kate Clark despised the establishment at the same time as she was manipulating it.

Sometimes, you needed to show that you could be more of a bastard than the average male executive. A breakdown in the water supply, like this one in the Forest of Dean, was the ideal opportunity. No one could really say that you were being too harsh with your juniors when sanitation was involved, when the health of children was at stake. If you were a little too forceful, the convenience and the safety of the public was involved, wasn't it? So your energy and ruthlessness could only be applauded. Thank goodness someone was taking action, people would say. Thank goodness someone cared enough for the public to be kicking arses on a Sunday.

It was a member of the public she had to see now, the head of a pressure group which was trying to gain assurances about the replacement of deteriorating water mains and sewerage pipes in Kidderminster. She had good news to give, which was why she was here on a Sunday. When you can only offer delays and evasions, get one of your deputies to do it: good training for them, surely. When you have good news to give, smile and relax and deliver it graciously yourself. Messengers delivering bad news didn't get shot any more, but they made themselves decidedly unpopular. And correspondingly, those with good news were often welcomed as if they had personally achieved their pleasant tidings.

She'd told her PA that there was no need for her to come in on a Sunday. 'We working women must stick together and I understand your family commitments,' had been her unspoken message. She now ushered Geraint James into her office personally and seated him in her most comfortable armchair. Then she forsook her desk and sat down in another armchair opposite him. 'We're very informal here, whenever we can be,' she said. 'Sorry there are no refreshments, but I didn't feel it fair to bring ancillary staff in on a Sunday. Well,

Mr James, you are a business person as I am, so I am sure that we will understand each other.'

It was unashamed flattery to imply that he was on the same level as she was. James owned a small office supplies business in Kidderminster. He was not in her league and both of them knew it. But she was telling him that they were equals; that both of them understood the sordid world around them and yet were in some mysterious way above it.

Geraint James tried to assert himself against this brisk application of charm. 'I'm here as the representative of a larger group, Ms,Clark. We have made out what we think is a very effective case for refurbishment work to be conducted in our area.'

'It's Kate, please. And I hope I may call you Geraint. No need for formalities between people who are on the same side.' She flashed him a smile which was all the more dazzling for being unexpected. 'You have made out a very effective case indeed. I congratulate you on your presentation. It is at once forceful and free of the distressing gobbledegook which seems to characterize so many of the documents I have to plough through and respond to. I would say, indeed, that it is a model of how such arguments ought to be presented.'

'Thank you. And I appreciate your taking the trouble to make the time to see me during your weekend. But the essential—'

'It is your weekend as well, Geraint. And I am well paid for my efforts, whereas I expect your time today is being offered in a purely voluntary capacity. But let us cut to the chase, as the modern idiom has it. I have good news for you.'

Geraint James had been mustering his resources for an argument against this formidable opponent. He was for a moment lost for words as he was bathed in another dazzling Clark smile. He managed a feeble, 'That will be very welcome to our group.'

'I am able to tell you that new pipelines in Kidderminster have been approved by the board as a matter of urgency. I have pressed hard for a date and I heard yesterday that work will commence at the end of July. That means that the work should be completed in early autumn, well before winter brings the problems which you described so graphically in your excellent request for action. Perhaps you would be good enough to relay to the members of your group our apologies for the trouble caused by pipework and other engineering which are over half a century old. Obviously these date from times long before Severn Trent took over. I'm afraid that the Kidderminster section, whilst adequate in its day, was designed to cater for a scattered rural population and a much smaller demand. That applies to many of our services, sadly. We are undertaking reconstruction all over our area, but of course Rome cannot be built in a day. The fact that your project has achieved priority is down in no small measure to the excellent work you have done in outlining the problem so effectively and bringing it to our attention so forcefully.'

It was a longer speech that Kate had intended, but she could see from Geraint James's face that it was successful. When you had good news to give you might as well make the most of it. And end with a shameless compliment to the man in front of you; so long as the news was good and the praise was lavish, no one was likely to be coldly objective.

James said, 'I shall certainly relay your sentiments to my group. And may I thank you on their behalf for the forceful-ness with which you have pressed our case. I am well aware of your efforts in this matter.'

Kate Clark shook his hand and contrived to look modestly embarrassed by his reception of her news. She knew from previous experience that she was rather good at looking modestly embarrassed. It was a good way of receiving praise without appearing too pleased with yourself. She saw James through the outer office and right to the door of the lift herself, there being no one else around on this bright spring Sunday morning. Never be too grand to show consideration and simple politeness; women were much better than men when it came to things like this. James would tell the men and women in his pressure group how gracious and helpful she had been. When she had risen further, to control the company and become a national name, they would be glad to claim this fleeting contact they had once enjoyed with her.

Kate went thoughtfully back into her office, locked the

door, switched on her computer and inspected the latest internet news. There was no new information on the skeleton which had been unearthed at Brenton Park. No definite date of death had been established and the identity of the corpse had not yet been discovered.

For the moment, she could relax.

The farmhouse was a hundred and eighty years old and built in Cotswold stone, mellow and solid. It was itself a replacement for a much older building on this site. It had been built just before the great agricultural decline of the nineteenth century made such spending impossible. The Corn Laws had had their effects here, ushering in a long period of rural poverty, with minimal profits for the farm owners and starvation wages for those unfortunate enough to work on the land. These stones had witnessed tragedies worthy of Thomas Hardy's pen.

But those sufferings were long gone and long forgotten now. The building, with its mellow stone, would have brought a handsome price as a private residence. But it was still the centre of a working farm, one of the few of its size to survive in Herefordshire. There was wheat shooting up vigorously in the field they had driven past on their way to the ancient cobbled yard. Free-range hens strutted and pecked on the square of green fenced off for them beside the farm. There was no sign of the caravan site which so many farmers had decided represented an easier form of income than working the land. The barn beside the farmhouse no longer housed hay, but it had not yet been converted into 'desirable residences of character'. It housed the tractors and other expensive machinery which many farmers left to take their chance in the open.

Jim Simmons was standing in the doorway by the time Lambert had parked the car. He was a powerfully built man, just under six feet and with the muscles which develop with daily physical work. He had thick brown hair without a trace of grey and wide brown eyes which narrowed a little as he assessed his visitors. 'I knew you'd be coming.' He voiced it as if it were an accusation.

'And now we're here. I'm Chief Superintendent Lambert and this is Detective Sergeant Hook. From the little we know at present, it seems highly probable that we are engaged upon a murder inquiry.'

Simmons nodded calmly. 'It's about the body found in the Jacksons' garden, isn't it?'

Lambert smiled, playing for time for a second or two, trying to weigh up this seemingly very calm man and decide what his attitude might be. 'Yes. The body which was buried on your land.'

Simmons returned his smile. 'Fair enough. I sold that land to Joe Jackson last November. Just a fifth of an acre, to make his garden much bigger. Good business on both sides: it made his plot around the bungalow much more spacious and I was happy with the price he paid me. But I went up there this morning and peeped over his new fence. The spot where that skeleton was dug up was definitely on my ground at the time it was buried.'

'And when was that, Mr Simmons?'

He grinned at them. 'Nice try, Chief Superintendent. I could have incriminated myself there, couldn't I? But only if I'd known the answer, of course. As it is, my reply is that I've no idea. I was going to ask you when and how that gruesome thing got there.'

'"When" is about twenty years ago. "How" is what we're trying to find out now.'

'And I can't help you with either. This shouldn't take long.' He gave them a smile which had little mirth and much challenge.

'You were one of the men on the spot at the time. We haven't so far discovered many of them.'

Before Simmons could react, the door of the room opened and an attractive woman, probably in her mid-thirties, Hook thought, brought in a serving wagon which contained a large pot of tea and home-made scones, butter and jam. 'You shouldn't have bothered,' said Lambert immediately, embarrassed not just by the fact that he had not been asked whether he required refreshment but by the extravagance of what was offered.

'Sunday afternoon,' said the woman with the wagon. 'You're working outside your working week and my husband is being quizzed outside his normal working hours. You both surely deserve a little pampering. I'm Lisa Simmons, by the way, Jim's wife.' A boy of around eight and a girl a couple of years younger tumbled into the room behind her in raucous pursuit, anxious to see who it was who was visiting at this hour of family relaxation. 'And these two are Jamie and Ellie, anxious to view the famous detective and no doubt to impede his progress. Out, please, kids, and take your noise and your toys with you.' The children obeyed, though not before the boy had shaken hands solemnly with John Lambert and the girl had introduced the toy dog she carried to Bert Hook.

'Sorry about that,' said Jim Simmons, looking affectionately at the door his wife had closed securely to prevent further interruption. 'Do help yourself to scones and jam.' He poured milk and tea carefully into the cups his wife had laid out and handed them a little clumsily to his guests. His movements said that he was a man too active to be accustomed to tea and scones in the afternoon.

Hook was much easier than Lambert in this situation. He bit into his scone appreciatively and said, 'How long have you been married, Mr Simmons?'

'Eleven years, now. I can't believe how fast kids grow.' With that entirely conventional sentiment, Simmons too bit into his scone, viewing it and its coating of home-made jam with approval.

This was altogether too cosy for John Lambert, who had not come here to witness pleasant domesticity, but to pursue a serious criminal inquiry. He said tersely, 'Were you in a serious relationship at the time when the corpse of the young woman was buried on your land?'

'It was not my land twenty years ago. I believe that you have already spoken to Daniel Burrell, the man who owned the land and farmed here at that time. I'm sure he was able to tell you more than I shall be able to do.'

So Burrell had rung him. Warned him, in fact. Why had he thought it necessary to do that? As if he read these thoughts, Simmons said, 'He still takes an interest in me, old Daniel. Thinks I need looking after, I expect. Thinks I'm still eighteen, as I was when I first came to work for him twenty-five years ago. I appreciate his concern, even though I learned to look after myself a long time ago. But he was always good to me, was Dan. He had a son of his own, who wasn't interested in farming and took a different course in life. I sometimes felt that I was like another, adopted son, because I took on the role on the farm which he had hoped his son would fulfil.'

'And how did that manifest itself? I suspect that you already know that we visited Mr Burrell in the care home this morning. He told us virtually nothing about you and the way the two of you felt about each other.'

'Did he? Well, that's Dan, I suppose – it doesn't surprise me. He'd let you form your own impressions, let me make my own way with you.' He smiled affectionately. 'I visit him regularly, you know. He still wants to know what goes on here, what changes I am making and whether I think they are successful.'

'Do you own this farm now?'

'Yes. I completed the payments five years ago. Not long before his wife died. Emily was very good to me too. I think she loved me.' He made that daring claim without hesitation, without the embarrassment a sturdy English yeoman should show in declaring such things. He was plainly proud of being close to the Burrells, of being trusted and liked by them. Bert Hook thought he could understand that; having seen and liked the former proprietor of Lower Valley Farm that morning, he could only think that a man who had acquired his trust and friendship must be a man of some quality.

Lambert apparently had no such thoughts. He said bluntly, 'This place must have cost you a lot of money.'

Hook thought Simmons might show the usual British outrage at being questioned about money matters – in his experience, many people were prepared to be surprisingly frank about sex, but regarded finance as sacred and intensely private. But this man spoke almost as though he had been prepared for the question. 'Not as much as you'd think. The farmhouse is tied to the land. It is covenanted as an agricultural residence, so it can't be sold as a private house. And small farms are cheap, because most people think they are on the way out. Salisbury Plain is full of huge factory farms. Herefordshire has a few idiots like me who think that we can still make a living from smaller units.'

Lambert nodded, studying his man closely, looking at him directly and unblinkingly, in that way which often unnerved people who were used to conventional social interchange rather than police interrogation. He had a feeling that Simmons was happy to speak of anything which would divert him from the period when the corpse had been hastily interred on the land which he had been working at the time. He said brusquely, 'Tell us about this place twenty years ago. Tell us about what you were doing then and who else was around these buildings then.'

'The type of farming was not radically different from what I am doing today. The great changes in British agriculture had come about well before then.'

'I don't want a lecture on farming history or modern methods. What I need is the clearest picture you can give me of what was happening in this particular place at that particular time.'

Jim Simmons looked at him steadily, measuring his opponent as clinically as he would have assessed the potential of an acre of land. 'Dan Burrell was emphatically still in charge. You did things his way or you didn't stay around for very long.'

'You must have found that irksome.'

'Not at all. I may have given you the impression that he was a reactionary. If so, I have done him an injustice. Daniel was very aware of tradition and he regarded himself as being in temporary charge of land which had fed people and provided employment for centuries. But he was open to new ideas. He knew that you couldn't hold back progress, even if you found it uncomfortable. He believed that you learned to farm by being in daily touch with the land, but he also sent me off to agricultural college to learn about the wider world and the ideas which were going to shape farming in the next generation.'

'You're saying that he was open to argument?'

Simmons smiled. 'We had a few of those, in our time. You had to choose your moments, with Dan. But if you did and you spoke sense, he would listen.'

Bert Hook said softly, 'And from what you said earlier, Jim, you had Mrs Burrell on your side.'

The farmer glanced sharply at him with this first use of his forename, but raised no objection to it. 'Emily was always good to me. She always wanted me to have the farm, once she realized that her own boy wasn't interested in it.'

Hook nodded. 'Even when you didn't seem the most likely candidate to take over.'

It was an intuitive stroke, the kind of thing he sometimes threw in unexpectedly; it stemmed more from his assessment of the individual in front of him than from any knowledge of the facts of the matter. And it worked on this occasion. Simmons apparently accepted that he had done some previous research, that he knew more than he actually did about the situation in this place twenty years or so ago. 'You're right there. It was Emily who made me feel that I could take this place on, who made me feel that I could organize myself and organize the finance and the labour I needed to take over this place from Daniel and make it a going concern. It took her at least ten years to do that.'

'Because no one would have thought that you had that in you when you first came here, would they, Jim?'

'No, they wouldn't, and least of all me.'

'So tell us about those early years, Jim.'

Simmons looked at the two CID faces opposite him, the senior one grave and suspicious, the other expectant and encouraging. He wondered quite how he had got here, how he seemed now almost to be volunteering this account of himself as a young man which he would have preferred to keep hidden. 'I was a bit wild, in those years. I was surprised Dan kept me on, at times.'

'But you had Emily on your side. I suppose she spoke up for you, at critical moments.'

'I'm sure she did. Neither she nor Dan acknowledged it, but I'm sure that it was Emily who kept me here, on one or two occasions. I'm not sure I'd keep a youngster on now, if he did some of the things I did then.'

'Drugs?'

'Yes. I was never in any danger of becoming an addict – I

hadn't the money, apart from anything else. But I dabbled and experimented, in the way stupid young men did and still do. One or two mornings I didn't turn up on time for work. One or two others I wasn't fit for work when I got there. You can't have that kind of thing on a farm.'

'Or anywhere else, Jim. People don't keep their jobs for long, if they're doing drugs.'

He nodded. 'I can see that. I only know farming.'

'No doubt you got into fights as well.'

Simmons smiled grimly. 'One or two. A few bloodied noses and hurt pride. Nothing that got me into trouble with you lot.'

Bert returned his smile. 'No. We check criminal records before we speak to people, whenever we can. I expect there were girls as well.' He didn't mention boys or men. You had to ask about those as well in most situations nowadays. For the moment, he'd ignore that, in view of the reason why they were here and the evidence of a happy marriage which they'd glimpsed earlier.

Simmons gave a brief nervous smile and snatched a glance at the door his wife had shut so firmly behind her. 'There were, yes. I'd been in a care home from twelve to sixteen. I was still finding my way with girls when I came here.'

Bert Hook was around the same age as the man he was questioning. But he felt almost avuncular as he said, 'I was a Barnardo's boy myself, Jim. I worked it out through sport rather than drugs. But I wasn't much good with girls, for a long time.'

Confession often prompted confession, in the right circumstances. It did that here. Simmons said, 'I did all right with the girls. It didn't do me much good. I got myself into a few scrapes with women. I tended to pick the easy ones rather than the ones who were best for me, when I was a young man. I was lucky to end up with Lisa.'

Hook nodded. 'And I was lucky to end up with my Eleanor. There's an awful lot of luck in these things.' He glanced at Lambert, but found that his chief was content to let him play his patient game. 'We think this mystery girl who was killed and buried here at that time was a drug user, Jim.'

'I knew nothing about her.' His features were suddenly set in stone.

'With respect, you don't know that, Jim. You don't know who she was, any more than we do at the moment. And you've just indicated that you associated with a variety of girls at that time in your life.'

He smiled bitterly. 'I like that term. "Associated with". I took them to bed, whenever I could. No, that's not correct. Most of them didn't make it to bed. Most of them were up against a wall, or in the woods, in the summer.'

'All this sounds pretty turbulent. You must have had arguments with some of them. Must have fallen out quite seriously, at times, I should think.'

'I had a few rows, yes. Girls don't take kindly to being ditched, do they? And I didn't even know how to be tactful, in those days. I was a bastard at times. I'm sure I deserved the names they called me and the slaps across the face I got from time to time.'

'And no doubt you retaliated also, from time to time. No doubt you hit back, as an impulsive young man.'

'No! I never laid hands on a woman. I got out as fast as I could when they turned nasty, but I never hit back. Not with girls.'

'Not even with a girl who was hooked on drugs? They can be very irrational, girls like that. Quite unreasonable.'

'Look, I know what you're about here because you've virtually told me. I didn't kill a druggie or any other girl. And if I had, I wouldn't have buried her here. Don't shit on your own doorstep. That's the expression, isn't it?'

Lambert came in now as he heard the man's voice rising. He said calmly, 'You might have had no alternative, if you wished to dispose of a body quickly. If you hadn't meant to kill her but had hit her a little too hard with a blunt instrument, for example. In those circumstances, you'd have had to conceal the remains as swiftly as possible, which would probably have meant locally. The furthest point of the farmland might have seemed to you an excellent place to dispose of a corpse. After all, it's taken around twenty years to expose the skeleton, and it might well have taken much longer.'

Jim Simmons nodded slowly, accepting the logic of this.

Then his face brightened. 'But if I'd buried a body there, I wouldn't have sold the land on, would I?'

'Probably not. But our information is that you'd sold two other plots for handsome sums before you sold the neighbouring plot to the Jacksons, who were the last people to move in at the end of the building development. It would have been difficult to refuse what Joe Jackson was offering you for a fifth of an acre of pasture land, wouldn't it? Everyone knew the sum was far more than the land was worth to you. And you'd already sold two similar plots for less than what Joe was offering. You couldn't have refused his offer without exciting suspicion, which was the last thing you would have wished to do. And had those bones been lying just a fraction deeper, they would never have been disturbed. It was only because a young man was doing very enthusiastic double digging that he turned up the skull. You could say that you were very unlucky.'

'No! You could say that the person who put that body there was very unlucky. I had nothing to do with that death and nothing to do with that burial.'

Lambert stared at him for five long seconds, assessing the man as much as his statement. Then he said tersely, 'Very well. You will understand that we cannot simply accept what you say at face value, in these circumstances. We need to establish the innocence of everyone who was around here at that time. We shall know many more details of the death in the next few days, and we may then need to question you again, Mr Simmons. In the meantime, we need the names from you of other people who were regularly around this farm twenty years or so ago. Particularly young men or women who might have associated with a girl who was around your age at that time.'

'There aren't any. Not that I can pinpoint for you. I'm no longer in touch with anyone who was around here at that time. My life has changed and so has theirs. They're not around here any more.'

'Nevertheless, we need to contact them and eliminate them from this inquiry. Give some thought to the matter, please. You will see that it is very much in your own interest to give us the names of people who may have been around then and who left the area shortly afterwards. They may have had good reason to leave quickly. Just as you have good reason to recall them and everything you can remember about them and deliver it to us. Here is my card. Ring this number at any time and someone will take the details of whatever you are able to tell us. Good day to you, Mr Simmons.'

It was Hook who drove the police Focus carefully down the track to the farm entrance and the lane beyond it. He had a sense that Lambert was planning to say something, but he had too much experience of the man to hurry him. The Chief Superintendent was too old now to change his ways, too respected by his team to be hurried.

Eventually John Lambert said unexpectedly, 'What did you think of the tea and the scones?'

'I thought they were excellent. And more welcome for being unexpected.'

'And carefully arranged. The man was showing us what a paragon of family life he is, with his pretty wife and his attractive children. It didn't take you long to burrow into his wilder past, Bert – congratulations on your technique. It makes me wonder exactly what it is that Jim Simmons is trying to hide from us.'

SIX

'I 'm sixty-eight now.'

Very few women announced that information. Occasionally people who considered themselves very old boasted about their age and the miracle of their survival; otherwise, women in particular preferred to conceal their years.

CID officers are normally expert in assessing ages. It is something which becomes second nature to them as they gather experience. Lambert would have put the age of this woman as a good ten years older than sixty-eight. If her statement was correct, she'd probably lived a difficult life.

It was Detective Sergeant Ruth David who had brought her into Lambert's office, and she wouldn't have done that without good reason. Ruth David said, 'It's in connection with the Brenton Park case, sir. Mrs Grimshaw thinks she may be able to help us towards an identification of the human remains discovered there.'

Lambert glanced from one to the other of the two very different female faces in front of him, which were united by their earnest appreciation of something of huge import. He said, 'I'd like you to stay for this, DS David.' Ruth's dark hair was cut short and was glossy black, in contrast with the unkempt wisps of grey-white hair which peeped out from beneath the hat of the woman who now sat down opposite Lambert. DS David's smooth oval face was very different from the lined and troubled one beside her.

Not many women wore hats nowadays, and still fewer donned them to come into a police station. This one was scarcely more than a beret, but John Lambert realized suddenly that the woman had made an attempt to present herself at her best to come here. The action was mistaken, but there was something very touching about it. He said gently, 'How can I help you, Mrs Grimshaw?'

'You can give me closure. You can confirm for me that this was my girl. That this was my daughter.'

The accent was unexpectedly educated. That was prejudice, Lambert realized. Why should you expect that someone down at heel and life-battered would be uneducated? Police experience, he supposed. The majority of people who were questioned here, who peopled the nation's prisons, hadn't had much education, nor had they enjoyed an even chance in life. But the police function was to see that the laws of the land were observed, not to campaign for social reform. And this woman might be no more than a crank; that possibility was far more important than any speculation about her background or her position in the community. 'What reason have you to think that this dead woman might have been your daughter, Mrs Grimshaw?'

'I know it. I feel it in my bones.'

He thought of those other bones, the ones he had seen being patiently assembled on the plastic sheet at the edge of the Jacksons' garden, and he flinched at the thought of what lay ahead for this suffering woman. 'What is your daughter's name, Mrs Grimshaw?' Always speak in the present tense, until you are sure of the corpse's identity. That was the rule. Those bones on the plastic sheet might yet have no connection with this woman. Her daughter might be living and breathing, in a different county or a different country.

'I'm Anne. Or Annie. I'd prefer that you call me that. And my daughter was Julie.' She was using the past tense against his use of the present; it was the reverse of the usual situation.

'All right, Annie. I realize that this must be very stressful for you. When did you last see Julie?'

'Twenty-two years ago. Twenty-two years and seven weeks, come tomorrow.' She smiled sadly in recognition of her accuracy.

'We don't think this girl has been in the ground for quite as long as that. Around twenty years, the experts think.'

It was meant as a comfort, a suggestion that this might not be her daughter after all. But Annie Grimshaw merely nodded her acceptance. 'That's right. I hadn't seen Julie for around

two years before she disappeared completely. I'd had occasional messages from her, every month or so; enough to let
us know that she was still alive. Then they stopped.'

'She went missing?'

'That's right. We registered her as a missing person. Mispers,
you call them, don't you?'

'Yes. Her details would have been entered on to the police
computer, along with those of the thousands of other people
who disappear from their homes each year.'

'Very little chance of locating her unless she chose to turn
up herself. She was an adult and could leave home if she
pleased to do that. That's what they told us, and that's how it
proved.' She spoke without apparent resentment. Perhaps the
years had dulled her reactions, and with them her capacity for
fury at the system's apparent indifference to human tragedy.

Lambert said gently, 'Who is "we", Annie?'

'My husband and I.' She looked suddenly surprised, as if
she had shocked herself with an unexpected and quite inappropriate joke. 'That sounds like the Queen, doesn't it? "My
husband and I." I was speaking of Paul, who used to be my
husband. We aren't together any more. We split up ten years
ago. Apparently it often happens, when you lose a child in
the way we lost Julie.' She spoke like one observing someone
else, as if the heartbreak had left her dry and barren long ago
now.

Lambert glanced at Ruth David and gave her the tiniest of
nods. She registered the signal: she should press on into this
vanished tragedy, to try to ascertain whether it had any relevance to the case on which they were engaged. His DS said,
'Where were you living when Julie left you, Annie?'

'In Birmingham. In Solihull. That's where we lived, in those
days.'

'And why do you think Julie might have ended up down
here? It's almost a hundred miles away, isn't it?' Her voice
was gentle, persuasive, understanding. Intensely feminine, a
contrast to Lambert's equally sympathetic but much deeper
tones.

'She was in a squat, in Gloucester. There for a year, we
think. She'd been in other places, before that. It took us a long

time to trace her, and by the time we found out, she'd disappeared again. Moved on, we thought. But now we know that she hadn't. Not this time. She'd . . .' The words ran out, just as she was convinced her daughter's life had run out at this point. They thought she might break down and weep, but the sharp agony of grief had died long ago, and the tears did not come.

'You think she was dead? That she'd been killed by person or persons unknown and buried where she was found last week?' Ruth David spoke as softly as she could, but there was no way of disguising the stark questions she had to ask and the pictures they evoked.

'Yes. I didn't know someone had killed her. Not until I heard the announcement on the radio and it said that foul play was suspected. But it makes sense. She was living in squats and she was on drugs. I don't know if she was an addict because she'd ceased all communication with us by then. But you meet odd people in squats, don't you? The attempts to make contact all came from us and they – they weren't successful.'

DS David said, 'We don't know that your daughter is dead, Annie. This may be a different girl entirely.' But she was catching conviction from the insistence of the shattered woman in front of her. The skeleton had been a drug user; they knew that. And she had been killed at around the time when a desperate couple had lost all contact with their vanished daughter.

Annie Grimshaw said, 'This is Julie that you've found. I've hoped for long enough that she will come back to me. She isn't going to do that. I want closure.'

It was her repetition of that phrase which made Ruth David say, 'Have you had counselling, Annie?'

A nod and a wry, raw smile. 'I've had counselling. Two or three times, over the years. How can they comfort anyone who's lost an adult child, unless they've lost one themselves? Even now, I wouldn't know what to say to anyone else who was going through it. I felt sorry for the last woman who was sent to see me. I ended up saying the things she wanted to hear, so that she could think she'd been useful to me.'

'Would you be willing to give us a DNA sample? It's quite a simple procedure and it would enable us to—'

'Yes. Tell me what to do and I'll do it. I want this over as quickly as possible.'

Lambert left David to take the saliva sample and went out quickly to consult with DI Rushton. The DI confirmed that routine DNA samples had already been taken from the remains retrieved from Brenton Park. This was done automatically and quickly, not just to provide samples for comparison and eventual identification, but to confirm that only one body had been put in that ground near the edge of the farm twenty years ago.

They brought Annie Grimshaw a mug of strong police tea; they wanted to make it heavily sugared, as convention dictated it should be, but Mrs Grimshaw refused all sweeteners and grimaced a little at the strength of her steaming drink. Ruth tried hard to make conversation with her, but she responded only with monosyllables and eventually asked to be left alone. They left her in an interview room, the only place where they could ensure privacy. She sat alone in that claustrophobic box, sipping her tea as she contemplated the blank green wall and what her life had come to.

Meanwhile, the forensic girl in the lab had been working frantically on the samples and came up with a match. It was Lambert who took this finding back to the desperate woman in the slightly ridiculous hat. Ruth David went with him, wanting to put her arm round Annie Grimshaw but knowing that police protocol dictated that there should be no physical contact.

Mrs Grimshaw looked up at them, reading what she had always known was the truth in their faces. 'It's Julie, isn't it?'

'I'm very sorry to have to tell you that it seems it is, Mrs Grimshaw. We have a match between the samples.'

'Don't be sorry, Mr Lambert. I knew it from the moment I heard the news on the radio. It will give me closure.' She repeated the phrase as if she had fallen upon some mantra which offered her consolation.

Lambert hoped indeed that it would. He couldn't think of what he could say to her now. He knew he mustn't offer counselling, and any of the other services seemed inappropriate or inadequate. He said, 'How did you get here today? I'm sure we can arrange transport to take you—'

'A friend brought me. She's gone to visit her daughter. I'm to ring her when I've finished here.' She fumbled in her bag, produced a mobile phone and stared at it as if seeing it for the first time. 'They're good, these things, aren't they? Very useful on occasions like this.'

'Very useful, yes.'

He hoped she was going to leave them quickly, and felt a coward because of that hope. She half-rose, then sank back on to her seat in front of the square table. 'Can I see her?'

'I don't think that would be a very good idea, Annie. Not in these circumstances.'

The old, jaded face set as stubbornly as a child's. 'I want to see her. I'm entitled, aren't I?'

'Entitled, perhaps, Annie, but believe me, this isn't a good idea. Your daughter's remains have been in the ground for a long time, for twenty years or more. This isn't the daughter you remember, with flesh and blood and a smile on her face. You'd be much better to—'

'I want to see her, all the same. I need to see her.'

'She isn't here, Mrs Grimshaw.' It was ridiculous, but he needed to say it: the woman was behaving as though those bones were in the next room.

'Of course she isn't. And it doesn't have to be today. But I need to see her. I don't need anyone else with me and I won't do any screaming and shouting. But I need to see her and say goodbye to her.'

It was two days before she saw the skull and the bones which went with it. They could dress up a normal corpse and make it look better, sometimes amazingly better. But they couldn't do anything with a skeleton. All along the line, people tried to persuade Mrs Grimshaw that she should not do this. But she was persistent and implacable, and in the end she had her way. And after a first sharp gasp, she was still and calm. She spent two minutes in contemplation of all that remained of her daughter Julie.

Annie Grimshaw had her closure.

* * *

Michael Wallington studied himself for a moment in front of the full-length mirror in the bedroom. The blue suit had been a good choice, he decided. It had been Debbie's choice rather than his; he always went for colours which were a little too bright. But this suit set off his dark hair and blue eyes rather well. The tie worked, too. A lighter blue, with widely spaced small diamonds of red. Discreet but not dull against his immaculate white shirt. Marks and Spencer, that was, and new for the occasion.

He presented himself for his wife's inspection, happy because he knew that she would approve. He was lucky to have Debbie, as he told himself at least once a week. She dextrously transferred the clean handkerchief from his top pocket to his side one. 'Too showy for tonight,' she explained. 'And much too conventional for a man who has made himself Chief Education Officer at forty-six.'

'Only in a small town. Only because I worked hard and kept my nose clean.' He spoke the words he had spoken many times before, enunciating them now to his wife as though rehearsing them for a more important occasion. But you didn't really make your way like that. You did work hard, and you were as able as the rest, though perhaps with a greater grasp of the possibilities of certain situations. But the really important thing was to have a greater degree of ruthlessness than the rest.

Debbie, sweet, innocent Debbie, was still preparing him for the evening to come. She was still preoccupied with the handkerchief she had removed from its flamboyant display in his breast pocket. 'You mustn't look like a man who is trying to draw attention to himself. You don't need to do that any more.'

'No. I shall be cruising among parents tonight. Trying to give them the impression that their kids – sorry, children – are in the best possible school with the best possible teachers making the best possible progress in the best of all possible worlds. Whereas in fact their little darlings—'

'Forget the facts. Always forget the facts when you can't do anything about them. You told me that.'

'Did I? What a fount of wisdom I am! That must be why

I got the job. That and my ability to sell myself as a local education Messiah possessed of all the answers.'

'You really do have most of the answers Mike. You're nothing like as cynical as you present yourself.'

But he didn't present himself like that at all, and he knew it. Not to the public. He mouthed all the correct and conventional education maxims, even when they were quite different from last year's magic formulas. When he'd begun his personal education odyssey, older education gurus were still talking about integrating the children of immigrants into the English way of life. Nowadays you had to be enthusiastically multi-cultural; the safe thing was to be a zealot for variety. Variety in dress, in religion, in cultural inheritance. Well, so be it. No use swimming against the tide, or against any other of the clichés which passed for enlightened thinking.

Michael Wallington, Chief Education Officer, must be at the forefront of progress.

He was greeted as a VIP at the parents' evening at the comprehensive which was the most important school in his largely rural area of responsibility. He was becoming used to this status now and he found it rather enjoyable. People deferred unthinkingly to your ideas, where they would once have argued. He pretended to find that frustrating, but it was really rather pleasant and undemanding. He found that the 'undemanding' was increasingly to his taste. There were enough problems in his office each day, with the economies imposed upon him by the idiocies of local councillors, without looking for them elsewhere.

He gave a brisk opening address to the group of parents impatiently waiting to quiz the teachers who were lined up behind him: the headmaster, his deputy head and the senior teaching staff. They were all in this together, he told everyone. They were steering young people on the ship of education through the rough waters of teenagedom and into the even rougher and more challenging waters of adolescence. Teachers needed their support and understanding. (It always paid to keep in with the staff whom you directed and appointed and occasionally disciplined. You needed them on your side. The poor sods who slaved at the chalk face were the foundation of all this.)

His audience applauded dutifully – some of them, Michael thought, even enthusiastically. Those would be the naive and enthusiastic parents who were attending one of these sessions for the first time. There were probably even one or two young teachers here who believed in his dynamism and in the creed he advocated. That wouldn't last long: experience in education brought cynicism, in his view. His own was a healthy cynicism, of course, the kind which asked questions to ensure that ratepayers and governments got value for money from the funds they poured in.

Some of the teachers developed a scepticism which questioned everything and achieved nothing. It would be better for all if these people left the profession and ceased to damage the young with their defeatist philosophy. Michael Wallington expressed that view forcefully in other places, such as council committees, where teachers or their union representatives were not present. His contributions there maintained his reputation for honesty and realism and ensured that he would go far. Local greybeards nodded in agreement, whilst he smiled modestly and shrugged his elegantly suited shoulders, in that gesture which acknowledged that whatever would be would be.

When the initial speeches of welcome were over, he circulated and smiled among the parents and teachers. He was delighted to hear one parent say how gratifying it was to see the Chief Education Officer here and taking an interest on an occasion like this, and to see others nodding their sage affirmation of that view. He spoke to the deputy head, a fifty-five-year-old woman with whom he had started his teaching career in a much smaller school, a professional for whom he retained a lasting respect. She was conscientious, efficient and absolutely honest. She was in fact the kind of practitioner who made him feel a little shabby as he played the system and made his way towards the top. Yet he told himself that he would make life better and more rewarding for teachers like Barbara Moss, once he had satisfied his ambition and was in control of a large authority.

Barbara retained an affection for the man whom she had assisted through the trials of his probationary year as a new teacher. Tonight she took him on one side and they discussed how they might rid themselves of a particularly lazy and inefficient teacher. 'He's letting down his colleagues,' Barbara said. 'They're the ones who have to cover for him every time he calls in sick when he isn't sick at all.'

'You know the problem,' said Michael. 'You've been around a lot longer than I have, Barbara. Unless this fellow touches little boys or the dinner money, it's very difficult to get rid of him.'

She nodded a reluctant agreement. 'And meanwhile the school's reputation and the children he deals with suffer. It's the kids who lose out at the end of all this. We can't give him examination classes, which means that the younger children he gets are missing out on the groundwork they should be building. And the unions spring into action to defend anyone who's a member, irrespective of their efficiency. They mouth off about standards and then defend people like him who don't have them.'

'I know. Look, you know the form better than most, Barbara. Document everything you can, give him a formal warning when it's warranted and then pass all the evidence on to me. Then the next time that he steps out of line or we get a formal complaint from a parent, I'll have him in to the education office in the town hall and give him an official bollocking. I'll suggest he considers a different career. I'll even push him towards early retirement, if all else fails.'

'He's thick-skinned as well as idle. You won't find it easy to embarrass him.'

'No, and I can't promise anything. But I'll have a go. I'm quite used to dealing with the thick-skinned and the idle. And I'm quite a good bluffer. If I can convince him that we're contemplating a serious attempt to sack him, he might take the easier option to avoid the publicity and the disgrace. I'll do my best.'

Barbara Moss went home from the parent–teachers' evening with her spirits a little lifted. She'd called in a favour from the man whom she had helped through his first year in teaching, called upon the man who was now a high flyer to do his bit for the classroom he had left far behind. And for his part, Michael Wallington too felt himself unexpectedly lifted by the exchange. He wasn't all cynicism and self-promotion, after all. He was still doing his bit for the children and the people who slaved away at the chalk face.

He had a quick word with the headmaster, who thanked him profusely for his attendance at the evening 'above and beyond the call of duty'. Then he slipped quietly out of the school. The evening would go on for a good ninety minutes yet, but the seventy-five minutes he had stayed seemed quite long enough to the new Chief Education Officer. He had seen and been seen, and the occasion had no more to offer him. Away home to his family then, and a little belated attention for his wife and his children.

He had his hand on the door of the BMW when he heard behind him first the footsteps and then the voice. 'We need to talk.'

He turned and peered at the face beneath the hood. 'I don't think so.'

'Oh, but we do.'

'Whatever we had to say to each other was said a long time ago.' He flung open the door of his car, then felt the urgent fingers upon his arm.

'They've got an identification. Her mother has been in to Oldford police station. She's spoken to that John Lambert, the one the papers call the "super-sleuth". She's been to the morgue. Viewed what's left. Said it's Julie. We need to talk, mate.'

Michael grimaced at that word mouthed in the darkness, which was dropping in early beneath the heavily clouded skies. He glanced like a hunted man to his right and his left in the school car park. 'Where?'

'We'll go to the pub. You can buy me a drink.'

A snigger beneath the hood, a reminder to Michael of how much he had disliked this man, how much he had needed to shake him off. 'Not here. I can't be seen with you here. It will have to be the Coach and Horses.'

It was a run-down pub in the town centre. It was almost

two centuries since it had been the coaching inn which had given it its name. Nowadays, it was a gathering place for the human detritus which accumulated around any industrial centre. Wallington told the man he had hoped he would never see again to sit in the back of the BMW. He drove as if he had been plunged into the centre of a very bad dream. Thirteen tense and silent minutes later, they left the car and slid like conspirators into the small, shabby room beside the main bar of the Coach and Horses.

Michael Wallington forgot about his family and began a conversation which he had persuaded himself he would never need to have.

SEVEN

Andrew Burrell was a very different man from his father. Even at the age of eighty-four and in the care home, Daniel Burrell had looked like a man used to hard physical labour, a man who had worked outdoors and lived willingly with the land and the seasons which visited it.

Andrew Burrell looked on the other hand like a man who lived by his brain, who worked indoors and would be scarcely conscious of what the weather was doing outside. He had narrow shoulders and a long, thin body which draped itself naturally into the armchair he chose to sit in for this exchange. He said, 'I'm happy to see you and give whatever help I can. But I can't even think what this would be about.'

Lambert looked at him sceptically, happily letting the tension stretch with the seconds, allowing the man to see how flabby this first reaction must appear in these circumstances. Finally he said, 'Really, Mr Burrell? I find that hard to believe. You have surely read about the skeleton which was discovered near the boundary of what was once your father's farm. The papers have been filled with the news of this discovery over the last few days.'

'I don't give much attention to the popular press. I find it unreliable and sensationalist.'

'As do most policemen, Mr Burrell. But it is difficult to be unaware of it. Are you claiming not to have heard about the discovery of these bones?'

'No. I am well aware of it. I have heard about it on both radio and television.'

'But you didn't expect that anyone would come to talk to you about it?'

'I hadn't given the matter much thought, to tell you the truth.'

'Do tell us the truth, Mr Burrell. It will make things much simpler for all of us. For instance, I find it very difficult to believe that you have not been giving this matter quite intense thought in the last twenty-four hours.'

Andrew stretched his long legs out in front of him and studied his slip-on brown shoes, anxious to give them the impression that he felt no tension. He glanced at the unthreatening face of Bert Hook and said rather dismissively, 'We academics tend to live in ivory towers, I'm afraid. It's one of the dangers of the intellectual life.'

They were sitting in his ground-floor tutorial room, one of the most spacious in the new block which linked the university library and its largest lecture theatre. Lambert was already irritated by this pretentious man. He looked out at the students calling to each other on the neighbouring path and at the largely industrial landscape beyond them. 'It's hardly the dreaming spires, though, is it?'

'The University of Gloucester has its advantages, Chief Superintendent. They might not be immediately apparent to busy policemen.'

'Not to me, perhaps. DS Hook has a degree which is at least the equivalent of your own, Mr Burrell. He would be able to offer a more informed opinion than I can.'

Andrew Burrell drew in his feet and folded his arms. He was shaken by what this tall CID man had said about the colleague who looked to him like PC Plod, but he didn't think it was a joke; neither of these two large men was smiling. He said stiffly, 'You're right, as a matter of fact. I have given the matter of your skeleton some thought over the last day or two.'

'More your skeleton than ours,' said Bert Hook thoughtfully. 'You were around at the time when that body was buried. I'd have been giving intense thought to those bones myself, if I'd been in your place.'

'But you surely can't think that I have anything to do with this, whoever the man might be.'

The introduction of the sex of the corpse was a mistake. It was so obviously contrived that its awkwardness lingered as the policemen let the words die in the quiet room. Then Hook said, 'You will need to convince us of that, sir. You will understand that, in what is now a murder investigation, we cannot accept anyone's word at face value.' He produced a ball-pen and a notebook, which he opened at a new page with obvious relish.

'And why should I have anything at all to do with this?'

Lambert was already tired of his evasions. 'Because you were around at the time of this death and interment, Mr Burrell. Because you very possibly had a connection with this murdered woman.'

Burrell started elaborately at the first mention of a female victim. 'This was a woman? The bulletins spoke only of a skeleton. I had assumed that it was a man – possibly a vagrant.'

'And why should you think that, sir? Had you an identity in mind for this vagrant? Someone you had seen around the farm or on your father's land, perhaps?'

'No. No, I don't know why I thought that. I – I suppose I hadn't given the matter much rational thought at all.'

'It seems not, sir. Let me now help you to be more rational. We have an identity for these remains. We now know that these bones are those of a Julie Grimshaw.'

Another, smaller start. Less theatrical, more genuine. Lambert thought that this strange man was possibly really shocked by this information. And frightened by it, maybe. It was possible that he had been fearing just this name. 'You knew this person, sir.' He made it a statement, rather than a question. 'She was a young woman when you were a young man, Mr Burrell. Almost certainly at the time when you were living at Lower Valley Farm. You would be most unwise to deny that you knew her unless that is in fact the case.'

All the confidence Burrell had exuded when they arrived, all the derision he had accorded to them as mere policemen in this place of learning, were suddenly gone. He ran a hand swiftly through his carefully parted yellow hair and looked hard at the carpet between him and his visitors, as if he feared now to meet their gaze and reveal what he felt in his heart. 'I knew Julie Grimshaw, yes.'

Probably his physical appearance derived from the mother who was now dead. He could scarcely have looked more different from the sturdy octogenarian they had spoken with in the care home two days ago. Almost as though he was sharing this line of thought with them, he said now, 'I wasn't

born until my parents were almost forty. They were in their
sixties by the time I knew Julie.'

Lambert studied the pale, drawn face for a few seconds
before he said, 'And what is the relevance of that to what you
are going to tell us now?'

Burrell glanced up at that, but he didn't query the assump-
tion that he was going to tell them things about Julie Grimshaw.
'There isn't much relevance, I suppose, really. I just felt that
if they had been younger they might have understood things
a little better. I'm probably wrong. I don't think Dad would
have behaved any differently if he'd been ten or even twenty
years younger. And Mum wasn't unreasonable about it. Not
really, when I look back on it. Now that I've got kids of my
own, I can understand how she felt and some of the things
she said to me. My twins are only nine years old, but you
want to protect them, don't you? I can understand now how
Mum and Dad felt about Julie.'

Lambert wondered whether the man was brandishing his
own children as a badge of respectability. He said tersely,
'You're divorced, aren't you, Mr Burrell?'

'Yes. I can't see that my divorce has anything to do with
this.'

'Neither can I, at the moment. But we like to know everything we can about people involved in a murder investigation.
You'd be surprised how often bits of people's private lives
suddenly suggest things to us.'

'My divorce had nothing to do with Julie Grimshaw.'

'I see. Well, you appear to be suggesting to us that you've
long since left behind the life you were living twenty years
ago. We need you now to revisit it and tell us all about it.'

'I'm forty-four now. I wasn't exactly a kid twenty years
ago, was I?'

'So how does that affect what you are now going to tell us?'

'It doesn't. I'm just saying that I wasn't a helpless adolescent
when my parents were trying to control my life.' A little of
the resentment of events long gone crept into the thin, pale,
too-revealing face.

Lambert said with his first sign of real impatience, 'Tell us
about your dealings with Miss Grimshaw, please. And take

care to leave nothing out. We shall be talking to other people who knew her at that time, as you would anticipate. It would be most unwise of you to attempt to conceal anything.'

Andrew Burrell's arms were no longer folded. He lifted them a little, then let his hands drop heavily back on to his thighs. 'This is all a long time ago now. It feels like part of another life.' He looked for a moment into John Lambert's implacable face. 'I expect you often hear people saying things like that.'

'We do. But they are usually able to recall that other life quite vividly.'

He nodded slowly, accepting what Lambert said rather than resisting it. 'Perhaps I should tell you what I know about Julie first, and then go on to outline what I felt about her.' He sounded as though he was planning his approach to an article in an academic journal.

'Do that. And while doing so, remember that as yet we know almost nothing about Miss Grimshaw, beyond the very little her mother has been able to give us.'

'I never knew Julie's mother. I can't recall her ever speaking of her mother.' He sighed and glanced at Hook and his open notebook, then spoke in a low, even voice. 'Julie was living in a squat in Gloucester when I first encountered her. When I look back now, I feel that gave her a certain grisly glamour for me. It wasn't very long after Fred and Rose West had been exposed. The details of their killings of drifters like Julie had become public and were much discussed in the area. I expect I felt that I was rescuing Julie from that dangerous sort of life; when you're twenty-three or twenty-four, you still think you can rescue people from moral and physical danger. I might even have been doing that, I suppose.'

'Except that in the end this girl wasn't protected or rescued. She was killed and hastily buried in a shallow grave. Not so very different from many of the Wests' victims, wouldn't you say?' Lambert spoke harshly, hoping to provoke some significant reaction.

'No, I suppose not. You must remember that I've only just heard about this. I'm still in shock. I'm still coming to terms with it.'

'Unless, of course, you knew all about it and are merely simulating surprise. It's a possibility we have to consider, Mr Burrell. CID officers are paid to be suspicious about what they hear. In the next few days, someone who knows all about how Julie Grimshaw died is going to tell us a pack of lies. If we can establish that you are not that person, it will help us as well as you.'

Apparently Burrell accepted their logic. He clasped his hands together and nodded twice, though still he could not bring himself to meet the gaze of either of them for longer than a couple of seconds. He said in a low voice, 'I met Julie in a pub in Gloucester.'

'Were you in search of illegal drugs at the time?'

'No! That's a ridiculous suggestion.'

'On the contrary, it's an entirely reasonable query. We know from the forensic reports on her remains that Miss Grimshaw had been a serious user in the months before her death. I can tell you that we are not interested in charging you with drugs offences from twenty or more years ago, even if we could assemble the evidence to do that. We are concerned only with the person or persons who killed her and buried her at Lower Valley Farm, where you were living at the time.'

'I dabbled a little with drugs. Most people did at the time. When you're young, you're curious and often rather stupid. It was mostly pot, but a little coke from time to time. I was never a dependent user. I never came close to being an addict.'

'And what about Julie Grimshaw?'

'Julie was a user. I thought she was in danger of becoming an addict. That was one of her attractions for me, I suppose. She was two years younger than me when I first knew her and I thought I could save her from dependency. When you're twenty-three, you think that the world is there for the taking and that you can work miracles.'

'Was she your girl friend?'

He looked as if he would like to deny it for a moment, then gave the slightest shrug of his shoulders, as if recognizing that he had no choice now in the matter. 'I made a date with her in the pub that night. Within a couple of weeks, I took her home with me to meet Mum. I was quite close to Mum, you know. I thought she'd understand. I thought she'd support me against Dad, if it came to it.'

'What was your relationship with your father at this time?'

He studied his fingers, watching them twine and untwine as if someone else was in control of them. 'Strained. That is the politest word I can think of. He'd sent me off to agricultural college and hoped I'd come back full of ideas and thrilled with the prospect of taking over the farm – he was planning to transfer responsibility gradually to me over the next few years. I came back knowing that farming wasn't for me and determined to pursue a different sort of degree and a different sort of career.'

'And your father didn't take kindly to that?'

For the first time in minutes, Burrell looked into the long, lined face of John Lambert. 'Dad was in his early sixties by this time. It must have come as a great disappointment to him to find his only son turning aside from the family inheritance. And when you're not much more than twenty yourself, you're not very sensitive to older people's feelings. Perhaps that's especially so when they're close family: your own emotions prevent you from thinking as clearly and as sensitively with family as you would do with others at a greater distance from you.'

Andrew Burrell spoke with feeling and a note of appeal. He really wanted to convince them of this, to make them see the way it had been at that time for him and for his parents. It was essentially a selfish thrust which was driving him. He felt in danger here, with these two experienced men studying him so dispassionately and weighing his every reaction to their questions.

Lambert now nodded his apparent acceptance of Burrell's latest thoughts and insisted, 'Our concern is with justice for Julie Grimshaw. Tell us how the situation in your home affected your dealings with her, please.'

'Dealings.' Andrew weighed the word and found it distasteful, but did not reject it. 'For my parents, Julie was just another sign that I was going off the rails. They found out about the drugs and thought she was a junkie. She wasn't – she was a user and I thought she was in danger of becoming dependent, but she hadn't got to that stage. I wanted to rescue her from dependence and bring her back to live a normal life with me. I can see now that the missionary aspect added to my zeal in the relationship. I didn't see that at the time.'

'Were you lovers?'

A bitter smile settled upon the wide, pale lips. 'Yes. She was a very attractive girl. I should have told you that at the start, I suppose. She was even more attractive when she wasn't taking horse. I think it was because I saw that, because I saw what she had been and might still be, that I was so attracted to her. I thought I wanted to marry her, at the time.'

'But your parents didn't want that. What did they do to prevent it?'

He shrugged. 'Everything they could, as far as I can remember. Dad wouldn't listen to any of my arguments. Mum wasn't quite as bad as that. I think she understood some of my feelings and sympathized with my motives, but her main concern was to safeguard her only son. Now that I have kids of my own, I can understand that. Mum thought it was all very well offering comfort to lost souls, but she drew the line against setting one up with her son. And she was even more terrified of drugs than Dad was. She was fearful that Julie would drag me down with her into that world.'

'So what happened?'

'I made the mistake of taking Julie to the farm when she'd just injected. It was obvious she was drugged and abnormal, even to someone as innocent as Mum. Julie behaved badly. She couldn't sit at the table properly and she spilled her tea. She said stupid things. Mum and Dad said they didn't want her in the house again and forbade me to associate with her. I said that I was over twenty-one and I could do as I liked. Not in their house I couldn't, Dad said. It was the usual kind of family row, I suppose, but when you're in the middle of it, it seems worse than that. I got myself a place on a history degree at Liverpool University and left the area. I hardly visited Lower Valley Farm after that; I came home for the odd weekend and for a week or so during the summer holidays. I made my peace with Mum before she died and patched things up with Dad. I wouldn't say it's any better than that

– we still treat each other like strangers when I visit him in the care home.'

Bert Hook looked up from his notes. 'I need to ask you this and to record your reply. Did you kill Julie Grimshaw?'

Burrell seemed neither surprised nor outraged by the question. It was almost as if he had prepared himself for it. He said quietly, almost formally, 'No. I had nothing to do with her disappearance or her death.'

'And have you any thoughts on who might have killed her?'

'No. She simply disappeared. I feared something might have happened to her, but assumed that if it had it would have been after she had left us. I think I assumed at first that she'd moved on to get away from me.'

'But the place where the body was found implies a connection with Lower Valley Farm and the people who were in the area at that time.'

'Yes, I can see that. That is why it was such a shock to me to hear that a body had been found there.'

'When did you last see Julie Grimshaw, Mr Burrell?'

A long pause. Then a weary 'Does it matter?'

'It does to us, Andrew. And it does to you, if you wish to see her killer apprehended. We need to establish a time of death. Then we shall interview anyone who was around and close to her at that time.'

He nodded, a long strand of yellow hair falling over his left eye. 'I couldn't be precise. She disappeared, as I said. I went into Gloucester to look for her, thinking she might have gone back to the squat. I couldn't find her. After a month, I accepted that she'd gone and wasn't going to come back.'

Hook was in his persuasive, understanding mode now. His gentle tones suggested that it would be far easier and healthier to tell him everything you knew than to attempt to deceive him. 'How could you be certain of that, Andrew? Squats are strange, enclosed places. They don't welcome outsiders. How could you be certain that she wasn't somewhere in this underworld labyrinth, that she wasn't just refusing to see you or to have any further dealings with you?'

The blue eyes looked hard at Hook, then glanced for a moment at the watchful Lambert. Burrell looked in that moment like a hunted man, wondering how much he could get away with before these two observant, experienced men. He decided that he had better be honest in this at least. 'I told you I was doing drugs a little at this time. I got my coke in the form of rocks from a dealer in Gloucester. I saw him, bought from him, and then asked him about Julie. I knew that he'd been trying to make a dealer of her – offering to deliver her own supplies to her free, so long as she sold whatever he chose to allocate to her. It's how they get new dealers, and for Julie it would have been another step along the road to addiction. But I expect you know that.'

'And was this man able to tell you where she'd gone?'

'No. He convinced me that she wasn't still around, though. He said that she'd left the squat without saying anything to the people there. In fact, she'd apparently not taken away even the few pathetic things she possessed. Her coat was still there, he said. Nothing else – anything of any value would have been snatched up by the others in the squat – but I don't think Julie had much. I didn't go into the squat myself. They're not safe places for those who don't live there.'

'What was the name of the man who sold you drugs and was trying to recruit Julie to become a dealer?'

'I don't know. I never knew. You didn't ask for names, if you knew what was good for you.'

Burrell looked drained. This venture into the past he thought he had left for ever had left him physically shaken. Hook allowed him a few seconds of respite before he said, 'Can you give us the names of any other people who were in the squat at that time? We shall obviously make every effort to contact them and question them. We have means at our disposal to discover the present whereabouts of people who have long since moved on to other places and to other modes of life.'

Andrew Burrell shook his head miserably. Then, unexpectedly, he said in a low voice, 'There was Kathy, of course. I never found out her second name. People in squats don't care for anyone who pries.' He smiled grimly at the recollection, then said suddenly, 'It might have been Clark. I think I heard Julie call her Kathy Clark. But I couldn't be certain. And a lot of people in squats didn't use their own names anyway.'

'You said, "There was Kathy, of course" as if this was someone you knew quite well, whereas you can't identify for us any of the other members of that squat. Can you explain yourself, please?'

Another pause, then a sad shake of the head. 'She was a friend of Julie's – not that you could have normal friends, when you were in the squat and on drugs, as I think both of them were at the time. Kathy came along with Julie when I first dated her – I suppose that was a sort of insurance. I didn't see her much after that, but Julie Grimshaw often spoke of her. It was Kathy who came out of the squat and told me that Julie had left without speaking to her. and without taking her belongings. I've no idea where Kathy is now, or even whether she's alive.'

Hook made a note of the name, then stared hard into the anxious face. 'We've had to drag this information out of you, haven't we? Exactly what else are you concealing, Andrew?'

'Nothing. I've told you everything now.'

'What was the state of your relationship with Julie Grimshaw when you last saw her?'

This time it was Burrell who paused, recognizing the seriousness of the query and the response he would make to it. 'We knew by then that we weren't long-term. I was still keen on her, but she'd rejected the idea of marriage as ridiculous and she said that any protracted relationship was impossible. The way my parents felt didn't help that.'

'It seems odd that you didn't make further efforts to trace her when you found she'd disappeared from the area. It's almost as if you knew that she had in fact disappeared from this earth.'

Burrell gave a little gasp, but didn't rush into any denials. He said only, 'No, that isn't true. I realized that our relationship had run its course. I went off to Liverpool and completed the degree I'd always wanted to do and began another life.' He lifted his hands palms upwards and then dropped them again, as if he wished to indicate the academic world in which he now existed and cite it in his favour.

'Who else do you know who was close to her in the weeks before her death?'

He shook his head hopelessly. 'There were the people in the squat with her. But I didn't know them. And there was Jim Simmons. He knew her.' His lips set for a moment in a tight line, but he said nothing further about the man who now controlled the farm which had once been destined for him. And he offered them no other names. 'That time seems to me now like part of another life, as I said. I can remember Julie vividly, but not much else. I suppose I've spent most of the time since then opening the door on a new life and closing the door on that one.'

Andrew Burrell sat very still for what seemed to him a long time after his CID visitors had gone, staring unseeingly at the telephone number on the card John Lambert had left with him. Then he opened the top drawer of his desk and extracted a pile of student essays. He began reading them resolutely, writing the occasional comment vigorously into the margins. He strove hard to concentrate, forcing himself back into this world which was now his real place, and away from that world where a girl no older than many of his students had died twenty years ago.

EIGHT

Steve Williams was anxious. He didn't let anyone know that. It wasn't his way and it would have been bad strategy to acknowledge to anyone that he had anything to fear. But as the days dragged past, he felt more on edge than he had done for many years. He thought that he had perhaps lost his capacity to deal with danger; he would never have been as tense as this in the old days.

The fact that he was sixty-six now didn't help, he supposed. The police had come to the house within thirty-six hours of the skeleton being discovered. Just a couple of uniforms, doing the standard house-to-house stuff. Nothing to be worried about there, just the expected questions. Did he or Hazel remember anything about a young woman around these parts twenty years ago? They'd had a son at that time, hadn't they? A lad who must have been about the same age as the girl who had died.

The uniforms, one male and one female, had been young and studiously polite. He'd explained to them about Liam being killed in a road accident and being no longer with them. He told them that it would be better if they stuck with him and didn't question the boy's mother. He could tell them everything they wanted to know, answer all the standard questions they had on their sheet, and it would upset his wife terribly if she had to talk about Liam to them. She'd never really accepted that he'd gone, you see, not completely. Liam's room was still preserved as a shrine, with the same posters of footballers and sports cars he'd stuck on the walls before he'd gone out and been killed in the accident. Hazel didn't allow anyone else in there to clean: even he had to tiptoe around and touch nothing, on the rare occasions when he insisted on going into the room.

The plods had been very understanding. They'd nodded sympathetically and made a note of the date of Liam's death.

They'd put a series of ticks and crosses on their sheets, added notes to two of Steve's replies and said that they were sure they had everything they needed. It might be that more senior officers would need to come and speak to him in a day or two, but that would depend on how the investigation progressed and what information they gathered from other sources. Just following normal routine, the plods assured him at least three times.

It was two days now since they'd told him that and nothing had happened. It was the very absence of action which was making him nervous. Steve Williams was a man used to controlling his own life, to dictating to others what would happen in the coming days. He didn't like being passive and waiting for things to happen at the behest of others.

Moreover, he knew quite a lot about police procedures. He knew that there would be furious activity in the days following the discovery of that skeleton two hundred yards from his door. There was nothing in the papers or on the television beyond the initial statement about the discovery of remains and the fact that it was being treated as a suspicious death. But the fuzz would be like swans, cruising about with their feet working frantically under the water. There were lots of things going on; all kinds of information was being gathered, and none of it was available to him. Steve didn't like that.

On Wednesday morning, he took the dog out again. Dogs always made you look innocent: he'd realized that years ago. Especially if you took your polythene bag with you as a poop scoop and behaved like a responsible citizen. There was no better badge of respectability than a dog. Not a pit bull, of course. Even he didn't approve of pit bulls and still less of the young thugs at the other end of their chains.

But Ben was a Labrador. Always cheerful and everyone's friend. Mischievous, of course, and likely to mount anything in sight on one of his energetic days, but people quite liked that. The dog-lovers in the woods and on the sports ground where Steve walked him liked Ben, anyway. They were a tolerant and long-suffering lot, dog-lovers, with a good sense of humour where canines were involved. An unsuspicious, mainly elderly, group, who exchanged harmless thoughts about the weather and the latest inanities of celebrities and politicians. Lately, of course, they'd swapped thoughts about the sensational discovery of the skeleton beyond the edge of the sports ground. Steve had listened to whatever they had said, but he hadn't picked up any more information about what the police were doing at present. It was all speculation, and less informed speculation than he would have been able to offer himself, if he had chosen to comment on the matter.

He put Ben on the lead and took his leave of his fellow dog-walkers. The way home took him past the spot where the bones had been discovered. He walked as close as he could to it and looked across at it for a moment. The ribbons and screens which denoted a scene of crime were still there, but he doubted whether much was going on behind them this morning. The police and the pathologist would have reassembled the skeleton during the hours after the discovery at the weekend. He had no doubt that they would have recovered almost everything, but he didn't know how much they would have been able to discover from things which had been hidden from the world for twenty years. It was that uncertainty which disturbed him.

They had a lot of resources, the police; more than he'd ever been able to employ, even in his heyday. They operated on a wider front than he had done, of course, so they needed those resources. But they weren't inefficient, as a lot of the criminal fraternity chose to think they were. It didn't pay to underestimate the pigs. He knew a lot of people who'd done that and were now locked away.

The filth gave it everything when they got their teeth into a murder. It was a matter of professional pride to them that fewer murders went unsolved in Britain than anywhere else in the world. An increasing number of gangland killings went undetected, as you'd expect. But the police, although they wouldn't say so, weren't too worried about those. That was villains killing villains, as far as the filth were concerned, and leaving that many fewer bad buggers in the world.

This wasn't one of those deaths. They'd be on the case in a big way, sniffing hard after scents which had long gone cold. Steve wondered what success they were having and found his ignorance disturbing. He shifted his cap a little on his bald head, tugged Ben away from the fence and went back to his house.

Hazel was finishing the breakfast washing up, setting the dishes carefully on the drainer in the pattern she always followed. He gave her his ritual, 'You should have left that for me. I have time for these things, now that I'm retired.'

'Semi-retired, you said.'

He smiled at her. 'I have to keep one hand on the tiller. You wouldn't like it if the money stopped coming in. But there's no reason why we shouldn't take holidays, now. You only have to say the word and we'll be away. This country or abroad, it's your choice. The world is your oyster. You only have to speak.'

'I don't want to go away. Any more than I want to move house. I've told you that often enough.'

'It might be good for you to get away. I'm sure you'd enjoy it, once you'd made the effort. You used to enjoy holidays, in the old days.'

The old days. They were skirting round Liam, as they always did. He didn't know whether Hazel wanted that, or whether she just didn't want to talk about it with him. He didn't know a lot of things about her nowadays. It was true what they said, those anonymous and annoying millions who made up 'they'. Money didn't necessarily bring happiness. Perhaps he didn't deserve happiness. But he'd never accepted that what you deserved had much to do with what you did in this life.

He watched Hazel hang up her apron, then went across to her impulsively and stood close behind her. She stood still and stared ahead of her, awaiting his next move. He slid his arms gently around her waist, stroking the top of her stomach, feeling against his body the curves which had excited him as a young man. He kissed the top of her head softly and whispered into her ear, 'It would do us good to get away from here for a while, my love.'

She detached his hands from her waist and said firmly, without turning to look at him, 'I don't want that.'

He said impulsively and unwisely, 'I can get other women, you know.'

She didn't turn to look at him as she said, 'I know that. You always could. You always did.' Then she went out of the kitchen and shut the door behind her.

He hadn't known that she'd been aware of those things when he'd done them. It was the first time that she had ever acknowledged that she'd known. But of course she'd known: she wasn't stupid, Hazel. He realized suddenly how much he wanted her to love him. And in the same instant, he realized that she was now never going to do that.

He went into the room which he called his study and tried to read the newspaper. He had a phone in here, but he let Hazel answer in the sitting room when it rang. He could hear her calm, unemotional tones, but not the words she said. She came and spoke to him through the open door of his study, without entering the room.

The police now knew the identity of the skeleton they'd dug up at the weekend. The man in charge of the case would like to speak to Mr Williams. He would come here with another officer at two thirty this afternoon.

'Our Customer Services Director will see you in two minutes. The cancellation of an appointment has left her with a fifteen-minute gap in her schedule. You are fortunate to be able to see her at such short notice, Detective Inspector Rushton.'

The PA stared disapprovingly at the handsome, dark-haired policeman with the document case in his hands. Disapproval was part of her job. She built up the status of her boss by being the dragon at the desk in the ante-room outside her office, a formidable sentry guarding the entrance to that holy of holies. She was more zealous than she had ever been about this aspect of her work, because Ms Katherine Clark was a woman, the first female boss she had ever had. The sorority must stick together; men underestimated abler women like Katherine, so anything her PA could do to compensate for that must be done.

She eyed the soberly clad policeman with an automatic disapproval. It was a good thing he had at least come here in plain clothes: it wouldn't do to have policemen marching about the place in uniform and sparking off all sorts of speculation.

He had his job to do, she supposed, but she couldn't think what possible business he could have with a board member of Severn Trent. Meanwhile, he should be made properly aware of how privileged he was to gain such a swift audience with a senior executive of one of the great national utility firms.

Kate Clark welcomed Rushton with a warm smile, reserving her position, ready to turn on the charm with a man perhaps ten years younger than her if that seemed the best tactic. This was probably some police inquiry into the conduct of a company employee. She would sacrifice him – or her – if they were junior and unimportant. If this was about the misdeed of a more senior employee, she might need to exercise her full diplomatic skills to plead for leniency. In the complex power games which were played out behind the doors of the boardroom, it never did you any harm to have senior colleagues owing you favours.

Kate gave him a broad, frank smile and threw out her hand. 'Detective Inspector Rushton, I believe. And I'm Kate Clark. No time for coffee, I'm afraid: you've been pushed into a very small window in my day, in the interests of urgency. Now what can I do for you? Is this the peccadillo of one of our many hundreds of employees? Not speeding, I'm sure, because that wouldn't warrant the presence in my office of as senior an officer as yourself.'

'No. It's not speeding. Nor driving without licence and insurance. We should be taking direct action against the individual in the case of traffic offences. But I'm CID, not traffic.'

She caught his slight wince of discomfort that she should consider it a possibility that he might be traffic and said, 'Of course. A senior CID officer implies something much more serious, though I find it difficult to see how I might be the person to help you. But of course I shall do whatever I can. If this concerns some offence by a senior colleague, I can assure you that we speak here in strict confidence. Anything you say will not be repeated outside these four walls without your approval.'

'We wish this to go no further, at this stage. That is why I have come here in person to speak to you.' Chris Rushton had been determined not to be overawed by authority, but he found himself speaking stiffly and formally. Despite his resolve he was awed by the easy manner of this attractive, supremely confident and successful woman.

Kate glanced at her watch. 'We had better get on with this,' she said briskly.

Rushton was much more at home with briskness than with charm. 'This concerns you, Ms Clark. And I should say at the outset that you are not accused of any crime.'

'It's Kate. And that's a relief.' Her smile gave him the full benefit of some very expensive dental work. It also masked her first twinge of apprehension.

'This is nothing to do with the past few weeks or even the past few months. I'm here to enquire about your whereabouts in 1995.'

She'd been preparing to sit down opposite him in the comfortable armchairs which dominated one end of the large room. Now she sat down abruptly behind her desk with the window behind her. 'That cannot possibly be of interest to you. I was not engaged in any criminal activity.'

Chris's assurance increased with the decline of hers. 'No one has so far suggested that you might have been. But we are investigating what we now know is a very serious crime. We need your cooperation.'

'I've already offered that. What is it you want of me?'

'Last Saturday, a skeleton was discovered in a shallow grave in Herefordshire. You may have read about that.'

Kate was sure that her face had gone white. She hoped that with the light behind her he wouldn't see that. 'I don't read about crime in the papers. I'm too busy, for one thing. And the details sometimes upset me. But I heard the police bulletins on the radio when I was in my car.'

Rushton nodded. 'We now know that this woman died about twenty years ago. It's our job to find out exactly how she died. To do that, we need to discover as much as we can about the life she lived in the weeks immediately before her death. We think you may be able to assist us with that.'

'And what makes you think so?' She felt like an actress in a bad play, without any key lines herself, merely speaking a series of cues to prompt action from others.

'Can you tell me where you were twenty years ago, Ms Clark?'

She wasn't calling upon him to address her as Kate any more. She was floundering, wondering if there was a way to escape from this, to handle it without compromising her present exalted position in the firm. 'Twenty years ago isn't easy to recall at the drop of a hat, DI Rushton.'

'Allow me to help you, then. Were you at or around that time living in a squat in Gloucester?'

A significant pause, whilst Kate thought furiously of her options and decided that there was no easy way out of this. 'I might have been, I suppose.'

'Our information is that you were in a derelict house in Fairfax Street in the city at that time.'

She wondered furiously where their information had come from. But there was no future in that. She said quietly, 'You agreed earlier that this would be confidential. Can I rely on that assurance?'

Rushton allowed himself his only tiny smile of their meeting. 'I think it was your assurance, rather than mine. But yes, all our enquiries are conducted in confidence. Unless of course you should eventually be called as a witness in a court of law, when things would obviously be outside our control.'

He rather enjoyed that addendum, feeling himself reversing dominance with this powerful, confident woman. For her part, Kate was trying not to show the very real fear she now felt. 'I admit that I was in the place you mentioned for a short period at around that time. So where do we go from here?'

'The man in charge of what is now a murder inquiry is Chief Superintendent John Lambert. He will wish to interview you with a colleague of his within the next two days. You may wish to suggest where that interview might take place.'

She took the card with Lambert's number, promised to ring him during the next few hours. Whenever she could fit the call in with her busy schedule, she said.

DI Rushton let that little piece of vanity go. Kate Clark might need all the trappings of authority she could muster, in the weeks to come.

*   *   *

You didn't let the police into your house without showing resentment. Steve Williams had spent his life fighting the filth. That wasn't going to end now, merely because he was sixty-six and finished with most of the things which had divided them. He made his ritual protest as he led them into his large and well-fitted sitting room. 'This feels like persecution. I had nothing to do with that skeleton. I've already told your wooden-tops that.'

They were old foes, he and John Lambert, though they hadn't crossed swords for many years now. 'If you'd no connection with this death, then you've nothing to fear. You'll be treated like other, more innocent, members of the public. The law says we have to do that, whatever our private feelings might be. Unlike you and the people you employ, we have to abide by the law.'

'Used to employ, John. Those times have gone. I'm retired. As you should be by now. I know you must be around ten years younger than me, but coppers retire early on fat pensions. Bastards like you should be piling shit on your roses.'

It was the first time in his life he had used his opponent's forename. Both of them noted it; both of them determined to show no reaction. Lambert said sourly, 'Until the Brenton Park estate was built, you were the nearest householder to the spot where this body was found. Of course you're going to be investigated. Even someone without your record would be asked the questions we are going to ask you.'

Williams waved a hand at the largest of the sofas and adjusted the alignment of an armchair carefully so that it directly faced them. He had so far given no more than a single glance at Hook. He knew him too from way back; they had tangled when he had been dishing out beatings and Bert had been a raw young constable. But he was not going to acknowledge that. Bert studied him objectively and with no embarrassment. CID officers have no need for the conventions and niceties which people are accustomed to in their normal social exchanges.

Hook saw a man who was ageing but still vigorous. Williams was almost completely bald now. He had lost the use of one eye after a brawl conducted in his twenties, but you would scarcely have known that without studying his face very closely, which not many people were bold enough to do. He was broad-shouldered and powerful, but now carried a paunch which had not troubled him in his younger days.

At this point, there was the noise of a slight movement in the room above their heads, which all of them heard but chose to ignore, save for swift glances at the ceiling from the policemen. Steve said roughly, 'You'd better ask your damned questions and get out of here. Leave innocent folk to get on with their quiet lives.'

Bert Hook flicked open his notebook without taking his eyes off the big man's face. 'Did you know a young woman called Julie Grimshaw?'

'Yes. Shapely young tart, she was, twenty years ago. Wouldn't have minded an hour or two between the sheets with her, if I'd had the chance.'

He was being deliberately offensive and they all knew it. This was an answer he had prepared and considered long before they came here. 'And did you get that chance?'

A smile which degenerated quickly into a leer. 'No. These young girls don't want to know the things an experienced man could teach them, do they? And you know me: I was far too much of a gentleman to force my attentions upon her, wasn't I?'

'We have reason to think Miss Grimshaw was on drugs at the time of her death. What can you tell us about that?'

'Bugger all. I was never into drugs and never wanted to be. You know that.'

It was true. Prostitution and loan-sharking had been Williams's main sources of income, in the days when he had operated chains of pimps and lenders in three counties. Hook said, 'You'd have had access to drugs, if you'd wanted them. You could have provided her with whatever she wanted, if you'd chosen to do that.'

'That is a wicked accusation. You are fortunate that I choose not to take it up. I shall be tolerant with you, for old times' sake.'

He was playing games with them. Safe games. He was on firm ground here, because he hadn't ever been accused of dealing in drugs. He'd never been convicted of anything in court, in fact, though every CID officer in Gloucestershire, Herefordshire and Somerset knew that Steve Williams was a villain. Hook watched him carefully as he said, 'So you knew her. Did she come to this house?'

Williams looked round the room he had used for thirty-three years as if he was seeing it for the first time. 'Yes, she did. A few times, I think. She ceased coming here rather abruptly, as far as I can remember. I've no idea why. Well, I hadn't, until you walked in here today and told me that someone had killed the poor bitch.'

'And why did she come here?'

'Think I had designs on her, do you? Would I have brought her into my own house if I had? Don't shit on your own doorstep, DS Hook. That's as true now as it was then. You should remember it, if you're planning a crafty shag on the side.'

Hook was annoyingly unresponsive. He made a note of Williams's reply. His face betrayed not a flicker of emotion.

It was Lambert who now said tersely, 'The girl was on drugs. She was vulnerable. She was the kind of female you used to recruit to work in your brothels. You liked vulnerable girls.'

'Piss off, Lambert! I had nothing to do with Julie Grimshaw. And I've no idea what you're trying to pin on me when you mention brothels.'

The barefaced lies were usually the best, he'd always found. They took people aback and most of them didn't know how to react. But these weren't fellow villains. These were CID, used to dealing with lies, barefaced or otherwise. Lambert regarded him steadily. 'It's difficult to accept the word of a man with your record. I'm sure you realize that. We may need to speak to your wife about this.'

'You're not speaking to Hazel! She's not well. She's not fit to be badgered by coppers.'

Lambert continued as if the big man in the armchair had never spoken. 'We may need to check what Mrs Williams remembers about Julie Grimshaw. People's recollections are sometimes very different, twenty years on. Even those of people with nothing to hide. And you're giving me the distinct impression that you have something to hide.'

That wasn't true. It was just that you automatically exploited any sign of weakness in an enemy, and he certainly listed Williams as an enemy. He doubted at this moment whether the man had anything to do with this death, but he would check that out thoroughly before he accepted his innocence. And he wasn't going to make any concessions to Steve Williams. They looked challengingly at each other across the ten feet or so which separated them and he saw with some satisfaction fear and hatred in the one good eye of his opponent.

John Lambert knew he couldn't force an interview with Hazel Williams. As far as the law of the land went, these were good citizens who were helping the police voluntarily with their investigation. He didn't want to accuse a disturbed woman of obstructing the police in the course of their enquiries, but he would certainly do so at a later stage in this strange case if it became necessary. He said quietly, 'You had a son living in this house twenty years ago. A son who must have been about the same age as Julie Grimshaw.'

'Yes.' For the first time since he had brought them in here, Williams was edgy rather than truculent. 'Liam had nothing to do with this.'

'But we can't speak to him. He's no longer around.' Lambert's tone had softened a little, for the first time.

'Liam was killed in a traffic accident eight years ago. RTIs, you call them, don't you? There's no such thing as an accident, as far as the filth are concerned.'

'I'm sorry you lost your son, Williams. But I need to know about his relationship with Julie Grimshaw.'

'He knew her. Same as he knew lots of other girls.'

'But he brought her here.'

'Same as he did lots of other girls. There was nothing special about Julie Grimshaw.' He was tight-lipped, determined to be unemotional.

'Are you sure of that?'

'Quite sure. Liam had lots of girls. Too many, to my mind. But I was probably the same, at his age.'

'If Liam was here now, do you think he'd be able to help us to find out exactly how this girl died?'

Williams looked with open hostility at Lambert, hating the question but knowing he must answer it. He would have lied unthinkingly and automatically on Liam's behalf if he had been alive and in the next room. For some reason he would never to be able to explain, Steve found it more difficult with the boy no longer here. Liam would have been forty-one now, but his father could never picture him as more than the thirty-three he'd been when he'd killed himself on the road a mile from here. For most of the time, he remembered him as a young, irresponsible, attractive lad, the age he'd been when Julie Grimshaw was around. That wasn't helping Steve now. He said carefully, 'Liam knocked around in a crowd, a group of lads and a group of girls. Julie Grimshaw was one of the girls.'

'Was he getting drugs from her?'

'No. Liam wasn't a user.' He was furious and he wanted to say more, but he didn't trust himself with words. Not on this.

And Lambert, who wanted to press him, knew that he wasn't going to get any further today. They told him ominously and unsmilingly that they would be back. They treated him as they left as a known criminal who had frustrated them over many years, rather than as the grieving father he had been for the last few minutes.

They didn't know it, but Liam Williams's room had been the one immediately above the door of the solid red-brick house. As Hook reversed the police Mondeo, Lambert glanced up at the window of that room. He saw the white face of a permanently grieving woman, watching them depart.

NINE

J im Simmons told himself that he was luckier than most people involved in the case. He worked on the land. He could use the eternal rhythms of weather, seasons and soil to sooth the fears he felt over what was happening around him.

The cornfield was doing well this year. Green was dominant still, but he fancied he could see the first tinges of gold as the low early-morning sun shone almost horizontally on the slope of the land. The small herd of cows was proving a success, despite the pessimists who had said you needed huge herds or nothing. The Herefords were looking healthy and there was enough growth in the pasture now to keep them amply supplied without the need for expensive feeding supplements. The milk yield had increased over the last two weeks. Hopefully the negotiators would screw a decent milk price from the supermarkets in their present meetings, and make dairy cattle less of a suicide venture for the small farmer. The cows mooed at him as they saw him standing there; their udders were full as they assembled outside the milk parlour for the evening milking.

It was in the twilight that he walked out alone to look at the place where the skeleton of Julie Grimshaw had been found. That was over the fence at the end of his pasture field, the poorest land on the farm. Old Joe Jackson, the man who had bought the land from him to add to his small garden, had put up a fence, but not a high one, to mark the new boundary of his garden plot. The scene-of-crime tapes and the screens which had masked that sinister square of ground were gone now. The spot looked once again quite innocent – like the newly dug vegetable plot it had been intended for, in fact. He wondered if old Joe would feel like growing stuff there now, after what had happened. Jim decided that he wouldn't feel like planting cabbages there himself, in view of what had been dug up from that ground when Joe had begun to work it.

Jim Simmons couldn't see Joe Jackson using that land if he wouldn't himself. Jim had been brought up to work the land, to get used to it containing all sorts of things, both useful and unpleasant. It was only soil, after all. In fact the man who had taught him most of what he knew, Daniel Burrell, would have said with a grin that rotted human remains would have made the soil all the richer, all the more likely to produce excellent vegetables. Jim smiled at the memory of old Dan and his sturdy common sense. He could hear Burrell's voice now, telling him that he'd received a good price for a small, almost useless patch of land, and that this finding merely proved that he was well rid of it.

Simmons frowned as he gazed at the place where the skeleton had been found, wondering for just a moment whether Daniel Burrell could possibly have known anything about how those bones had got there. But old Dan surely wasn't that sort of fellow. Jim wondered how much they would talk about the skeleton when he next visited Dan in the care home. Then he shook his head and turned away, walking slowly and with a sudden weariness back to the farm and Lisa, and to Jamie and Ellie and that other, more innocent world in which children lived.

Kate Clark, MBE, was more shaken than she cared to admit by her short meeting with Detective Inspector Rushton. She had a good relationship with her PA and she often swapped irreverent thoughts with her about the people who had come to see her, but on this occasion she said nothing.

She had a full day before the meeting she had arranged by phone with Chief Superintendent Lambert. Usually time fled from her all too quickly, but these hours seemed to drag by in a long series of anxieties as she wondered what they would ask her, how she should respond and how much she could afford to conceal. She was used to exchanging ideas. She enjoyed challenging herself, whether it was with senior colleagues, more junior employees or members of the public. She was pretty good with people, she thought, and exchanges normally stimulated her and made her work and her life interesting. But she could talk to no one about this. She was alone with her thoughts, with her guilt, and with her speculations about how much the police knew and how much they would have to know.

Harry Purcell was coming to her place tonight. They usually managed one night each week with each other and they tried whenever possible to alternate their venues. They were both divorced, both wary of the commitment of a second marriage. They were moving closer together, but they were quite a way yet from even living together. Kate felt that; she wasn't quite sure how Harry felt.

Harry had tried to push things on when they'd met at his place last week. She'd said, 'It's working well as it is. Let's just leave it to take its course. Give it another few months – until the autumn, say – and then we'll review it. Meanwhile, we've both got busy lives and we're both ambitious. This friendship should help us along, not get in our way.'

He'd accepted her logic, or appeared to accept it. Kate had been flattered by his desire to get closer to her. She wished she'd told him that, once she was back here with time to reflect upon the matter. Men needed reassurance, didn't they? Especially men who'd been hurt once, as Harry had. She didn't know how much the failure of his marriage had wounded him, how deep were the scars it had left behind. That was the kind of thing you discovered when you lived with someone, she supposed. She was finding that she didn't know quite as much about life and its workings as she knew about business.

Now, when her thoughts were full of the police and what they might or might not already know, she almost cancelled Harry's visit. It would be easy enough: she could say that she had to be away for some business meeting that had been arranged at short notice. But she didn't like lying to Harry. That was surely a good thing, wasn't it? A sign that there was mileage in their relationship? When he rang her on her mobile at four o'clock to check that tonight was still on, as he usually did, she told him that it was and that she was looking forward to it. She spoke quite formally; even though they were both on their private phones, she was never convinced that only he could hear her. She never breathed sweet nothings or sexual encouragements on the phone, even in response to the outrageous things Harry Purcell sometimes said.

It was a strange evening. She didn't want to tell him about the police and that erected a barrier between them. Couples all had their secrets; all people kept some things strictly to themselves. But her fear of the coming police visit was so great and so immediate that she felt guilty concealing it. Their conversation during the evening seemed to her stilted, though Harry didn't seem to notice anything unusual. There were rumours of an American takeover of his company, and he spent quite a long time talking about that. Asking her advice, in fact, which Kate supposed was flattering. He was very much dominated by his work and his worries about it. They were two of a kind really, she thought wryly.

The sex was good, as it always was. She forgot about the police and gave everything to it, in her usual way. She was quite abandoned in bed, screaming out her pleasure, ordering him to do things violently (which she knew he was going to do anyway), flinging out the four-letter words of command which she never used elsewhere. She wondered sometimes whether she used sex as a counterbalance to the rest of her life, to the rational decisions and the rational accounts of them which occupied most of her days. It was the only time in her life when she enjoyed being subject to anyone else, when she enjoyed pleasuring a man and indulging his every physical whim.

Harry Purcell loved it. Perhaps even loved her, Kate thought, as he lay panting with his head upon her breasts. She stroked his head gently as her spirit crept unwillingly back into the real world. She'd been lost in her own wild, scatological demands, but she was pretty sure that he'd said somewhere in the early stages that he loved her. That was surely a good thing. Yet she didn't welcome it. Not now, when the problems she had cast aside were reasserting themselves.

Harry had to leave early in the morning. She was glad of that. She knew she wouldn't have been good at conversation over the breakfast table, with the day she had to face. He left after hurried toast and coffee, taking with him her assurance that they would meet at his place as usual next week. She wondered as he left what her position with the police would be by then, what the next seven days might have in store for her.

She had a meeting in Oxford at ten thirty. She was as usual well prepared for it, but she went over her papers again before getting into the car. It was a good thing that she had this meeting to occupy her, she told herself unconvincingly, as she fought her way through the Oxford traffic to the venue. It would keep her thoughts off the interview with the police in the afternoon, prevent her from going over and over the same ground that she had covered so thoroughly yesterday.

The meeting followed its agenda and was from her point of view quite straightforward. She made a few contributions, rather more muted than usual. Then, more quickly than she wanted to be, she was driving the Mercedes coupé back along the A40 and into Gloucestershire. She stopped first for lunch at a small place she'd used before in Burford. The food was good and the owner was friendly but didn't insist on making conversation whilst you were trying to eat and rest.

Today the woman was more attentive than usual. 'You're sure that all you want is soup and a roll? We have some tasty sandwiches. Baguettes, if you prefer them; most people seem to, nowadays.' And then when Kate replied in monosyllables and forced a smile, she said, 'You look very pale today. Not sickening for something, are you?'

Kate was back in her flat in Tewkesbury long before the police were due. Give yourself plenty of time to get ready for any important meeting: that was her policy. Except that for this one there was no agenda, so how did you set about preparing yourself? Two thirty, they were due to arrive. She wasted three quarters of an hour in useless speculation about the attitude they would take and the direction in which the conversation would go.

Two big men, one very tall and the other burly and powerful. The older and taller one introduced himself as Chief Superintendent John Lambert and his companion as Detective Sergeant Bert Hook. She'd heard of both of them, John Lambert as the man the papers called a 'super-sleuth' and Sergeant Hook as that rare police phenomenon, a man who'd taken an arts degree with the Open University. She told them that: it gave people a lift and got you off on the right foot when they realized that you'd heard of their exploits and their claims to fame.

On this occasion, it didn't seem to help her.

Lambert said bluntly, 'We're here in connection with the discovery of human remains in the grounds of a bungalow on the Brenton Park housing estate in Herefordshire. I don't suppose that surprises you, Ms Clark.'

His last words were a challenge which she chose to ignore. 'I read about the skeleton which was dug up there. I can't imagine why you would wish to speak with me about it.'

'It is because we think you may be able to give us information about those remains. I should tell you that we are now speaking of a murder victim.'

She was already finding his unflinching scrutiny disconcerting. She was used to dominating face-to-face exchanges. More often than not it was not she but the people she spoke with who dropped their eyes or looked away from her. Kate said, 'I'm sorry about that. The murder, I mean. But I don't see why you should think that I have anything to offer to you in the way of information. Do you know who this woman was?'

'She was a young woman who was twenty-one when she died. Her name was Julie Grimshaw.'

Kate was studiously untroubled. 'Can you be sure of that?'

'We can be quite positive. We have a DNA sample from a parent which confirms the identity. Modern DNA analysis tells us quite certainly that a body which was buried under a car park in Leicester was that of Richard III. In the light of that, you will appreciate that we are absolutely positive about the identity of this woman. Now we have to discover who killed her and buried her body in that spot in the Brenton Park development.'

'I want you to discover who killed this woman. That goes without saying. Until now all I knew was that the skeleton was that of a youngish woman.'

'And now you have an identity. This is a woman whom we

have reason to think you knew quite intimately at the time of her death.'

There was no escaping the challenge this time. She said as firmly as she could, 'I think it is high time you enlightened me about exactly what you're thinking, Mr Lambert.'

She had deliberately omitted his police title, but he gave no sign of irritation. He did not respond directly to her request. Instead, he threw another question at her. 'Where were you living twenty years ago, Ms Clark?'

'I cannot recall that precisely. I don't suppose many people can.'

'But I think that in your case you know exactly where you were. Our information is that you were at that time living in a squat at seventeen Fairfax Street in Gloucester. Do you deny that?'

Kate tried hard to remain calm. She had been over this a dozen times as she anticipated their visit, but it seemed more stark and infinitely more damning as it emerged like an accusation from the mouth of this calm, experienced man. 'Who is the source of your information?'

'We don't reveal our sources. I'm sure you wouldn't expect us to. Just as whatever you are going to tell us this afternoon will not have your name attached to it if we need to use it elsewhere. Unless you are about to provide us with a confession, of course.'

This should have been said lightly, Kate thought, with a small laugh to follow it to indicate that it was not intended seriously. But this grave-faced man delivered it as if he thought it was a serious possibility. Kate Clark gathered herself to give of her best, to give the performance of her life which she felt was now needed. 'I have come a long way since those days, Mr Lambert. I think you will understand why I do not care to recall my time in that squat. It would provide salacious material for the popular press if they found out that one of the women who has broken the glass ceiling and entered senior management with a great national company lived in a squat as a twenty-one-year-old.'

She had put on her most formal grey suit for this meeting, in a futile attempt to gain the respect which such dress seemed to bring to her in her normal working life. It did indeed seem amazing to the CID men that this formally suited and patently efficient woman could ever have been one of the pathetic and often criminal creatures who usually peopled squats. Yet they too were professionals. They would behave as if this were a situation they met regularly, even expected.

Lambert said, 'We have no wish to expose your days in Fairfax Street to your present colleagues. Some people would say that it is very much to your credit that you have progressed from there to here. But that is neither our business nor our concern. We are interested only in the assistance you can offer us in a murder inquiry.'

'I don't remember much about those days in Gloucester. I think perhaps I have deliberately shut them out as I have made my way to my present post.'

Yet her very clear grey eyes and the agile brain so obviously at work behind them belied that. If she put her mind to it, this woman could remember all sorts of details about the life she had lived in the squat and the people who had lived it with her. Lambert watched her as intently as ever as he said, 'We have been told of a Kathy Clark who was a leading figure in the squat. A friend, in fact, of Julie Grimshaw. That was you.'

'I suppose I was a friend of hers, yes. I'd still like to know who told you that. It might help me to remember other things.'

Lambert ignored the blatant attempt to trade information. As a woman now well experienced in business dealings, Kate Clark must recognize that she was playing a very weak hand here. 'How long did you spend in that derelict house in Fairfax Street?'

'I couldn't be sure. Months, I think. Certainly not years. I moved on to another place in Bristol when the pigs made it too hot in Gloucester.' She gave them an apologetic smile. 'Sorry. I stopped thinking of you lot as pigs a long time ago now.'

'And was Julie Grimshaw with you throughout the time you spent in Gloucester?'

She paused, apparently anxious to be as accurate and helpful as possible in her reply. In fact, her brain was working furiously to decide how much she had to tell them and what she might safely conceal. 'I knew Julie. I can just about remember her. We weren't bosom friends. You don't have bosom friends, in a squat.'

'I appreciate that. Our information is that you were quite close.'

'Then your source is ill-informed.'

'Were you on horse or cocaine at the time?'

She was shaken by the question and by its matter-of-fact delivery, as if it was taken as read that she had been a user. 'I wasn't on anything.' Then, as she saw the disbelief on their faces, she added, 'You picked up whatever you could in a squat, and Fairfax Street was no exception to that. Food from wherever you could, drink from wherever you could. Even water from wherever you could.' She shuddered involuntarily at the memory of it, and congratulated herself on doing so. Her shudder must have added verisimilitude to an otherwise less than convincing narrative, she thought. 'Occasionally you picked up drugs – mostly just pot. The occasional spliff was very welcome, if it helped you to forget reality for a few hours. And in the squat, you were like scavengers – like carrion birds, really, picking up whatever enabled you to carry on living. If you got the chance of drugs, you didn't refuse them, simply because you scavenged by habit.' She shuddered again, this time by design rather than instinct.

'Julie Grimshaw was a regular user. In danger of becoming an addict.'

'You seem to know a lot about her. Far more than I can remember as I strive to assist you. Now that you have reminded me, I remember that she was on horse. Maybe a little coke too, when she could get it. But she wasn't an addict; not when I knew her.'

'But in danger of becoming one. Was it you who introduced her to drugs, in your days as Kathy Clark?'

'No! Emphatically it was not. I resent the suggestion.'

'We think that at the time of her death someone was inducing her to become an agent. Probably to secure her own supplies free in return for selling her quota of illegal drugs to others. That is a common method of recruiting new dealers, as you are no doubt aware.'

'I didn't try to get Julie to sell drugs. I wouldn't have done that, even then. And I wouldn't have known how. I had no connections with drug dealers.'

'It is difficult for us to accept that. We know that drugs were being used in that squat. And we've been told that someone was trying to persuade Julie Grimshaw to become a low-level dealer. You're too intelligent not to have known most of what was going on.'

'Perhaps I didn't want to know. Drugs are dangerous things, life-threatening things. I think I realized that even then, however stupidly I was behaving otherwise.'

Lambert nodded, studying her as unemotionally as if she were a rabbit being used for research. 'How did you come to be in a squat, Ms Clark? Neither your family background nor your previous education is typical of a squat-dweller. Any more than a career such as the one you have enjoyed in recent years normally springs from such beginnings.'

Kate shrugged. This was safer ground and she was willing to speak more freely about it. 'How does anyone arrive in such a place? I'd completed my degree and couldn't get a job in the weeks that followed. Those were the years of boom and bust and I ran straight into bust when I graduated. That recession didn't last long, but there weren't many jobs for new, inexperienced graduates. Especially female ones. I had a big row at home and decided I couldn't spend another night under the parental roof. Things are very black and white, when you're twenty-one going on twenty-two. A bloke took me to the squat because he thought he'd get inside my knickers. He didn't and he pissed off pretty smartly. Whereas I, who'd thought I'd be in the squat for a couple of nights, was there for months.'

'And I believe that during those months, you were much closer to Julie Grimshaw than you have so far allowed.'

She stared at him with open hostility for a moment, then dropped her gaze to the carpet. 'I went with her to Lower Valley Farm when the son of the farmer invited her there. I didn't tell you earlier because I wished to distance myself from a death with which I have no connection.'

It sounded like a statement she had prepared for this fall-back position and it probably was. It was Hook who said to her persuasively, 'You were friendlier with Julie than you told us you were earlier. I understand your wish to distance yourself from this, but that isn't possible. It's time to be frank, Kathy. I use that name because I think that's what people called you in that squat in Fairfax Street.'

She'd glanced up sharply at him with that 'Kathy', as if it had brought back a wealth of unwelcome associations. 'I got to know Julie quite well, I suppose. As well as you get to know anyone in a squat. We looked out for each other and each other's possessions. The women were mostly on the first floor and the men down below. We told each other which men wanted it and which ones were harmless. You're right: the bloke who fed us drugs in drips was trying to recruit Julie to the trade. But I don't know his name – I'm not sure I ever did. I told her to steer clear of him.'

'And did she do that?'

'I don't know whether she did or not. She simply disappeared. She went out one day and never came back.'

'And have you any idea where she went?'

'No. You don't ask many questions, in squats, if you know what's good for you. But she didn't even take her few possessions with her. That seemed odd, even at the time. Now I realize that she'd probably gone out and got herself killed.'

Her voice didn't break, even on that thought. For a woman involved in a murder inquiry, she was remarkably composed. Lambert felt like a man who had lost on points in a closely fought contest. He glanced through the door into the kitchen as he prepared to leave and said, 'Do you live here alone, Ms Clark?'

She said, with a smile which was suddenly relaxed and attractive, 'Yes. I enjoy my independence, Mr Lambert.' Then she followed the direction of his glance and saw the two cups and two plates on the drainer beside the sink. She frowned and added, 'I allow myself occasional visitors. I'm not a complete workaholic.'

She felt a quite irrational irritation when he had gone, simply because he had scored that final tiny, irrelevant point in their confrontation.

TEN

Michael Wallington found meetings of the town education committee the strangest of all his assignments. He was an employee, but as Chief Education Officer he was the expert here, among town councillors who varied from the well-meaning to the venal and who all had their own agendas. Some made their intentions obvious from the start. Some only declared themselves as people spoke up during the meeting. They were a strange lot, local councillors, varying from committed liberals to the rightest of right-wing fascists, but they were in most cases easy to read.

The important thing for Michael was that they could be manipulated. They saw things in terms of headlines in the local press; by hinting at what might be printed, you could swiftly modulate their opinions. Today they were discussing music in schools. There was a shortage of properly qualified music teachers in the area and the sole independent councillor on the committee was concerned about children in primary schools being deprived of musical guidance at a vital stage in their development.

'We cannot provide what we have not got,' said Michael firmly. 'In an era of scarce resources, we have to prioritize. The absence of music, as of certain other educational luxuries, may be seen as regrettable, but we have to remain clear-sighted. Our main duty is to provide our children with a sound basic education and to meet the demands of the national curriculum. Our head teachers are aware of this and working diligently to achieve it.'

'But there is a demand for music. How do we explain our failure to provide it?'

Michael smiled tolerantly, the professional among struggling laity. 'That is up to you, of course. I am only here to advise. But I think we should make people aware of the virtues of our policies, rather than dwelling on any negatives. We are keeping down class sizes rather than allocating money to desirable but peripheral areas of education.'

Councillors liked a few big words to justify their decisions. Long words and technical jargon showed the punters that they were thinking, dealing with issues which were beyond the comprehension of a mere Joe Public. Wallington watched the retired builder next to him writing down the word 'peripheral' and struggling with the spelling.

The chairman nodded appreciatively. 'And how do you think we should present this to the main council meeting, Mr Wallington? They asked us to examine the possible provision of primary school music teaching in this meeting.'

Another deprecating smile, signifying that he was only here to serve, and in particular to serve their interests in the greater context within which they all operated. 'You are far more experienced in such matters than I am, Mr Turner. But again, I think we can put a positive slant on this. We were asked to make economies, were we not? Told sternly to do so by the council, in fact. I think they reminded us that education was the biggest spender and that they expected us to act accordingly and make the biggest cuts – in terms of gross expenditure, not percentages, of course.'

He waited for the nods of confirmation and then continued. 'I think we can present the absence of specialist music teachers in our primary schools as a decision we have taken with great regret, in order to accommodate their instructions to us. We are aware of the national situation and of government directives to cut down on Council Tax. In view of these, we have taken a tough and unwelcome decision to cut out music for the present and to concentrate our attention upon the essentials of primary school achievement in the basic subjects.'

It was Michael's longest speech of the education committee meeting and he was pleased to notice much furious scribbling around the table. The chairman nodded his gratitude and spoke approvingly of the three Rs. They were always popular with councillors, the three Rs. Wallington never mentioned them himself, but he provided lots of opportunities for councillors to come in and nod sagely about the need for them. You couldn't go far wrong with the three Rs, as he'd learned very early in his career in education administration.

After the meeting several men and women congratulated Wallington on his clear-sightedness and thanked him for his help. He was pleased to see that they came from all political parties. You had to cater for swings in the vote. It was no use being a bright young man with the group which had suddenly lost power: that could actually work against you. Useful to all but servile to none was the impression he needed to give. Efficient but humble, an aid but not a threat. All councillors liked that. When he moved on from here to something bigger, the goodwill of councillors would be important to him. The reputation he was working so hard to establish here would go before him; people often underestimated the efficiency of the local government grapevine.

At the end of the afternoon, Michael Wallington sat in his car and relaxed. He'd handled the meeting well, but these things took more out of you than you realized at the time. He was finding it more difficult to relax than he had done in the past. Stress of the job, perhaps; he wasn't prepared to admit to himself that it was this other matter which was troubling him. He sat for a full five minutes before he turned on the ignition and started the BMW. It wasn't typical of him to rest like this; his colleagues, junior and senior, thought he was hugely energetic. And they were surely right, for most of the time, he thought.

He drove slowly home, patient in the rush-hour traffic – not that you should really even speak of a rush hour in this pleasant rural area. The news bulletin gave him the latest on what the media were now calling 'the skeleton mystery'. The remains were those of a young woman who had now been identified. Police were anxious to speak to anyone who had lived in a squat in Fairfax Street, Gloucester, in 1995. Anyone who had known occupants of that squat, either at the time or subsequently, should also get in touch with the police and deliver whatever information they could provide.

Michael drove the car carefully into his garage at home and sat there for a moment, listening to the shrill, carefree voices of his children on the wide lawn at the rear of the house. Then he went into the kitchen and told Debbie that he was finished for the day and at his family's disposal. She brought them gin and tonics and sat with him whilst he unwound from the day's tensions in the conservatory.

They had almost finished their drinks when Michael said quietly, 'There are things I haven't told you about my past, darling. Things which may shock you a little.'

It was almost seven o'clock on Thursday evening when Lambert and Hook visited the house in Fairfax Street, Gloucester, which was Julie Grimshaw's last known abode. They had been assured by the local beat officers that the house still existed, though the whole street was scheduled for imminent demolition and replacement with modern terraced houses which would be suitable for first-time buyers.

John Lambert wanted to see the place where the dead girl and her desperate companions had lived. There would be no traces left of them now, of course, but sometimes empty buildings carried echoes; sometimes the idiosyncrasies of construction suggested questions which might be asked. Bricks and mortar, dust and neglect, could sometimes be as evocative as music.

Even squatters had forsaken this place many years ago. The house would have been long gone, had not the prolonged recession stemming from the sins of international bankers delayed the planned development. It is human failure which peoples squats, even more so in 2015 than twenty years previously. But not even the most desperate of outcasts would have considered using seventeen Fairfax Street now. The roof was almost completely gone; a few of its broken slates lay on the floor of what must once have been a lobby. A few scraps of flowered wallpaper were still visible, but in many places the plaster had fallen away. Not a single pane of glass remained intact in the windows. Most of the wooden frames were missing too, used long ago as fuel by the house's final denizens. Only ragged holes were left in the walls, like the sightless eyes of some slaughtered beast.

The two men moved cautiously through what had once been a front door and into the dirt and decomposition which were all that the grimy bricks concealed from the world. There was not enough of the staircase left for any sane attempt to climb to the first floor, but the pair gazed upwards and thought very similar thoughts. Somewhere up there, on one of the floors now dimly visible through shattered interior walls, Julie Grimshaw had walked and crouched and slept and lived the strange life of the squat.

And incredible though it seemed as they stood here and smelt the decay, that exotic creature they had spoken with only a few hours earlier, now the Customer Services Director of a great national company, had lain beside her and offered comfort in their mutual distress. That was if Kate Clark's account of those times was to be believed, of course. It was hard to accept that that expensively clothed human powerhouse had ever been here and fought for existence in this dim and threatening place. They had only her account of those times to go on, at present. Ms Clark had seemed so much in control of herself that she had no doubt presented the story she chose and withheld what it suited her to withhold.

Who else had been here? Lambert kicked aside plastic bottles and flattened cartons and took a further cautious step towards what had once been a kitchen. Here pipes without taps stood jagged above the spot where there had a long time ago been a sink. Something scurried away beneath the remains of skirting board and into the blackness by the far wall. A rat, presumably, but they saw nothing. What other, human, presences had there been on this filthy ground floor two decades ago? Was there here the ghost of someone who had seen fit to remove a twenty-one-year-old woman from the face of the earth?

Hook was glad when they stepped out of that grim place. It seemed to him a dangerous rather than a useful visit. In less than a week now, this place would be gone for ever. And good riddance, in his view. But Bert conceded that the vision of the place would add something vivid to any future interviews they might conduct with those as yet anonymous beings who had inhabited seventeen Fairfax Street two decades ago.

At the same moment that John Lambert was standing in the Fairfax Street squat, his opponent of many years was thinking about that very place as he consumed his evening meal and tried to make conversation with his wife.

Salmon and new potatoes and mangetout peas. Cooked to perfection; he told Hazel that. She smiled bleakly, staring down at the potatoes she had pushed to one side of her own plate. 'Cooking was never a problem. I used to enjoy it, once. And I enjoyed eating then, as well. I don't seem to have much of an appetite now.'

It was an effort for her to talk and both of them knew it. Steve was grateful for that effort, but she seemed like a stranger attempting to say the polite, conventional things. And what was he? For much of the time, he felt no more than a stranger here. He had to tread carefully in his own house, with his own wife. He was treating her better now than he had ever treated her. Certainly he was far more considerate of her feelings than he had been when he was making millions and doing as he pleased. He'd been out for most of the time then and taking women as the fancy seized him.

Yet he wanted Hazel now more than he had ever wanted her. Needed her more than he had ever needed her, perhaps. He was moving in his own home like a man treading on hot coals. His companions of the great days would laugh at him if they could see him now, behaving so carefully with a woman. It all came back to Liam, of course. The boy came between them as if he was in the next room, instead of being dead and buried these many years.

Steve said, 'I have to go out tonight. I won't be very long.'

'That's all right.'

Steve willed her to ask him where he was going, what he was about. But she began piling the dishes together. In a moment she would be gone to fetch the dessert. Their first strawberries of the summer, which he'd brought back from the market in Oldford. He said quickly, 'I'm going to see Jack Dutton.'

'That's good.' But she'd no notion whether it was good or bad, and she didn't care.

'He's dying, Hazel.'

'I'm sorry about that. But I hardly knew him, did I?' There was only one death which affected Hazel Williams, but that ruled her whole life.

Steve went out and threw himself into the seat of the big maroon Jaguar. He'd enjoyed driving until recently, but tonight it was a chore, merely a method of transferring himself from point A to point B, as most journeys recently seemed to have become. He found a space easily in the hospice car park and stumped heavily into the quiet building. This was a place where people came to die. Happily, for the most part. Hospices did a wonderful job; everyone said that, and Steve was sure that it was true.

He hadn't thought to bring anything with him. He couldn't recall the last time he had visited anyone in hospital. He could still remember very vividly identifying Liam in the morgue, but that was quite different. He couldn't recall when he'd last visited anyone in a hospital bed. And even this wasn't a normal hospital, where people had surgery and then got better. The man he had come to see would be dead within the week.

But dying men sometimes went in for confessions, and this one mustn't say anything damaging in his last few days.

Steve would scarcely have recognized Jack Dutton if he had not been directed so precisely to his bedside. The thin frame beneath the blankets must be less than half the weight of the man who had worked for him and done his bidding so unquestioningly all those years ago. Steve had to tell Dutton who he was, then watch the grey face nod without interest.

So this was death, the universal enemy whom no one could defeat. Everything here was done to take the grimness away from the reaper, but he would come for his harvest nonetheless. 'Doesn't seem long since I was paying you good money, Jack,' said Williams awkwardly.

He couldn't remember making conversation with a dying man before. It seemed inconceivable now that this man had been one of his 'heavies', employed emphatically for brawn rather than brain. It was one of the first things you did when you established yourself in the shady businesses of brothels and loan-sharking. You paid other men to do your enforcing; you didn't do any of the rough stuff yourself. Apart from the fact that violence was risky and could land you in court and in clink as soon as it went wrong, employing other people to do your roughing up and your retributions showed that you'd made it, that you were a big player in the criminal world.

The man dying beneath the bedclothes had shed plenty of blood and broken plenty of bones in his time. He'd done all kinds of dirty work for the ageing, bald tycoon who sat beside his bed. And he'd been paid handsomely for it. Reliable and trustworthy hard men didn't come cheap.

No point in reminding him of that now. Men didn't show gratitude or many other emotions when they were measuring out their lives in hours. Steve Williams didn't think the police would work things out and get here in time to question Dutton. But he wasn't going to take any chances on that. He'd cover the possibility, if he could. And he thought he knew the way.

Jack Dutton, like many violent men, was a devoted family man, kind and considerate within the walls of his own home. Steve went quickly through the truisms of cancer being a bastard and there being neither rhyme nor reason in whom it chose to attack. He waited until he received a wan smile from the sick man, and then said. 'And how's Beth?'

The invalid showed his first flicker of animation. 'She's all right. She's a good lass, Beth. She comes every day, in the afternoons. She's preoccupied with the grandchildren. We've got six of them now. I'd have liked to see them grow up.'

'I'll see her right, you know, Jack, if – if anything happens to you.'

That ashen smile again. 'We all know what's happening to me, Mr Williams. But thanks for that.'

'It's Steve now, Jack. And I've got a bob or two laid by, as you'd expect. I'll look after Beth. I'll see she wants for nothing.' Dutton nodded weakly. 'I'd better be going now, Jack. The nurse said I wasn't to tire you out.'

He stood up, wondering if he had really achieved what he had come here to do. Was Dutton too far gone to appreciate why his silence was being bought with the promise of money for his wife? Then, as Williams turned to go, he learned that he had succeeded. The feeble voice from the bed behind him said, 'I know nothing about that skeleton they found last week, Mr Williams.'

*   *   *

The dark shadows of Fairfax Street were still vivid in Lambert's mind as he watched the opening headlines of the television news at ten o'clock that night. The phone shrilled suddenly beside him, startling him because it seemed louder and more urgent with the lateness of the hour. Christine answered it, as she normally did in their home, prepared to defend it against the intrusions of the more brutal world which her husband's job sometimes brought here. She listened for a moment, then passed the instrument without a word to John.

The duty sergeant was highly apologetic, wary of the earful which might come his way for contacting a senior officer at home at this hour. 'It's a woman on a mobile, sir. Probably a nutter, but she insisted that you'd told her to contact you personally if she had any thoughts on the skeleton case. I can tell her to—'

'What's her name?'

'Clark, sir. Ms Katherine Clark, she says. I wouldn't have bothered you, but she was so insistent that—'

'Give her my number, please.'

He waited with the phone in his hand until it shrilled again a few seconds later. A nervous voice in his ear said, 'Is this all right? You told me you wanted to know immediately if I'd any further thoughts on that squat.'

'I appreciate your taking the trouble to ring me. I've been to Fairfax Street this evening. Seen the place for myself.' It was irrelevant, but it seemed somehow that it might encourage frankness in that nervous voice.

'I remembered the name of one of the men who was there. Well, only the first name. But you said anything would be welcome.'

'It is. We've got the local police in Gloucester following up on that squat. But twenty years ago isn't easy. There aren't too many coppers around who were on the beat then.'

He'd meant it as a vague threat that they'd ferret things out, that there was no point in her holding anything back. But she wasn't listening to him. She was wondering how to phrase what she had to tell him, concerned only with giving him this one fact and then switching off her phone. 'Most of the men came and went quickly. So did the women, apart from Julie and me. But there was one man who I think was there throughout my time in that squat.'

'And his name was?'

'I don't know his surname. His first name was Mick.'

He thanked her, said that she would hear in due course how the inquiry was proceeding, emphasized that if a surname should come back to her he would want to have it immediately.

Kate Clark scarcely heard him, waiting only for the moment when she could cut the contact and relax. She hadn't given him much, but it was all she could safely offer. Please God it would take the attention away from her and the things she needed to conceal.

ELEVEN

Michael Wallington told himself that it was good that he was meeting the CID in his own office. He would be in control here, much less nervous than if he had been on their ground at Oldford police station, the alternative venue they had suggested. He told himself that repeatedly.

They came precisely at half past ten, the time they had specified. A tall, watchful man with a slight stoop who identified himself as Chief Superintendent John Lambert and a shorter but more powerful man who looked much less threatening, introduced as Detective Sergeant Hook.

'Your reputation goes before you,' said Michael effusively. 'I'm sure everyone in the town hall has heard of the achievements of John Lambert. Coffee, please, Mrs Barrett! And a few biscuits, if your skill and influence can conjure them up for us.' He turned his automatic beam on his PA and dispatched her to the task he had already agreed with her half an hour earlier. Then he seated his visitors in the chairs he had carefully positioned for them before they arrived and sat down opposite them. 'This is quite intriguing. I can't think what help the education department can offer to you, but it goes without saying that we are willing to offer whatever assistance we can.'

Lambert gave him a grim smile, watched Mrs Barrett set the coffee tray down on the table beside him and said, 'It is not your department but you personally who will be able to help us this morning, Mr Wallington.'

The PA was studiously calm and inscrutable, but her boss was not. He did not like this being said in the hearing of Mrs Barrett, but it was hardly specific enough for him to object to it on the grounds of confidentiality. It was, as Wallington suspected, carefully calculated on Lambert's part to counter the urbanity of his reception here, and it succeeded in that. The man who ruled here was discomfited, in spite of his

determination before they arrived to remain calm and in control
of things.

Michael waited until the PA withdrew and then said with a
forced grin, 'That only makes this more intriguing. Please
elucidate for me.'

That was a phrase he used with junior employees and
sometimes with town councillors. The four-syllabled word
often intimidated them. It did not intimidate this man. The
unsmiling Lambert was only too willing to elucidate. 'I can
be quite specific for you, Mr Wallington. Indeed, I am anxious
to be so, in the hope that such precision will prompt your
accurate recall of events now twenty years behind us.'

'I was told when this meeting was arranged that it was in
connection with your investigation into the discovery of this
skeleton which was unearthed near Hereford last weekend. I
can't think how—'

'We wish to know everything we can discover about events
which took place at seventeen Fairfax Street, Gloucester, in
the spring and summer of 1995.'

Lambert's grey, unblinking eyes held those of Wallington
as unerringly as a mesmerist's, though Michael was conscious
of Hook turning unhurriedly to a new page of his notebook
on the left of his peripheral vision. 'I – I think I was in
Gloucester in 1995. It's difficult to be certain of dates so long
ago. And that particular address doesn't—'

'Seventeen Fairfax Street was at that time a squat, illegally
occupied by a constantly changing group of people, as such
places commonly are. We have good reason to believe that
you were there throughout the months which interest us.'

Michael glanced automatically at the door, thinking of the
ordered world beyond it and the contrast with his life of twenty
years ago. 'I had various experiences in my younger days, as
many people do before their lives take on a pattern. I think I
was what my revered parents would call "a little wild" at the
time you mention. You will forgive me if I cannot be precise
about what I was doing at particular times, but I can assure
you that it was nothing which—'

'Let me try to assist the workings of your memory, Mr
Wallington. One of the occupants of that squat remained

constant through the comings and goings of others. He went by the forename of "Mick". We have reason to believe that this person was you. Are you telling us now that this was not so? Are you asserting that this "Mick" was some other person entirely?'

Michael's mind raced though the options, but he couldn't assess them coolly one against another, as he was used to doing now in his daily working life. He didn't have enough information for that. He didn't know what would happen if he denied all knowledge of Fairfax Street. How much did these men know? He had thought that he was finished with those days in the squat and everything which had gone on there. He had believed that he would never again need to confront this section of his past. But he was no fool. The police had a lot of resources, when they chose to use them. And in the case of a suspicious death, they used everything. Money was no object then; he often pointed out the richness of police resources when his own education budget was under fire.

If he said he was somewhere else at the time, could they disprove that? Innocent until proved guilty, after all. But if they had proof that he'd been in Fairfax Street, they could make life very difficult for him. His whole career was at stake here. He said dully, 'I was in a squat in Gloucester at that time. I don't recall the address – we didn't deal in addresses. You didn't receive any post when you were living in a squat.'

It was an attempt at a joke. But it didn't relieve the atmosphere in this room, which now seemed to him stiflingly hot. He noticed that they'd finished their coffee while he was speaking. He lifted his own untouched cup, trying desperately not to spill its contents. He said feebly, 'There's more coffee in the pot. Please help yourselves. And likewise with the biscuits.' He didn't feel able to pass them round. They'd probably end up on the carpet at his feet if he tried to do that.

'So you admit that you were the "Mick" who was living in this squat?'

He rallied briefly. 'I'm not sure that "admit" is the right word, is it? It makes me sound as if I was guilty of something, rather than just being a member of a desperate and ever-changing group living from hand to mouth in a derelict house.'

Lambert gave him a brief smile and returned to the attack. 'It seems quite an appropriate word in this case, Mr Wallington. Our information is that the person known to our informant as "Mick" was a drug dealer.'

'Then it couldn't have been me, could it? There were drugs around, in the squat. In my very limited experience, there always were in such places. Pot is one way of escaping from the real world and a lot of people in squats want to do that. There were the harder drugs, as well. Horse and coke, mainly. That's how some people had sunk low enough in life to end up in a squat. But I had no—'

'How did you come to be there, Mr Wallington? You had a degree from Bristol University at that time. Neither your background nor your education were those of the normal squat-dweller, if there is indeed such a person.'

'I don't think there is. My experience is very limited, as I said, but all kinds of people seem to end up in squats. They range from those who are well-nigh illiterate to those with public schools and universities behind them. A lot of squat-dwellers seem to drop out without completing their degrees; I suppose I was atypical in that respect.'

He was desperately trying to disappear into generalities, to lead them away from the specifics of what he had been doing in that squat in the summer of 1995. But they were too experienced for him. They saw his attempt at diversion immediately for what it was. Lambert nodded at Hook, who said immediately, 'Tell us whatever you can remember about the other people in the squat at that time, please.'

The Wallington brow furrowed impressively. It was a tactic he used extensively when he was about to make key suggestions in both formal and informal meetings; it now came automatically to him in these very different circumstances. He could surely handle this plodding DS like a local councillor. He said with a returning urbanity, 'I'm afraid I can remember very little about that constantly changing human detritus, Detective Sergeant Hook.'

'That's a pity, because we now know that the skeleton you mentioned at the outset of this meeting was a companion of yours there. Her name was Julie Grimshaw and we now believe that she became a murder victim during the summer of 1995. It is entirely possible, even probable, that her murderer was one of the people who lived with her at seventeen Fairfax Street. I'd say that it is very much in your interests to recall and pass on whatever you can about the people who were with you in that squat.'

Michael stared at Hook with real distaste. It was nothing personal: the bearer of bad news has been vulnerable for thousands of years. Wallington had at that moment no idea of the expression on his face. His mind was wholly preoccupied with what he had just heard and how he was going to cope with it. He eventually said dully, with the air of a man acknowledging defeat, 'I knew Julie Grimshaw. I remember her in that squat.'

'Then you must give us the benefit of your presence there. You must tell us everything you can remember about Julie and your other companions. Don't leave out even the smallest details; none of us knows at this moment what will prove to be significant.'

This was Bert Hook at his most persuasive, assuming for the moment the innocence of the man in front of him, treating him as if they were all on the same side in this. It wouldn't stop Hook weighing the evidence in due course, deciding with John Lambert how reliable or how devious Michael Wallington had been in the defence of his own interests.

Wallington's voice seemed to come from a long way away as he said, 'She was a pretty girl, Julie.'

'So you were attracted to her?'

'Yes, I suppose so. I didn't shag her.' The harsh four-letter word fell like a stone into the still pool of his recollection.

'But someone else did.'

Hook made it a statement, not a question, trying with his certainty to convey the impression that they knew more of the events in that dark place than they did. Wallington looked at him now not with hostility but with a kind of wonder. 'I expect so. She was a pretty girl, when you cut through the dirt and the torn clothes and the way she'd chosen to live.'

'Who, then?'

'I don't know. Not anyone in the squat, I think.'

'Tell us about the drugs.'

Michael felt no shock. Perhaps he wasn't capable of shock any more. His world was falling apart around him, but no one save he and these two men knew about it as yet. 'I think Julie was on drugs, yes. A lot of them were. It's difficult to remember much about it at this distance of time.'

Lambert had never taken his eyes off the man. He was trying to decide now how uncertain Wallington really was and how far he might be using his own stupefaction as a shield against their questions. He said quietly, 'Take your time, please. You can remember a lot more than you have told us so far and we need your help in this. Was Julie Grimshaw hooked on drugs?'

Michael turned his head very deliberately from one to the other of the two men opposite him, as if it demanded a physical effort to refocus. 'I can't remember enough about her to be certain. I'm pretty sure she was a user, but it wouldn't be fair for me to say more than that.'

Lambert nodded grimly. 'We're beyond the point where we need to concern ourselves with being fair to Julie, Mr Wallington. Someone was so unfair that he killed her and hid her body from the rest of us for twenty years. Someone whom you might have known and lived with at seventeen Fairfax Street. Forensic examination of what is left of her has shown that she had used considerable quantities of heroin in the final months of her life. What can you tell us about that?'

'I can't add to it. You already know more than I do. I remember that she was a user, but that's all.'

'Where did her supplies come from?'

'I don't know. I don't know where she went when she left the squat. I don't know where any of them disappeared to when they went out. It didn't pay to enquire into what the other squat occupants might be doing. They were a strange and unpredictable crew. Their behaviour wasn't consistent. They could be friendly and talkative one day and hostile the next.'

'But things are coming back to you now. Your recall of these events is much clearer than you thought it was going to be ten minutes ago.'

Michael wondered if that was congratulation or criticism.

He felt that he couldn't be sure of anything with these two any more. That unnerved him, because he was used to being sure of himself and of exactly what he must do in the situations which confronted him as Chief Education Officer. 'I'm battering my brain and trying to remember what I can. There were drugs around in that squat. I've absolutely no idea where they came from. I wasn't a user myself or I might have known.'

'Tell us about the other people at seventeen Fairfax Street in 1995. We've got the local police on the job, but someone who was in the place will know much more.'

Was that a warning to him? Had the local plods told them a lot more than they were admitting to? Were they trying to trip him up? What were the penalties if they could prove that he'd been trying to deceive them? Obstructing the police in the course of their enquiries, they called that, didn't they? But he'd no idea what the punishment for it might be. Michael Wallington was used to operating in a civilized world, where he knew the rules and could usually operate them to his advantage. Now he was being thrust back into the feral world of the squat, where dog ate dog and the weakest went to the wall. Was he mixing metaphors there? When he least wanted it and could least afford it, pedantry thrust itself into his teeming brain.

'I'm trying desperately to remember what I can of that squat. It's difficult for me, because I've spent the best part of twenty years trying to forget about that section of my life.' He looked at Lambert for a word of sympathy, but the man stared hard at him and said nothing. 'People came and went. I can't remember those who merely passed through and were only there for a day or two. There was another girl, I think. A friend of Julie's. I didn't see too much of them because they were on the first floor. The men mostly stayed on the ground floor.'

'Name?'

'I can't remember that. She was rather pretty, I think. She had darker skin and darker hair than Julie, who was almost blonde – I don't know whether that was her natural colour or not, though. This other girl had long dark hair at first, but not later. She cut it off herself while she was in the squat, I think.

What was her name?' His brow furrowed again and he stared at the floor. 'Kathy, I think. I'm pretty sure we called her Kathy. I don't know her other name; as I told you, we didn't indulge in those.'

Hook gave him the encouraging smile which Lambert had denied him. 'Clark, would it be? Could she have been Kathy Clark?'

Michael's features were studiously blank. He wasn't going to give them any more. Even if they knew more and were trying to trap him, he couldn't see what they could do if he blanked them resolutely from here on. He'd given them a little, and they surely couldn't prove that he remembered more, whatever they suspected. 'She might have been called Clark. But I wouldn't have known if she was, any more than she'd have known my name.'

Lambert said suddenly, 'Were you supplying the drugs in that place?'

'No! That's an outrageous suggestion. I wasn't a user and I don't know where the horse and coke and ecstasy which changed hands in the squat came from.'

'I see. We had to ask that, just as I now have to ask you whether you killed Julie Grimshaw.'

'No! Again, the suggestion is outrageous and I must register my—'

'Do you have any idea who might have killed her?'

'No. There were all kinds of people in there. It might have been one of them who killed Julie, I suppose, but I have no idea which one.'

'Give it some urgent thought, please. You are the nearest we have to a first-hand witness of the events leading up to the death of Miss Grimshaw. Any further recollections of your companions at seventeen Fairfax Street will be gratefully received.'

Then, abruptly, they were gone. Michael Wallington stared at the empty coffee cups and the biscuits, but did not call in Mrs Barrett to remove them. He felt unprepared for any kind of human contact. He might give away far more of himself than he could afford to reveal, even in this office which was so emphatically his own preserve. He was the strong man here, the ruler of his own small empire, and that situation must at all costs be preserved.

He tried to review his clash with the CID rationally – for clash it had undoubtedly been. It had felt during the latter stages of the confrontation as if they held all the weapons, as if he was hopelessly beaten. But when he reviewed the exchanges more coolly now, Michael decided that he had come out of it quite well – certainly as well as could be expected, in this dramatic and difficult situation.

He'd told them what he had to tell them. He'd admitted to knowing Julie Grimshaw and her friend Kathy, but he'd surely managed to convince them that he remembered a lot less about events at seventeen Fairfax Street than he did. Or he hoped he had done that.

Andrew Burrell searched the newspapers and watched the television anxiously. There seemed to be nothing new being revealed about the Julie Grimshaw murder.

On Friday morning he conducted a seminar with a group of third-year degree students, insisting that they came up with their own opinions rather than waiting for him to lead them, forcing himself to concentrate on the mores of the seventeenth century rather than those of the twenty-first which had so dominated his thoughts during a troubled night. His colleagues noticed his tenseness. They thought it was worries about work which were disturbing his sleep; he had been happy to foster that delusion.

At lunchtime he refused an invitation to eat in the refectory with his fellow tutors and sat brooding alone in his room. Eventually he pulled out his mobile phone and dialled a number. This would be the time to get Jim Simmons. He would be eating with his wife in the farmhouse. You were a creature of habit when you worked on a farm; the nature of the work determined that you had to be.

Jim Simmons was clearly surprised to hear his voice. The academic had to identify himself. 'It's Andrew, Jim. Andrew Burrell. Long time no see. Or hear, for that matter. I should have been in touch, but time slips away, what with work and divorce.'

'Yes.' Jim paused, staring at the phone, wondering what this could be about. 'Is it your dad? He was fine, when I saw him last week. I'm sure he'd appreciate a visit from you, though.'

'No, this is not about Dad. But you're right, it's time I went to see him. I'm very busy here, but I must make the time. I wanted a word about this skeleton someone's dug up on your land.'

'Not my land, Andrew. It's someone's garden now. It was sold off some time ago.'

'And at a very good price, from what I heard.' Andrew almost bit his tongue off; he hadn't rung up to offer barbs like that, to revive old animosities. He needed Jim Simmons's cooperation, not his resistance. 'Sorry. That's nothing to do with me. Good luck to you, I say, if you can get people to pay you good money to extend their gardens. It's just that I was wondering what the police had been saying to you, about Julie Grimshaw.'

It was a clumsy change of gear. He could almost hear the cogs grating. Simmons must surely have caught his anxiety. But how could you even pretend to be casual about something like this? He could picture Simmons in the farmhouse at this moment, taking his time, weighing this query in his measured, deceptively intelligent way. That had always been one of the irritating things about Jim: he was much sharper and more perceptive about people than farmers were supposed to be. But then the modern farmer had to deal with all sorts of government 'initiatives' which had not been around in his father's day.

After a few seconds Simmons said, 'They wanted to find out everything they could about Julie. They didn't even mention her name, but that was their concern. I told them she'd been here. Not much more than that.'

'And what did you tell them about me?' Andrew Burrell felt feeble in showing his anxiety, but he needed to ask that.

'Virtually nothing. They were more interested in me. I told them I'd been wild, got into a few fights at that time, dabbled a little in drugs. They were interested in what I might have done and in my dealings with Julie, not yours. I think I was the first one the senior men had spoken with at any length. They probably know a lot more now than they did then.' Jim rather enjoyed saying that.

'Yes. They gave me the impression that they knew quite a lot when they spoke to me on Tuesday. That's one of the problems when they're questioning you, isn't it? You don't know how much they already know.'

'Not a problem if you've nothing to hide, is it?' Jim was both asserting his own innocence and turning the knife a little in the man who had lived here with him when they were both young.

Andrew wished he hadn't treated him loftily as the hired hand so often in those days. He forced himself to ask the question he needed to ask. 'Did they mention Liam?'

'No. And I didn't mention him either.'

'That's good. No need to raise all that stuff if we don't have to, is there?'

Simmons didn't comment directly on that. He could hear his old enemy breathing heavily into his phone. Jim said slowly, 'Well, Liam Williams isn't here to speak for himself, is he? That must make it difficult for the CID. But they don't give up easily, do they? Not when they get their teeth into a murder.'

TWELVE

Lambert got the message he had been expecting from the Chief Constable late on Friday morning. By two o'clock in the afternoon he was sitting in front of the CC's desk, feeling a little like a head prefect called into the headmaster's study.

One thing felt odd for a start. All his previous chief constables had been older than him, but Gordon Armstrong was a good ten years younger. And to Lambert, Armstrong, with his sharp suits and short, perfectly cut brown hair, looked even younger. Armstrong had been gracious and studiously polite towards him so far, but Lambert couldn't help feeling that the CC would like the older man out of his way, would like to make his imprint on CID by appointing his own man to head it.

Armstrong waited for him to refuse any refreshment, then said breezily, 'I thought we should have a quick word about this "skeleton mystery", as the media have decided to call it, John. I'm getting a lot of queries about our progress, as you can imagine.'

'I can, sir. I'm grateful to you for keeping the press at bay. I don't enjoy their bloodlust as they look for a sensational quote.'

Armstrong grinned at him and for a moment they were companions, united against the feckless media, allies who understood each other's problems in the face of the amateur and irresponsible world outside. 'I've given them all the usual guff. Enquiries are proceeding satisfactorily. We have several possibilities in view, and all are being thoroughly investigated. Various people are helping us with our enquiries. No, we do not yet have a leading suspect and no one has been taken into custody. But I can only fend them off with such things for so long, as you know. If I can't give them something to bite on in the next few days, it will

be "Police baffled" and "What are our overpaid flatfoots
doing to earn their money?"'

And you're new here and anxious to appear on the ball with
the Fourth Estate: quite understandable and one of the reasons
why I wouldn't sit in your seat for the biggest pension in the
land. Lambert didn't like the way pensions were intruding so
often nowadays into his thoughts and vocabulary. He said, 'It's
more difficult than usual, sir, with a corpse that disappeared
twenty years ago and a crime committed at that time.'

'I know that and you know that, John. Even the hacks with
the tabloids know it, but sympathy and patience are not notable
press virtues. The time lapse is the next line I plan to use, but
I'm sure they'll treat it as an evasion – they might even be
right, I suppose. Meanwhile, whatever I reveal to them, I need
to be kept absolutely up to date on the case. DI Rushton has
fed me everything he's filing, but I thought I'd like to have
the latest from you – including your private thoughts and
speculations, which can't be filed.'

At that Armstrong gave him a conspiratorial smile and
Lambert responded with a weaker one of his own. 'I've been
involved in a lot of murders over my CID career, sir. This is
the first one where I've been involved in a case which began
with remains buried twenty years ago.'

'I appreciate that, John. But I can hardly feed your inexperi-
ence to the press. They've spent the last few years fostering
the impression that their "super-sleuth" knows everything and
is prepared for anything.'

'You asked me to be frank, sir. I'll tell you privately that
I felt for a couple of days that we were really floundering. If I
look at the case as dispassionately as I can, I suppose we have
made decent progress over six days. I can't say we're on the
verge of a solution. We've turned up a number of suspects
who need further investigation. I'm not sure we've even got
a comprehensive list of those; we may still add to the number.'

'I think you should give me your thoughts on whatever you
have. You must rely on me to decide what might be released
to the media vultures.'

'Probably very little at the moment, sir, if we don't want
suits for defamation of character. There are some quite

powerful people involved, most of whom will no doubt prove to be quite innocent of murder.'

Armstrong sighed. That was exactly what he had feared. But such things came with the job. 'Start with the victim and what she was doing at the time of her death. Then pinpoint a few suspects and give me your thoughts.'

'We had an identification as early as Monday morning, sir. Thanks to a grieving mother and DNA confirmation we didn't need to trawl dental records. The victim was Julie Grimshaw, aged twenty-one. Her last known residence was a squat in Gloucester: seventeen Fairfax Street. The place is about to be demolished. I visited it with DS Hook on Thursday evening, but as you'd expect at this distance of time there was nothing to be learned there.'

'Can you be certain that this was her last residence? Mightn't she have moved on to some other, perhaps similar, place?'

'We can't yet rule that out. But it's my opinion that she was murdered whilst still living in that squat. She disappeared abruptly. That isn't unusual for squat-dwellers, but she didn't take any of her very few belongings with her. Even her coat was left behind; I think that's significant, because warmth is always a prime consideration for those living on the edge of existence in squats.'

'How many of the people living with her in the squat have you located?'

'Two so far. As you know, there is a constantly shifting population in squats. These were two of the few who seem to have been there for a lengthy period. Both of them were around at the time when Julie Grimshaw disappeared and died.'

'So both of them are suspects?'

'Until we can clear them, yes. Both deny guilt, as you would expect, and both claim to have no knowledge of how Julie died.'

She sounded more like a real girl who had lived and loved and died when Lambert called her just Julie, thought Gordon Armstrong. Policemen became attached to victims if they spent long enough on a case, and it sounded from his tone of voice as if the grizzled and hugely experienced Lambert was developing an attachment to this one. That was no bad thing, because it made you more determined that her death would be avenged and her killer put away. 'These are the two that DI Rushton itemized for me. Remind me please of their backgrounds, John.'

Lambert smiled grimly. These weren't going to be welcome details for a chief constable. People in high places often had influential friends. Diplomatically, it would be much easier for Armstrong if these two were clerks or artisans. 'The female is Katherine Clark, MBE. She is the Director with responsibility for Customer Services at Severn Trent Water. She has left seventeen Fairfax Street a very long way behind her. She is one of the new breed of female executives. She's riding the tide of female emancipation in senior management circles and I expect she is also highly efficient. I suspect she has aspirations to chair a major company. Not surprisingly, she is very anxious that her way of life in her early twenties does not become public knowledge.'

'You described her as highly efficient. Would her efficiency include a certain ruthlessness?'

'Almost certainly. I can't see how she could have risen as quickly as she has to the board of Severn Trent without that quality. You're asking me whether she would have had the nerve to kill Julie Grimshaw if the girl had stood in her way. I would say yes. I have as yet no evidence to support such a theory.'

The Chief Constable smiled wryly. 'This is why I needed to confer with you, John. I spend a good four fifths of my life listening to what people think it is safe to say. DI Rushton gives me all the facts. I need your opinions and speculations to flesh them out.'

'Kate Clark – she will tell you to call her that, if you have occasion to speak with her – was Julie's friend in the squat. She claims to have been surprised and baffled by her disappearance. We've no reason as yet to doubt her statement on that. What our second squat occupant has told us tends rather to confirm it, though he claims to remember very little. I think it suits him to do that. He has so far shown a very selective recall of his experiences at seventeen Fairfax Street.'

'You're speaking of this man Michael Wallington.'

'Chief Education Officer of Stainford in Worcestershire, sir. An able man, no doubt. Perhaps he just rubbed me up the wrong way, but I wouldn't trust him as far as I could throw him. For what it's worth, DS Hook, who normally tends to be more charitable than I am, thought exactly the same. But as I say, Wallington is probably very able.'

Armstrong frowned. 'Not a good combination, that, from our point of view. Able and unscrupulous.'

'And highly rated in Stainford, sir, which makes things even worse, in terms of PR. If we have to say anything to besmirch Mr Wallington's reputation, we'd better be very sure of our ground.'

'Thank you for the warning,' said Armstrong. 'What else can you tell me about him?'

'Not a great deal, as yet. We've got the local police in Gloucester on the case, but twenty years can be a surprisingly long time when it comes to bobbies on the beat. And I'm afraid the habit then was usually to ignore squats as far as possible, unless property owners made things hot. Neither Ms Clark nor Mr Wallington has any criminal record, which is probably a good thing from our point of view: we don't need to embarrass them with official records of past crimes. But it makes it difficult to find out exactly what they were doing in that squat, beyond what they choose to tell us.'

Armstrong nodded philosophically. '"We've unearthed several promising lines of enquiry and these are being thoroughly explored." I can probably fob the press boys off with that and similar well-worn phrases for another day or two. Who else do you have in the frame?'

'I'm not quite sure they're in the frame yet, sir. But we have four other people who will remain suspects in my mind until they can be eliminated. The most obvious one is the man who owned the farm where Julie Grimshaw was buried in 1995. Daniel Burrell is now eighty-four and in a care home. He has suffered some physical decline, but he is still fully alert mentally.'

'Motive?'

'His son brought Julie Grimshaw home as his girl friend. Father and son were already at loggerheads because Andrew, the son, had been lined up to take over the farm and had decided by 1995 that he no longer wanted to do that. Julie was into hard drugs and perhaps in danger of becoming an addict at the time of her death. Andrew's mother – now dead, which is unfortunate for us – and father were solidly against the liaison and they put pressure on Andrew to finish it. Old Daniel Burrell is salt of the earth and solid English yeoman stock, but he was used to getting his own way on his farm. Parents do strange and sometimes violent things in defence of their children and what they see as their children's interests. Miss Grimshaw seems to have died from a blow to the left temple, so it's possible that her killer acted in a fit of temper and didn't intend to kill her at the time. The forensic pronouncements on wounds inflicted twenty years ago are obviously not as precise as they would be on wounds inflicted last week.'

'What about the boy himself?'

'Andrew Burrell went off and did an arts degree at Liverpool University instead of obtaining the agricultural qualifications his parents had envisaged. He is now a lecturer at the University of Gloucester. A little precious about his work there and a little evasive about his exact relationship with Julie in 1995. That doesn't make him a murderer, but I want to interview him again when we've gathered more information from other sources. He agrees that there might have been a certain amount of missionary zeal in his attempt to rescue Julie from the squat and from drug addiction. Young people on drugs are notoriously moody and unpredictable. Julie's death could have been simply the result of a lovers' tiff. Or Andrew might have taken it badly if Julie said she'd had enough of him and proposed to end the affair.'

'Or she might have ditched him for someone else and brought the green-eyed monster into play.'

'Exactly. These are all possibilities until we can eliminate them. At the moment we only have Andrew Burrell's word for it that his girl friend simply disappeared and that he knew no more about her until her skeleton was unearthed last Saturday. We need to check whether other people who were around at the time agree with him on that.'

'You have these other people available?'

'Some of them. Two of the most vital are already dead: Andrew Burrell's mother, Emily, and a boy of around Julie's own age who had some sort of association with her, the exact nature of which has yet to be confirmed; I'll come to him in a minute. There is also a contemporary of Andrew Burrell's, James Simmons, who lived with him at Lower Valley Farm in 1995. He was at that time an employee of Daniel Burrell, who was still running his own farm. Simmons was favoured by Daniel when he found that his own son was not interested in taking over the farm.'

'James Simmons is the man in possession at Lower Valley Farm now.' The Chief Constable recalled the name with some satisfaction. It was always good to show your senior staff that you'd read their briefings and were on the ball. Armstrong had been blessed from childhood with a good memory and he had found it more and more valuable to him as he had advanced through the hierarchy of the police service.

'Yes. In fact Jim Simmons now owns Lower Valley Farm. Daniel Burrell was happy to sell it to him, as a favoured employee who wished to carry on working the land on the lines he had been following himself. That is a considerable compliment, because the Burrells have farmed that land for well over two hundred years – since it was the home farm of the great house which disappeared along with many others in the nineteen twenties.'

'Are you suggesting that this death was connected with the farm in some way? I know that land, with its uses and tradi-tions, can be a huge force in the lives of those who live on it and work it.' Gordon Amstrong, sharp-suited bureaucrat who thrived on the machinery of urban life and now directed the operations of four hundred police officers and numerous civilian employees, had begun life as the son of a pig and poultry farmer in Wiltshire.

Lambert's smile contained more frustration than humour. 'I don't as yet see how this death can be related to the farm, but we're keeping open minds. Jim Simmons now lives in the farmhouse with his wife and two children. I felt he was rather anxious to parade himself as a paragon of family life when we spoke with him on Sunday, but I may be too cynical.'

'You're paid to be cynical, John. We don't broadcast it, but cynicism is part of the CID equipment. We're going back twenty years here. Simmons might have been a different and more irresponsible man then.'

'He agreed when we questioned him that he'd had his wild moments in his youth, which more or less coincided with the days when Julie Grimshaw was around the farm. She was brought there from the squat by Andrew Burrell and she wasn't a popular visitor with Daniel Burrell or his wife. I'm not sure how close Jim Simmons was to Julie, or what motive he might have had. Was he a rival to Andrew Burrell for her affections? Could he even have got rid of her as a favour to Daniel Burrell, his employer and the farm owner? Was the transfer of the farm to his ownership a few years later a pay-off for favours rendered? He's now running it very efficiently and with a happy family installed there, but as you say I'm paid to accept nothing at face value.'

'You said you had four other people who were of major interest to you, in addition to Katherine Clark and Michael Wallington, the two who'd been in that squat with the murdered woman. I make that three so far.'

Lambert gave his chief another mirthless grin. 'I suppose I've left Steve Williams until the last because he's an old adversary of mine. One who's won most of the rounds between us so far.'

'We're all aware of what Steve Williams is, John. A known villain, mostly in prostitution and gaming and loan-sharking, who's seen off his lesser rivals in our area and surrounded himself with all the trappings of a successful crime boss, including heavies to do his dirty work and crafty lawyers who make sure nothing nasty sticks to him. The kind all coppers hate and most criminals admire and fear.'

'Fear is one of our problems, sir. It's been difficult to get anyone to give evidence against Williams and his activities. Understandably – because the only person who did so during his early years disappeared without trace and was never found. These things get around. I can hardly claim to be unbiased, where Williams is concerned. As he'll be only too happy to point out, if we get anywhere near him.'

'Let me deal with that, if it comes to it, John. But you know as well as I do that we'll need a cast iron case before we take him to court. The Crown Prosecution Service won't be interested in anything less than that. They've burned their fingers too often before with men like Williams. It's the old story: the worst people in our society can afford the best lawyers.'

'Steve Williams may of course be as guilty as hell about all kinds of things in the past and as innocent as snow in this case. I've no evidence as yet to connect him with Julie's death and I can't see it being easy to find any.'

'Why do you even think there might be a connection?'

'I've no more to throw against him at the moment than his proximity to the site. At the time when that body was buried, his was the nearest residence. The grave was at the edge of Lower Valley Farm, but the farmhouse and farm buildings are much further from the spot than Williams's house.'

'But would you choose a burial site so near to your own house?'

'Not if I had the choice. But if I'd killed a woman, perhaps without prior intent, I'd be anxious to get rid of the body as quickly as possible. It's only about two hundred yards from Williams's house, but in every other respect it was a pretty remote spot at the time. The housing estate has been built there now, of course, but it must have seemed a safe enough site for a shallow grave at the time.'

'But you're a fair man, John – well, perhaps not where Steve Williams is concerned, because he doesn't deserve fairness. But let's say objective. I don't see you pursuing Williams just because of the proximity of his house to the burial place.'

'There'd be no future in doing that. He'd laugh at us. But when I talked with him on Wednesday, I sensed he wasn't confident. He tried to be his normal truculent self, but he couldn't carry that through. The problem for us is that there are two people we'd like to interview and can't. One is Liam Williams, Steve's son. He's the lad I mentioned earlier who had some sort of relationship with Julie in the weeks before her death. But we can't talk to him about it, because Liam was killed in a road traffic incident eight years ago. The other one is the boy's mother, Hazel Williams. But she was so devastated by the death of her only son that she's become a virtual recluse. Her husband doesn't want us to talk with her and we haven't enough material to force an interview. The Williamses are voluntarily helping us with our enquiries and if she refuses to talk we haven't sufficient grounds for compulsion.'

'So what do we do?'

'Try to get more evidence. We now have a much clearer picture of the life Julie Grimshaw was living in the squat, and elsewhere, than we had six days ago. I need to see the people I've just discussed with you again and probe for more details. It could be that none of them is responsible for her death; women in danger of addiction are vulnerable in all sorts of areas. But I have questions which need answering.'

'I'm glad to hear it. I know as well as you do that in complex cases the principal CID task is to establish the questions which need answering. That must be even more true when the crime was committed twenty years ago. I wish you luck with it.'

It was only John Lambert's second private meeting with the new Chief Constable. He had suspected when the appointment was arranged that the new man was seeking for opportunities to be rid of him, that he was regarded as a survival from an earlier age by a man surging forward on the tide of new ideas. That was probably inevitable when a man ten years younger than you was put in charge of things.

For his part, Gordon Armstrong had feared that his most senior CID officer might be a man cocooned in the mores and practices of a previous generation, resistant to change, perhaps making sour and damaging comments to others when the newly installed CC was not around to look after himself. He had found in John Lambert only a man anxious to solve crimes, a man who wished to avoid the machinations and jockeyings for position which dominated so much of his own life. Like most chief constables, he had been a CID man himself; he understood the challenges and frustrations of detection and recognized a man who handled them both with integrity.

Each man had been cautious. Each man left this meeting with a higher opinion of the other.

*   *   *

In the early part of Friday evening, Michael Wallington was on the golf course at Ross-on-Wye. He was playing with a head teacher of about his own age whom he had helped to appoint four months earlier, in his role as Chief Education Officer.

The pair were trying to unwind after what had been a trying week for both of them, as they had agreed in the dressing room while donning their golf shoes. Tony Proctor, the head teacher, had endured problems with the supply teacher replacing a woman on pregnancy leave, with inexperienced young teachers who were having difficulty keeping order, and with a senior member of his staff who had finally given up on her Lothario husband and was enduring the stresses of a belated divorce.

Mike Wallington also had problems. He didn't specify what these were to his golfing companion. He merely told him that it had been a difficult week and that he was looking forward to a relaxing few holes.

They had perfect conditions for recreation. It was a peaceful early summer evening, with the sun still warm as the shadows lengthened and the birds bade their farewell to the day. The forest trees were in full, fresh leaf now, with multiple shades of green to delight the eye and define and individualize each hole. The course was in perfect condition and the putting surfaces were like green velvet, fast and true. An elderly foursome ahead of them called them through on the second hole, and from then on they had the green acres of the course to themselves.

They congratulated themselves three times during the progress of the round on being exactly where they were. There were few better places to be on a June evening than in Britain in a setting like this. Mike had been playing golf for three years now. Golf in a setting like this was part of his reaction against those wild early days which he had now left far behind him, an assurance to himself as well as to others that Michael Wallington, Chief Education Officer, was not only an important and influential person but part of the respectable middle-class establishment.

Having decided to give his time to the sport, Michael had

caught the golfing bug. He was genuinely very keen on the game now. He'd had lessons and he'd been looking forward to the summer evenings, when he would be able to grab a few holes and improve his game in preparation for the greater challenges of weekend golf with the titans of the club. His handicap was coming down steadily; he felt that all he needed to do to reduce it even further was to play lots of golf.

But tonight he couldn't concentrate. He exchanged the usual banter with Tony Proctor as they swapped holes and moved rapidly round the course, but his heart wasn't really in it. Proctor was too intelligent a man to miss that. He asked what was worrying Mike and offered to provide any help he could. By way of reply, he received only a weak smile of gratitude and an assurance that nothing was wrong. Wallington departed after a quick beer with a token assurance that they must do this again.

Mike was too late to read the bedtime story to his children, to his secret relief. He congratulated his son on his gold star from school and planted a gentle kiss on the forehead of his five-year-old daughter, who was already almost asleep. He went softly down the stairs and poured a glass of white wine for Debbie, but only water for himself. They sat quietly in the conservatory and watched the sun descending to leave a crimson sky over the Welsh hills. His wife was eight years younger than he was and he was sure he was genuinely in love with her. He certainly gave more of himself to her than he had believed he would give to any woman.

He had told her things about his past over the last few years. Not everything, but more than he had thought he would ever concede to anyone. He didn't regret that. Honesty was part of giving, one of the things you had to practise if you wished to love and be loved. You had to reveal yourself to your partner and learn intimate things about her, if the two of you were to be close. There were moments when he'd felt tempted to tell Debbie everything, to shock her with all the details, to unburden himself completely of the guilt he felt about those days.

But he was glad now that he'd held the worst things back. It wouldn't have been fair to overwhelm her with that degree of knowledge about him. She was such an innocent, Debbie: that was one of the things he loved in her.

He watched her now and smiled at her as she sipped her wine. Then he thought of the sinister figure from his past who had contacted him after the meeting at the school on Monday night and wondered again how much Debbie would discover about him in the days to come. He said quietly, 'If the police come asking questions, you may need to be discreet. It will be much better for us if you pretend to know nothing about some of the things I have told you.'

THIRTEEN

Chief Superintendent John Lambert was a townsman, bred on urban life and urban ways. Not a bad thing, because the vast majority of criminals were city-based. Murderers were a special case, of course: they came from all classes and all sorts of backgrounds. They could be illiterate or highly educated, crude or sophisticated, and they might come from any one of the complex sub-divisions of the British class system.

Detective Sergeant Hook was from a different background, which was one of the many reasons why they complemented each other so well as a detective duo. Bert as a Barnardo's boy had been bred on communal life in a closed environment and taught to be grateful for whatever good things came to him, in an almost Victorian ethic. All his early work placements had been rural. He had grown up knowing and respecting the long hours and hard, unrelenting work of country life. And he had been a doughty minor counties pace bowler for Herefordshire, one of the most rural of English counties, for seventeen years, running in rhythmically to surprise public-school batsmen with his pace, which was always a little sharper than it looked from the pavilion.

It was Hook who looked at the varied acres of Lower Valley Farm as the pair drove up the long lane to the stone farmhouse. It was Hook who gave the verdict on what they saw as Lambert parked his ancient Vauxhall on the cobbled farmyard. Poultry no longer roamed here as they might have done when Bert had done his very first farm stint as a wide-eyed twelve-year-old boy. Hook looked around and said, 'This place is doing well, unlike most small farms. This man knows what he's doing and what's required.'

The man in question was Jim Simmons, and he was nowhere to be seen at this moment. Nature does not work to man's calendar; Saturday is not a day off for farmers. Jim's wife

Lisa was apologetic. 'He knew you were coming and he knew the time you'd agreed. He gets so wrapped up in the problems out there that he forgets all about time, sometimes. I'll try his mobile.' She said this last a little self-consciously, as if demonstrating that this farm was not set in the old ways; that was a perpetual theme of her husband's. But seconds later, she had to report failure. 'He switches it off when he's on the tractor,' she said. 'I'll get Jamie to go and fetch him for you.'

The bright-eyed eight-year-old was dispatched to look for his father, though he would much rather have stayed and gazed with open mouth at the great detective John Lambert. His companions at school had been much impressed by his account of the previous visit of the great man, and Jamie had been looking forward to retailing every detail of a second episode to them.

Jamie was back with them in three minutes exactly, bouncing like an ebullient monkey on the tractor beside his father, waving enthusiastically to the CID men as Simmons parked beside the old Vauxhall Senator. 'Dad was on his way here!' he said by way of exculpating his errant parent. 'He forgets the time when he gets to the wheatfield.' Like many a boy of his age, he retailed with an air of original wisdom the things he derided when his mother said them.

Lambert wondered as Jim Simmons led them into a quiet room at the front of the house whether this little cameo had again been designed to present the farmer as a pillar of happy family life, a man who could not possibly have been responsible for dark deeds twenty years earlier. As he had agreed with his chief constable on the previous afternoon, it was part of his job to be cynical, wasn't it?

He smiled away Simmons's apologies for keeping them waiting and said, 'We need a further talk with you about the body buried on your land in 1995. After talking to a variety of people who were around at that time, we now know a lot more than when we spoke with you six days ago.'

He made it sound like a warning, as though they had spent the entire six days since they had last seen him assembling material which would prove him a liar and thus the leading suspect for this crime. Jim Simmons said defensively, 'It wasn't my land in 1995. And it wasn't my land when those remains were dug up last week.'

'Technically correct. Does that matter to you? Let's agree that the body of a healthy young woman, Julie Grimshaw, was buried just inside the boundary of this farm almost exactly twenty years ago. Is that satisfactory?'

Jim wondered whether to query the assertion that Julie had been a healthy young woman, on the grounds that at the time of her death she had been seriously into drugs and in danger of sinking into addiction. But that would argue more detailed knowledge of her condition and habits than he cared to admit to here. He said carefully, 'I think I told you everything I knew about this matter when you were here last. I was hoping that you were now close to an arrest.'

'Were you, indeed? Well we aren't, I'm afraid. We wouldn't be here seeking further information if we were close to an arrest, Mr Simmons.'

'I'm sorry about that. I hope Julie is avenged, if that's the right expression. We had our differences, but she should never have died like that.'

'Those differences interest us, Mr Simmons. We'd like you to enlarge upon them. We'd like you to add to what other people have now told us. We need to hear your side of the story.'

Jim glanced instinctively at the door he had shut so carefully when they came into this small, quiet room. How much did they know? What had other people told them about him and Julie? It was a police tactic, this exploitation of your ignorance, this making you tense by playing on your fear of what other people might already have told them. You might need to defend yourself against what they had said, or you might be better saying nothing – but then you might seem evasive, and that wouldn't help you if, as they said, they were searching desperately for someone to arrest for this crime long gone. Dead and buried, that crime had been, he thought grimly, but it had now returned to disturb the lives of those who had shared those months with Julie Grimshaw in 1995. He said carefully, 'I knew Julie quite well for a short period.'

'No, Mr Simmons. You can do better than that. I believe

you can remember more than you told us on the day after her bones had been discovered. Let's say that more details have probably come back to you during the six days since we last spoke with you.'

It was delivered in firm but superficially polite tones. It said, come clean with us now whilst there is still time, so that we do not need to treat you as a hostile witness. Jim wasn't in court, but he felt at this moment very much as if Lambert were a prosecuting counsel. He said, 'You were vague yourselves when you were questioning me about the skeleton on Sunday. We were all shocked.'

'Perhaps. But you knew more than we did. We didn't even know the identity of the victim. You pretended to be as ignorant as we were about how the body had come to be in the ground on your territory. It's my belief that you must at least have suspected who this woman was.'

Jim forced himself to take his time. He wasn't used to dealing with words; he didn't have to use them very often, nowadays. But he knew he wasn't bad with words when he needed them – just a little out of practice, perhaps. 'I suppose I thought that skeleton might have been Julie's – feared might be a better word. The thought hit me as soon as I heard about the discovery of bones there. That wasn't because I knew anything about how they came to be there. It was because I knew a young woman who had disappeared suddenly at that time. When you hear that remains have been discovered all these years later, your thoughts naturally fly to who was around here at that time and who it might have been. Julie Grimshaw vanished from our lives during the summer of 1995. It was natural that my thoughts should fly to her.'

'But you didn't see fit to communicate her name to us last Sunday. We would have waited much longer for an identification if her distraught mother had not come to see us on Monday and provided us with a DNA sample for comparison.'

'I'm sorry about that. But it was less than twenty-four hours after the skeleton had been unearthed when you spoke with me on Sunday. My mind was reeling with the shock of finding out that a body had been buried near the boundary of this farm. And there were others who knew her, as well as me. I didn't want to implicate them and open a can of worms. It was still possible then that the skeleton might have been that of a complete stranger, unknown to any of us.'

Hook had established an easier relationship with this man than Lambert had achieved, at their previous meeting. They had similar backgrounds, with Hook having been a Barnardo's boy and Simmons having been in care from twelve to sixteen. Bert now looked up from his notes and said, 'Your initial instinct on Sunday was one of self-preservation, was it not, Jim?'

Simmons looked at Hook's rugged outdoor face suspiciously, then softened a little as he remembered their previous exchanges. 'I told you I had a wild youth. I told you I'd got into fights and all sorts of scrapes at that time. I told you I'd had my share of girls and treated a lot of them badly. If a dead girl had been buried on our land at that time, I felt you were going to have me down as a leading suspect. Don't you think it understandable that I would tell you as little as possible?'

Hook allowed himself a relaxed, avuncular smile. 'Understandable, perhaps, but ill-advised nonetheless, Jim. Withholding information leads to far more suspicion than revealing it, for the innocent. You are innocent in this, aren't you?'

'Yes, of course I am.'

'Then convince us of that by giving us all the help you can.'

'I want to do that. Believe me I do.'

'We're policemen, Jim. We're here as professionals. You need to make us believe you. Tell us about your own relationship with Julie Grimshaw. Tell us about how Andrew Burrell felt about her and treated her.'

He looked up sharply with the mention of his contemporary; his wide brown eyes showed his alarm. 'It was Andrew who brought her here. He had a thing going with her, for a while. I'm not quite sure how serious it was.'

'But his parents thought it was serious, didn't they? And they didn't like it.'

'No, they didn't approve of Julie. We thought they were out of touch and didn't understand youth, at the time.' He shook his head and ran a hand briefly over his rather untidy brown hair. 'Now that I've got kids of my own, I can imagine how they felt. You want to protect your kids, don't you? Andrew was a young man by then and wanting to assert himself. But your kids are always kids to you, aren't they? You feel the need to protect them, whatever age they are.'

Hook reflected that this was a boy who had been placed in council care between the ages of twelve and sixteen and then left to make his own way in the world. Not much parental care there. But that probably made him even more anxious to do his best for his own children. Bert, the Barnardo's boy who had fought his way through to his present professional position and a happy marriage, certainly felt extremely protective of his own two boys, now in their early teens. He knew he'd have to relax the bonds of love as they got older, but he knew also that he wasn't going to find that easy, that he'd find Eleanor telling him firmly that he must let go. He felt suddenly quite close to this successful farmer of almost his own age. He was unprofessional enough to hope deeply for a moment that they wouldn't conclude the case with an arrest of Jim Simmons. He said quietly, 'So the Burrells didn't approve of Julie. Tell us all about that, please.'

'I think they'd have been quite prepared to help her, if Julie had been prepared to accept help. Emily in particular was a very kind woman, and not at all the old fuddy-duddy we thought her at the time. And Daniel Burrell knew the score, far more clearly than we thought he did. There's an arrogance about youth, isn't there? It's one of its least attractive qualities. I read that the other day and I agree with it, when I look back at those times.'

'Tell us about Julie. She's a murder victim and we need to know all we can about her. You knew her in the weeks before her death. There will be something which happened in those days which is directly linked to her killing.'

Simmons looked shaken, as if he was confronting this thought for the first time. 'I'd dabbled with drugs myself, like most of my set. I knew enough about them to realize immediately that Julie Grimshaw was a user. Not pot, like me, but coke or heroin. There was one day when she was completely out of it. I think Emily must have seen her on an occasion like that. From being sympathetic to a girl living in a squat and struggling with life, she turned right against her. I think she was frightened of what she saw and what might follow if things got worse. She'd never done drugs herself and the thought of horse and scag terrified her. She didn't want Julie under her roof any more. I remember Emily using exactly that phrase.'

'But it wasn't solely the drugs, was it? Daniel and Emily were worried about Andrew's relationship with Julie.'

'Yes. I think for Andrew there was something romantic about Julie's circumstances. He liked the idea of lifting her out of the squat and rescuing her from drugs and making her a pretty and successful young woman. There was a certain missionary zeal about his attitude when he brought her here. That's another annoying thing about youth: you think you can work miracles where others have failed.'

'But his parents didn't want this?'

Jim Simmons frowned. He didn't want to denigrate Daniel and Emily, both of whom had been very good to him. 'They wanted to help Julie. But she didn't seem prepared to help herself. She turned up here completely stoned once, and I think they saw that as a direct challenge to them. Daniel wasn't going to stand for that, for a start. Farmers are very proprietorial on their own patch, you know. They're used to ruling the roost and not being challenged. It's probably something to do with the place where you work also being the place where you live.' He grinned suddenly at Hook, recognizing the implications of this for himself. 'But the thing which really mattered to Dan and Emily was Andrew's relationship with Julie. They didn't want their son lining himself up with a druggie – a girl who might even become an addict. I could see their position at the time. I can sympathize with it a lot more now, when I have kids of my own.'

Again the emphasis on himself as a family man, on his feeling for his children. Genuine emotion, or an attempt to divert attention from the man he had been in 1995? Bert said, 'So they feared that Andrew might be dragged into the world of drugs by Julie Grimshaw?'

'I doubt whether they really feared that. I think they just

felt he was taking on more than he could handle with Julie. They might have been right. No one wants an addict in their family, or even close to them. Addicts can ruin other lives as well as their own.'

'So what did the older Burrells do about the situation?'

'They said they didn't want her in the house again. I think there'd been some sort of incident. I didn't see it. I was out working the land at the time. But I think Julie was stoned and insulted Emily. Dan wasn't going to stand for that.'

Hook smiled grimly. 'Jim, I need you to be very honest now about people I know you admire. Do you think either Dan or his wife did anything more violent than that? Do you think either of them might have had any involvement in Julie's death? Not necessarily a planned or even a deliberate involvement. We could be looking at manslaughter rather than murder. Do you think one or both of them might have been provoked into violence by her conduct or by her relationship with their son?'

'No. I've thought about it during the last few days, as you might expect. But Emily simply wouldn't have been capable of that sort of reaction. And Daniel, despite his demand to rule the roost here, could never have been violent towards a woman. He was old-fashioned in that respect. I'm sure when I first came here as a lad he'd cheerfully have thrashed me with a belt, if I'd stepped seriously out of line. That was the impression he gave me and I'm grateful for it now. I don't deny that I was frightened of him at the time. But the fear was good for me: I might have gone seriously off the rails without it. But Daniel would no more have been capable of physical violence against Julie than his wife would, however much he might have wished her out of his sight for ever.'

Simmons was breathing hard now, vehement in his description of his benefactors, determined to convince the CID men that the dead Emily and the man now in care at eighty-four had had no involvement in this death. His defence was the more convincing in that he must have known that it left him more exposed as a suspect in the case. As a young man not much older than Julie Grimshaw, who admitted to knowing her well at the time, Simmons was too intelligent not to know that he must be one of the CID candidates for murder.

Lambert had never taken his eyes off the man during Hook's gentler interrogation. He now said tersely, 'The man most closely involved with Julie, according to your account, was Andrew Burrell. What was your relationship with him?'

Jim was thrown for a moment by the question. It was a diversion from the themes they had been pursuing, the condition and behaviour of Julie Grimshaw when she had visited this farm twenty years ago. He had expected to be asked about Andrew and Julie, not about Andrew and himself. And he had expected the questions to come from Hook, not from this intense older man who he sensed was more hostile to him. 'We were contemporaries. We got on all right.'

'You can do better than that. Did you like each other?'

'We didn't dislike each other. We were two very different men. We were both young and both still finding out what we wanted to do in the world.'

'Did you see yourselves as rivals for this farm?'

'No. I think Daniel wanted to see it that way. I think he wanted to prod his son into thinking his inheritance was being taken away from him. And I was certainly conscious of taking over the role which Daniel and Emily had intended for their son. I felt in a difficult position. I enjoyed farming and I was being trusted with more and more of the day-to-day work and even the farming decisions, but I knew that the intention had been that the farm would pass to Andrew. There was tension between Andrew and his parents, but not really between Andrew and me. He came back from agricultural college without completing his course there; he'd decided that farming wasn't for him.'

'So you took over this place quite smoothly?'

'I wouldn't say that. I was in quite a difficult position, as I said. Andrew sometimes seemed to despise me, simply because I was interested in this place and in what he regarded as dull and menial work. And I regarded him as a wimp, because he wanted to go off and do an arts degree rather than taking this opportunity in the real world. I can see now that the world he's working in is the real one for him, but when you're young you think the path you want to tread is the only valid one.'

'So you had your differences. Did you fall out with each other?'

'No. We were very different personalities, so we weren't likely to be close friends. But what happened here in 1994 and 1995 was opportune for both of us. I remember Andrew eventually saying to me after a row with his dad that it was a good thing that I was around. Daniel and Emily would channel the ambitions they'd had for him into my career here. If I played my cards right I'd get the farm, and he wouldn't resent it because it would get him off the hook of their expectations.'

'You must have been glad to hear him saying those words.'

Jim looked round at the small, comfortable room, at the prosperous farm he could glimpse through its single window. He thought of the other rooms beyond this one, of his wife and two children and the satisfaction he got from being in this ancient house and from working hard on this land. 'It wasn't as straightforward as you seem to be assuming it was. It took Daniel a long time to accept the idea that his son wasn't going to take over. It took him several months to accept that I was a possible alternative. Emily liked me and was kind throughout my time here. I'm sure it was she who eventually sold the idea to Dan that I might take over here.'

'So how do you get on with Andrew Burrell nowadays?'

How persistent the senior man was! It was almost as if he knew that Andrew had phoned him on the previous day, asking him to keep quiet about Liam. But Lambert couldn't know that Andrew had been in touch, surely? 'We have very little to do with each other. He lives his life and I live mine. They don't overlap at any point. His mother tried to keep us in touch, but she's been gone for quite a while now.'

'So you haven't been in contact about this matter?'

Jim felt his pulses quicken at that. Did they know about Andrew's phone call to him? Had the man told them himself, without letting him know? He spoke as casually as he could. 'Andrew rang me yesterday, as a matter of fact. Wanted to compare notes about the skeleton, now that we know who it is.' He glanced at the two very different faces in front of him

and forced a smile. 'Only natural, I suppose; I'm sure you'd
agree with that.'

'What did you decide after you'd conferred with each other?'

'Nothing. We were both shocked. We each knew as little
as the other about how Julie's body came to be where it was
discovered.' He wouldn't mention Liam. He owed that much
at least to Andrew.

'Give me the most accurate description you can of Andrew
Burrell's relationship with Julie Grimshaw at the time of her
death.'

Lambert hadn't raised his voice; he seemed the calmest one
of the three in that quiet room. But his tone was brusque and
this was a command, not a question. Jim tried to speak confidently; this at last was ground he'd expected to cover. 'I think
the affair was coming to an end in the summer of 1995.'

'Which of them had decided that?'

'I'm not sure – especially at this distance of time. You'll
need to ask Andrew. But you will, won't you? Perhaps you
already have. You want to know what I think, whether it tallies
with his version of things.'

'At least one person and quite probably more than one will
lie to us in the days ahead, Mr Simmons. It's our job to expose
the truth. You would be most unwise to attempt to conceal it
from us.'

'I realize that. When I say I'm not certain about things, I'm
being as honest as I can. Julie was a druggie. Not an addict,
but a regular user. That meant that she was erratic in her
behaviour. She could be quite different from one day to the
next. Andrew was still seeing her after his mum and dad had
banned her from this house. I know that. But by the summer
he'd secured himself a place at Liverpool University and he
was determined to go up there at the end of September. Whether
he ended the affair because of those plans, I don't know. It's
equally possible that Julie decided she'd had enough of it.'

'Or it's possible that there was no mutual agreement to end
the association. It's possible that they argued over its termina-
tion. It's possible that Julie Grimshaw's death was a result of
that argument.'

'I suppose so. I can only say that I don't believe it was. We all thought when Julie disappeared that she'd simply decided to move on. Perhaps to another squat, perhaps to change her life back to something more normal.'

'How upset was Andrew Burrell when she disappeared?'

'I can't tell you that. Not at this distance in time. I remember only that he was excited by the new direction his life was taking with the degree he planned for himself. I can remember arguments between father and son over his deserting the farm. I can remember Emily trying to placate Daniel, because she'd accepted by this time that Andrew was never going to be a farmer. But as far as I can remember, the arguments about Julie were finished by the end of the summer. Perhaps all three of them were relieved that she'd moved on. But I can't speak for Andrew; you must ask him for his version of 1995.'

Lambert gave him a taut smile. 'We shall do that, of course. Thank you for your help, Mr Simmons.'

As the two big men stood up, Hook said, seemingly as an afterthought, 'You were aware that Julie was a regular user of illegal drugs at what we now know was the time of her death. I'm sure you know that regular users are often recruited as dealers by those who operate the drugs trade. Often they receive free supplies for themselves in return for selling a certain quota of Class A drugs. Do you think it possible that Julie had been approached to become a dealer?'

'I've no idea. Is it relevant to her death?'

'It could be, especially if she refused. People who fall out with the drug hierarchy often die swiftly and obscurely. It's a possibility we need to bear in mind.'

They were gone a moment later, leaving the sturdy Jim Simmons feeling more limp than he had done for years. He went into the kitchen and picked up the family phone book, checking Lisa's neat figures beside the names. He rang Andrew Burrell from the privacy of the room where he had spoken with Lambert and Hook. 'The CID came again, as you said they would. Grilled me about how we felt about each other at that time, about your relationship with Julie. I didn't give them much. I didn't tell them about Liam. I avoided all mention of him.'

FOURTEEN

The best way to shut out nightmares is to ignore them. The more you immerse yourself in the innocent concerns of daylight, the less threatening the unreal fantasies of darkness will seem. It is all a matter of setting things firmly in proportion; healthy daytime activity will do this for you. Michael Wallington tried hard to convince himself that this was the simple solution to his problems.

Saturday would be his family day, for this weekend at least. His wife and children must have his whole attention on Saturday. Michael had not always been so solicitous; indeed, he could not remember when he had last been so determined upon a family day. But on this Saturday he was determined to implement this worthy ethic. 'We're going for a ride on the Severn Valley Railway tomorrow!' he told his children on Friday night. Then he showed them the picture of the great GWR steam locomotive which dominated the publicity pamphlet.

Debbie loyally supported his contention that this was to be the outing of the year for them, though she knew that a boy of eight and a girl of five were in truth a little short of the ideal ages to appreciate the railway. Mother and father were bowled over by the poppy meadow near the railway, with its poignant remembrance for the adults of the poppy fields of Flanders a century earlier. But Tom and Jane were anxious to reach the station, the railway and the promised delights of Thomas the Tank Engine at the other end of the ancient line.

They were not as impressed as their father felt they should be when he told them that the tracks had been laid here in 1862 and had now been here for over a hundred and fifty years. They waited impatiently at Bewdley station for something more to childish tastes. Tom was duly impressed when the 4-6-0 steam locomotive *Erlestoke Manor* drew into the station with an impressive screech of braking wheels and a plaintive note in its whistle. Jane retreated in panic as a huge exhalation of white steam hissed noisily ahead of its wheels, but was eventually persuaded by her mother to board the chocolate and cream carriage.

They rattled happily through the sixteen miles of the green and restful Severn Valley to Bridgnorth, with the steam from the engine flying away above their heads towards the hills and the great river running below them. Michael tried to immerse himself in the landscape and in his family. The children, with the vagueness about time appropriate to their years, thought that Dad had surely travelled about the country in trains like this as a young man, with firemen enthusiastically shovelling coal from the tender on to the fire and blackened drivers peering anxiously down the line to check the signals. Mike explained laughingly that trains like this had ceased to function before his time, that even in Granddad's time there had not been many of them left working. Jane then became anxious: if the engine and the carriages were as old as that, mightn't they run off the lines and fall off the big bridge she'd seen in the picture? They might all be killed!

The small girl spent most of the trip cradled nervously in her mother's arms but perked up when the journey was complete and they could inspect Thomas the Tank Engine in the siding at Bridgnorth. She was fully restored after refreshments in the garden of the Railwayman's Arms. On the return journey Debbie and Michael tried hard to enthuse the children with the exhibits in the Engine House Centre at Highley, but it was quickly apparent that they were too tired as well as too young to reap the full benefits of railway history.

It had nevertheless been a good day out, Debbie assured Mike happily as they drove homewards. The fact that the children, securely fastened into child seats in the rear of the BMW, were asleep within five minutes attested to that. 'We should do this sort of thing more often,' said Debbie. 'You're a slave to your work, you know. It does you good to get away from the job when you can.'

Michael assented weakly, affirming to himself how lucky he was to have the precious cargo he was now ferrying homewards. But home when it arrived seemed to him a threat rather than a relief. The familiar bricks of the modern detached house seemed to tower like a menacing cliff above him against the western sky as he carried Tom in from the car. He watched the sleeping infant face of Jane bobbing gently on Debbie's shoulder ahead of him and told himself firmly that the world was surely not too bad a place. If he could just get through this crisis, all would be well . . .

There were two messages on the landline phone when he checked. The first was from his father, telling him what time they should arrive for lunch tomorrow. The second was from DS Hook, that unthreatening plod who had taken notes when the two CID men had spoken with him on the previous day. They had now assembled a fuller picture of events at Fairfax Street in Gloucester in 1995. In the light of this, they would like to speak to him further on the morrow. He was sure that Michael would now be able to help them to complete the picture of life in that squat.

'I'm aware that four o'clock on a Saturday afternoon is not the most convenient hour for a meeting. Thank you for making the time to see us.'

'One has a public duty, Mr Lambert. And I'm sure it won't be too onerous for me to exchange notes with two intelligent policemen.' It sounded much too oily, but Kate Clark gave her visitors her full public relations beam and gestured towards the sofa in her sitting room in Tewkesbury.

She had dressed deliberately in an outfit which was as great a contrast to her formal costume of Thursday as she could contrive. This was Saturday, leisure day, her clothes said; she was relaxed and unthreatened, cheerfully making the time to see them during her weekend. But she also wanted to show them what a balanced character she was. They must note how she was taking in her stride their discovery that this woman who was now a senior executive with a great national company had once dwelt in a sordid squat in Gloucester.

That was all securely locked away in the past for her. She might be embarrassed by any revelation that she had once lived in such squalor, but it would cause her just that: embarrassment, not fear. She had tried various garments in front of the full-length mirror in her bedroom before settling for a pale blue mohair sweater and a darker blue skirt, with comfortable low-heeled blue shoes beneath her elegant legs. She had considered trousers, or even jeans, but she knew from long business and social experience that men were beguiled by female legs; even experienced CID men, who should surely know much better, might be distracted by the sheer denier of her best tights. It was worth a try, anyway, she thought, as she planted herself opposite them, drew up her knees and turned her cool grey eyes upon the darker grey ones of John Lambert.

She'd had her short dark hair expertly cut and styled since they'd seen her on Thursday, Lambert noticed; sharp observation, one of the tools of the detective trade, had become a habit over the years, instinctive to him now rather than a conscious effort. Appearance must be important to a woman like this, he thought – to women in general, in fact. It was another cross they had to bear. He had long since ceased to care about how he presented himself, save for a very few occasions in his working year. He said, 'We've been asking the older coppers in Gloucester for their recollections of seventeen Fairfax Street in 1995. As well as speaking with other occupants of that house, of course. We've come up with a surprising amount of information about the last days of our murder victim.'

'That's good. The police machine is very efficient, I know, when there's a serious crime involved.'

More PR. Lambert ignored it completely and added, 'And no doubt your own recollection of those days has been sharpened by two days of thinking about them.'

It was a deliberate challenge and both of them knew it. She could have reminded him that she had a strenuous business life, with many important considerations to occupy her, but she didn't bother with such irrelevancies. 'I can't say that I've remembered anything which might be helpful to you. But no doubt you will wish to jog my memory with some of the things you and your team have discovered.' She crossed her legs and gave him the encouraging smile she usually reserved for the more favoured among her juniors.

'There were drugs in that squat. You admitted as much to us on Thursday.'

'I don't like that word "admitted". I did my best to recall circumstances from twenty years ago, which I had been at pains to shut out of my life.'

'Sorry for the semantics. You gave the impression of being reluctant to discuss the presence of drugs in that house. Tell us everything which you now remember about the drugs and the people involved with them, both as users and suppliers.'

She was being treated almost as a hostile witness here, she thought. But perhaps that was inevitable, when she'd told them so little on Thursday. How much more did they know now than when they had spoken to her then? Kate said carefully, 'I'm not proud of my time in that house. I have a career to think of. I've genuinely shut out as much as I can of those days. I live in the present, not in 1995.'

'As we all do, Ms Clark. That's a truism. But we and you are now involved in the investigation of a murder which took place in 1995, and we have to examine your part in events which took place twenty years ago. Neither you nor we have any choice about that. Tell us about the drugs, please.'

Lambert was even, emotionless, uncompromising. His eyes had not left her since they came into the room. Kate Clark could not remember when she had last felt so disturbed; she could have handled this better if he'd been openly hostile. She tried to speak as evenly as her questioner. 'I wasn't a user, beyond the occasional spliff, which all of us took when we could get it. Julie Grimshaw was a user. I'm not an expert, but I don't think she was an addict. She was quite a heavy user, however, and she seemed sometimes to need drugs, as I never did. It's difficult to be certain, because I think there were times when most of us in that house were using anything we could to escape from the life we lived there.'

'Who supplied the drugs?'

She paused, then spoke as if the words were being wrung from her on the rack. 'Mick. As far as I can remember, he was the only one who brought drugs into the squat. I can remember Julie begging for him to give her horse, one day. I came in suddenly and went out again just as quickly. I didn't want to get involved.'

'And did she get the heroin she wanted?'

'I think so. I don't know for certain. I didn't want to know. I was scared of drugs, especially hard drugs. You pretended to be quite blasé in the squat, but you were frightened underneath. I was, anyway.'

'This Mick was the one who brought in the hard drugs?'

'Yes. If there was any other source, I didn't know of it.'

'Surname?'

'I don't know. I never knew. We didn't deal in surnames.'

'Describe him, please.'

'I can't do that. Not in any detail. He was medium height and I think he had dark eyes. I remember them as deep-set, but there wasn't much light in most rooms in the squat and I don't remember seeing him much during the day. He had either a beard or extensive stubble. But a lot of men were like that in the squat. I suppose shaving wasn't easy.'

'He sold drugs, you say.'

'I believe he did, yes. But mostly in other places than the squat. There wasn't much money there.'

'We now know from others as well as yourself that Julie Grimshaw was an extensive user. You think the drugs came from this man Mick. How did she pay for them?'

'I don't know how she paid for them. She didn't tell me.'

'Was she sleeping with him?'

Kate was trying to assess the importance of these questions for her, whilst appearing to answer quickly and helpfully. It wasn't easy. 'I don't think so. She had this thing going with Andrew Burrell. I told you, I went to Lower Valley Farm with her once or twice. I know people do desperate things when they want drugs, but I don't think she was dropping her pants for Mick. I don't remember him even trying it on with her. He probably thought he could do better than a potential addict.'

'Then how was she paying for drugs?'

'I don't know. I've wondered about that a little since we spoke on Thursday, but I haven't come up with anything. Unless . . .'

'Unless what, Ms Clark?'

'I wish you'd call me Kate. I don't know how she paid. She had some money when she came to the squat. And I think she sold her watch and a ring she had whilst we were there. I was trying hard to get her to give up the drugs, but she reckoned she needed them.'

'So she was using at the time of her death. How do you think she was continuing to pay?'

'I told you, I don't know. But as you suggested to me on Thursday, I did suspect that Mick might be planning to recruit her as a seller. Provide her with her own supplies in return for selling a certain quantity of coke and horse and E.'

'We know all about that. We also know that many of the people recruited to sell drugs on that basis become addicts and end up totally controlled by people higher up the drugs chain. Do you think that happened to Julie?'

'No. I didn't believe she was an addict at the time of her disappearance. I thought she was in danger of becoming one and I was trying to prevent that. I don't believe that she'd sold out to the drug suppliers in that way.'

'But you think this Mick might have been putting pressure on her to become a dealer?'

Kate shrugged her supple shoulders beneath the mohair and gave him a taut smile. 'He might have been. I never saw him approach her and Julie didn't tell me that he had. But it would have been a logical move, if he was looking for new dealers.'

'You say you've thought about this since Thursday. Perhaps you have also considered a possible repercussion. If this Mick fellow approached Julie to sell drugs and she refused to cooperate, might he or his agents have killed her? Drugs are a massive and highly lucrative industry, but those at the bottom of the chain are very vulnerable, if they refuse what is offered. If they felt that Julie was likely to reveal the offer made to her and the identities of the people who had made it, she might well have been quietly and ruthlessly eliminated by them. Do you think that is what happened?'

This time Kate did not shrug but shuddered. 'It might have been. Everything you say is correct. It's a possibility that those people killed her. I didn't see anything to support that theory of her death, but then I wouldn't have done, would I? The drug people are careful as well as fearsome. That's one reason why I never got into horse or coke. It's why I wanted Julie to finish with drugs. But I can't provide you with evidence that those people killed her.'

Kate was conscious of no exchange between the two, but DS Hook now looked up from his notes and took over the questioning. 'You reminded us a moment ago that you went to Lower Valley Farm with Julie. As you know, that's where her body was buried. Tell us what you remember about the people there, please.'

She managed a smile into the rubicund face of this less threatening figure. 'That's rather a wide brief, because there were a lot of people there, as I remember it. But I'll do my best. The old people who owned the place were quite kind to us, at first. I think Andrew had told them about how he was rescuing these girls from the squat in Fairfax Street, because they seemed quite sorry for us. I didn't go as often as Julie did and they still seemed to be sympathetic towards me. But when they realized that Andrew was serious about Julie and wanted to take it further, they turned against her. And Julie told me she'd gone there stoned and done unpardonable things. I wasn't with her on that day, but when we went there together again I could see that the older Burrells didn't want her around any more.'

'Emily Burrell isn't here for us to question: she died three years ago. Daniel Burrell, Andrew's father, is now eighty-four and in a care home. But he and his wife were vigorous sixty-four-year-olds at the time of Julie's death. They were very protective of their only son. Do you feel that either or both of them might have been involved in Julie's murder?'

'No. I never got to know them well, but I don't think either of them would have been involved in murder.'

'Or manslaughter? We don't know that the blow which killed Julie was meant to be fatal. It might have been the culmination of some altercation which strayed into violence.'

'I obviously can't discount that possibility. But you asked me what I felt. And I feel that the Burrells weren't the kind of people who would have done this and buried the body in secret at the edge of their land.'

'Thank you.' Hook glanced at his chief. 'It seems unlikely to us also, but we have to take every possibility into consideration. What did you make of Andrew Burrell in those days?'

It was said very casually, but Kate was well aware that she was being asked to assess a murder suspect. She was one herself, so this was competitive. She'd enjoyed competition as she'd risen through the ranks of industry – thrived upon it, in fact. But this was a life and death competition; she felt her pulses racing at that thought. 'I didn't see Andrew that often. I wasn't at Lower Valley Farm as often as Julie.'

'But you had time to form an impression. And Julie was your friend. She must have talked to you about him.'

Kate wanted to remind them yet again of how long ago this was. But that would have seemed defensive. It would have sounded as if she had something to hide. 'I thought him a bit of a wimp, I think. He even objected to being called Andy. Remember that I was living in a squat, so perhaps I despised anyone who seemed to be taking the safe option. He'd got himself a place at university and was going off to it in the autumn. Somewhere in the north, I think.'

'Liverpool.'

'Was it?' She was shaken by the reminder that they'd already spoken to Andrew and to others and knew all sorts of things that she did not. Was Hook reminding her that she needed to tell them the truth? 'Andrew seemed very taken with Julie, at first. She was a pretty girl, when she chose to show it, so that wasn't surprising. But I think he was attracted to the idea of saving her from the squat and from drugs; you get romantic notions when you're as wet behind the ears as Andrew was at that time. And when his parents disapproved, he dug his toes in all the harder, as young men do.' Kate Clark was happy to give the impression that she hadn't a lot of time for young men.

'Why did he and Julie break up?'

'I don't know that. I thought that for him the novelty had worn off. I warned her that his university place was the import- ant thing for Andrew and that he was going to ditch her when he went off to take it up. But that was just my view. I don't know what actually happened. It might have been Julie who ditched him.'

'Do you think they had a major row of some kind? Or did they part on good terms?'

He was cleverer than he looked, this detective sergeant. He made you offer your opinions; he encouraged you to speculate and reveal more than you'd intended. More than you'd intended about yourself too, perhaps. Kate determined to be careful. 'I've no idea. I just assumed they'd split up, when she went off so suddenly. Now we know that she hadn't gone off at all, that someone had killed her. Perhaps they didn't split up. But I thought that all wasn't well between them, from the few things Julie let out to me when we were trying to get to sleep in Fairfax Street.'

'I see.' Hook made a brief note and she wondered what he was writing. 'What about Jim Simmons, who was living on the site and working full-time on the farm?'

It was an abrupt switch, perhaps designed to catch her off guard, to make her reveal more than she'd intended to about Simmons. But she'd prepared what she would say about him before they came. 'He was polite enough, but he didn't seem very interested in Julie. Or me, for that matter. He was a good-looking man who didn't find it difficult to get girls. Perhaps he thought he could do better for himself than girls living in a squat. Julie and I and Andrew and Jim were all about the same age, but Jim was probably the most mature one among us.'

'Too mature to have got himself involved in murder, do you think?'

It was a competitive situation, this, as she'd already decided. Kate was reluctant to discard Simmons as a suspect; that might throw more suspicion on to herself. 'From what Andrew said, I gathered that Jim could be quite violent. He'd already been involved in one or two serious fights. When Julie turned up stoned and was very rude to Mrs Burrell, Jim Simmons took her by the shoulders and shook her very roughly.' She paused, wishing to give the impression that she was anxious to be fair. 'But that's very different from saying he was capable of murder or manslaughter, isn't it? He was very attached to the Burrells; he said they'd been very good to him. I gather that Simmons is now the owner of the farm. Perhaps he was playing his cards very carefully in 1995, with Andrew off to university and plainly uninterested in farming.'

Hook nodded slowly, as if he hoped that his agreement might lure more revelations from her. 'Was there anyone else around at the time who showed any interest in Julie Grimshaw?'

'There was Liam, of course, the boy from the house which was nearest to the farm.'

Kate Clark's face was open but unrevealing beneath the neat dark hair. There was no indication in her bearing that she knew that she'd just delivered a bombshell.

Jim Simmons was the visitor whom Daniel Burrell liked most of all. Jim took him out into the gardens of the care home whenever the weather allowed it, so that Dan could feel the sun on his face and the breeze around his ageing body.

But there was more than that to his enjoyment. They never had awkward pauses and desperate searches for things to talk about, as he had with most of his visitors, however well-meaning they were. He could talk to Jim about Lower Valley Farm, about the problems of cultivation and livestock, about the impact of the changing seasons, about the things which had preoccupied him and his predecessors for at least the last two centuries, since the boundaries of the farm had been defined.

They were sitting on this Saturday evening on a seat facing west, watching the vivid crimson over the Welsh hills which guaranteed them a fine day for the morrow. The corn was looking very good indeed, Jim reported, knowing how it had been a perennial concern of the well-wrapped old man beside him. He was hopeful of a record crop if they got good weather for the harvest. Prices as usual would be in other, more anonymous, non-rural hands, and prices would determine the degree of profit. The two had the ritual grumble over that which they had regularly exchanged when Dan had been in control of the farm and Jim had been his increasingly trusted acolyte.

Then they sat in a comfortable silence for a few minutes, watching crimson turn to purple over the scene, seeing the detail disappear as the mountains became silhouettes against the dying light, sharing the thought which neither of them voiced that this scene had not changed in many centuries. Eventually, Daniel said, 'It's not a bad place, this. Everything's laid on for you and the girls are kind.' Every female under sixty was a girl for Dan. 'But you miss things; they can't help that. You miss sitting down after a hard day's graft and knowing you've achieved something.'

'Aye. You've always been an active man, Dan. But you have to slow down sometime.'

Another pause, whilst the old man nodded slowly, resentfully. 'You can't do owt about age. No bugger can.'

'No. I expect you miss Emily, too. I know I do.'

Dan Burrell was more grateful than he could have imagined for the mention of his dead wife. People skirted around it, thought it would upset you when it wouldn't. He wanted to tell people how much he'd loved Emily, how much she'd meant to him. But men didn't go on about things like that, did they? Not his generation of men. He'd never have found the right words. Now he simply said, 'She was a good woman, Emily. Good to everyone, not just to me.'

'She was, Dan. Good to everyone. I still remember how kind she was to me, when I was a daft lad still looking to make my way in farming.'

Dan smiled. 'It was Em who said you should have the farm, you know, when it turned out Andrew didn't want it. Persuaded me that you'd keep it going and make a job of it.'

'I think I knew that. I'll always be grateful to her.'

'She was a wise woman as well as a kind woman, my Em. It was she who told me to let Andrew go without throwing him out of our lives.'

'She was right, you know. Andrew didn't want to fall out with you. He's just different from us. He doesn't feel the same way as we do about the land.'

'He's different, all right.' For a moment, an old resentment clouded Daniel's face. 'He comes to see me, sometimes. Not as often as he should, perhaps. But I don't blame him, because we don't have much to talk about. Not like you and me.'

'Thanks for letting me know that the fuzz had been to see you about that skeleton.'

'I didn't tell them much. Well, I couldn't.'

'It was Julie, you know, the skeleton. That lass Andrew brought home.'

'Yes. They didn't know that, when they came to see me.'

'Probably best you don't tell them anything more than you have to about Andrew and Julie. Or me and Julie, for that matter.'

'Aye. Probably best. But I don't remember anything, do I?' The old man smiled enigmatically towards the outline of the hills. 'Best go in now, I think. It's getting quite dark.'

Hazel Williams usually came to the cemetery at this time. Saturday evening on the edge of dark was the quietest time of all. A lot of people visited the graves during the day. There were fresh flowers on many of them and she enjoyed the freshness and the colours. But in the evening she had the place to herself.

She could still feel very close to Liam here, though she had to work at it more than in the early days. It was eight years now; people who cared for her sometimes reminded her of that. She knew that he wasn't really here, that the real Liam had left her and left this world some time ago now. But when she sat here on a silent June evening like this, she could forget that. She could convince herself that he was still here, still speaking to her, living on with her in this strange world which only she knew and which she did not want to leave.

'It's peaceful here, isn't it?'

She leapt as if the words had been pins stuck into her lean body. She hadn't known that there was anyone there, hadn't heard the footfall of any approach. But it was only Steve. Hazel didn't know why she thought 'only'. She didn't want him here, any more than she wanted anyone else. Less than she wanted anyone else, now that she thought about it. She said, as though he was a stranger, 'Why have you come here?'

'Because I want to remember our son too. Because I want to be with you.'

Both eminently reasonable things to say. And both ideas she wanted to reject. Liam was hers and this place was hers. She didn't want anyone coming here and interfering with that. Least of all Steve.

He reached out his hand and put it on top of hers. She stared at it for a moment and let it lie there. As soon as she felt she could, she slid her hand out from under his. She didn't want him next to her, didn't want the smell of him, didn't want to hear the sound of his steady breathing beside her.

Hazel wasn't sure how many minutes passed before she said, 'This is my place. Mine and Liam's.'

Steve Williams said, 'You've got to let me in.'

Another long pause while she calmly reviewed that claim. Then, 'I don't have to do anything, Steve.'

'I want to look after you. I want to protect you. I don't want those damned coppers disturbing you.'

'I don't need your protection, Steve. I'm not afraid of the police.'

They were simple statements. But they sounded to both of them like the most damning things she had ever said.

FIFTEEN

Mike Wallington's study was at the front of the detached modern house, insulated from the family noise of kitchen and playroom at the rear. He took the two CID men in there and shut the door carefully behind him. Everything was pleasingly ordered in here, with his computer containing the information which would once have been in a filing cabinet and the few paper files he needed stacked neatly upright on the bottom level of the well-stocked bookshelves. Mike had grown used to feeling safe in here, away from the shrill voices of children and the small, recurrent crises of family life.

He didn't feel safe now. He said, 'We shan't be disturbed in here,' and gave a small giggle which showed him and them how nervous he felt.

Lambert looked unhurriedly round the room, letting the silence stretch as he and Hook seated themselves carefully upon the upright chairs in front of Wallington's desk. He said, 'I trust you've now remembered some of the things you couldn't recall when we spoke on Friday, Mr Wallington.'

'It's a long time since 1995. A lot of things have happened in the world and to me since then. I've been determined to put that time in the squat behind me. That means that I've deliberately thrust those days out of my mind as thoroughly as possible.'

'I see. Other people who were in seventeen Fairfax Street at that time have put the same argument to us. But they've remembered a surprising amount, once they've put their minds to it and received a few reminders from me and the rest of our murder team.'

Michael forced a smile he did not feel. 'May I ask who these people are who have such eminent powers of recall?'

'You may not, Mr Wallington. Information revealed in the course of our enquiries is confidential. I'm sure you will find that reassuring, in the light of what you are going to tell us this morning.'

Michael looked hard into Lambert's cool grey eyes, wondering exactly what his rights were here. The detective was being offensive, in his controlled, laid-back way, but Mike didn't feel that he could respond aggressively. He knew that he was a private citizen voluntarily helping the police with their enquiries; in theory, he could withdraw his cooperation at any moment. But that wasn't really an option. It would make him look guilty and encourage them to concentrate their enquiries around him. With the things he needed to hide, he couldn't afford that. He said grudgingly, 'I'll help you all I can. But I don't feel that my recall of events twenty years ago will be either comprehensive or completely reliable.'

'I see. Well, we have established that some of the information you gave us a couple of days ago was not reliable. In the light of that I feel you should be aware that we have now spoken to other people who were in the squat, other people who knew Julie and met her outside the squat, and some of our officers who were policing the Fairfax Street area in 1995. You would be most unwise to conceal anything which might help us, and still more unwise to offer us deliberate lies. The law takes a very dim view of people who obstruct the proper conduct of a murder investigation.'

Wallington tried hard to show no reaction to this. He said as impassively as he could, 'What is it you want to know?'

'You need to tell us everything you can about Julie Grimshaw and her activities both inside and outside seventeen Fairfax Street. You need to tell us everything you can remember about the other members of that squat and their activities. You need to explain your own presence there and give us an account of the things you did there.'

'I can't add much to what I told you about Julie on Friday. She was a drug taker. Not an addict, I think, but I have no expertise in such matters.' He glanced at them to see if there was any reaction to this, but learned nothing. 'She had a friend, Kathy, whom I mentioned to you on Friday. I don't think there was any sexual association between them, as there was between some women in squats, because as far as I could see both of them were straight. But I didn't see a great deal of either of them, because the women spent most of their time on the first floor and the men on the ground floor in that house.'

'What do you know about the people Julie met outside the squat?'

It was a chance to spread the web of suspicion, to draw others into it as well as himself. He'd anticipated this, but he'd need to go carefully – he didn't know what they'd already picked up from the array of other people Lambert had mentioned. 'She was meeting a man. That was at the farm where she was eventually killed and buried, I think.'

'Where she was buried, Mr Wallington. We haven't established yet where Julie Grimshaw was killed.'

'No. I suppose you have to be careful about these things. But when all this is over and the facts are established I'll be surprised if it doesn't turn out that she was killed very near where the skeleton was found last week.'

'Will you, indeed? Well, perhaps you are better placed than we are to have an opinion on that. We shall need to keep open minds until we have more facts available. I suspect you know more about her life outside the squat than you have so far revealed to us. Tell us about the people she met away from Fairfax Street.'

'There was the farmer's son. I don't remember his name; I don't think I ever knew it. He fancied her and he bedded her, but I'm not sure whether they were ever an item – that was the term we used, I think. You'd need to ask him about that.'

'We already have, Mr Wallington. And we've asked others as well. There was certainly a close relationship between them.'

'Well, there you are then. A close relationship, some sort of bust-up, and death for the girl. She was unstable because she was on drugs; she might have done things to bring about her own death if she involved herself in a violent row. But that's your business, not mine. I don't envy you trying to establish the truth, at this distance in time.'

'It isn't easy, as you say. But we're lucky to have many of the leading players still around. Including you, Mr Wallington. Do you think your friend Kate or Kathy was involved in any way in Julie's death?'

He decided to ignore their description of her as a friend. Perhaps she'd told them things about him, if they'd managed to locate her. That wouldn't have been easy, surely – but they'd found him, hadn't they, so why not Kathy? 'I don't know. They were quite close in the squat and they went off to that farm together and saw men there. I don't know what men, beyond the fact that one of them was the farmer's son and that Julie was shagging him at the time.' He glanced up to check their reaction to the word. He found them again quite impassive.

Bert Hook, who hadn't spoken at all thus far, said, as if he was merely confirming something they already knew, 'You were trying to get between the sheets with Kathy yourself, weren't you, Mike?'

He forced a smile. 'Sheets were in short supply in the squat. But I suppose you're right. Things were pretty free and easy in places like that. You grabbed what you could where you could and when you could. So long as you didn't think you'd get the clap, you had a go at most women. Sometimes you got no further than a quick grope and a knee in the balls. But quite often you got a surprisingly good fuck.' He threw in another four-letter word; he had an obscure feeling that the most basic terms would make them think he was being more honest. 'I think I had a go at Kathy, yes. But she turned me down. Pity, really: I think she'd have been a very satisfying shag. And both Kathy and Julie scrubbed up well, when they chose to. But you can never tell with these things, can you – I expect you've found that yourself.' He grinned a little in appreciation of his own wit as he raised his eyebrows at the sturdy Hook.

'When was it that you asked Julie Grimshaw to sell drugs for you, Mike?' Hook threw the question in as if it were the next stage in a casual conversation.

'Now look here! I asked you to come here so that I could offer my full cooperation as a responsible citizen who holds a key post in our community. If I'd thought that you were going to make these—'

'You didn't invite us here, Mike, and you've so far shown very few of the qualities of a responsible citizen. You were selling drugs both in the squat and in at least two pubs in the Gloucester area. We know that and we have the evidence to bring charges if we choose to, even at this distance in time. Whether or not we decide to pursue the matter will probably depend on the degree of cooperation and assistance you offer us in the course of a murder inquiry. Your conduct so far would indicate anything but innocence. We have not cleared you of involvement in the death of Julie Grimshaw. In fact, your evasions are exciting our interest in you as a suspect. We know that you were the Mick who was selling drugs around Gloucester and that you were trying to recruit people to sell them. Julie was one of those people, wasn't she?'

Hook spoke with such conviction that Michael felt the man was very sure of his ground. They had unearthed other people in the squat, as well as members of the filth who'd patrolled the area, so they probably knew all these things for certain. He licked his lips and said, 'I've a hell of a lot to lose here, you know.'

Hook nodded. 'You have indeed. And you're going the right way about losing it at the moment.' He shook his head a couple of times. 'You may or may not be a good Chief Education Officer in 2015. That is quite irrelevant to this matter. Did you or did you not approach Julie Grimshaw to sell drugs at seventeen Fairfax Street, Gloucester, in 1995?'

Mike wanted to deny his involvement, but he didn't know how much others had already told them about him. He said heavily, 'Yes. Julie was a heavy user and she hadn't the money to sustain the habit. That was the sort of person we recruited – when I say "we" I mean the people higher up the chain than me. I didn't have much choice in the matter.'

'Except that it was you who identified Julie as a suitable recruit to an evil trade. Give us the details.'

'I offered to provide her with her own supplies in exchange for her services as a seller. That's what you did. You found people who were heavy users, but preferably not addicts. Addicts are totally dependent on you for their supplies, but they're unreliable. They might try to sell while they're stoned and get reckless.' He was for a moment back in his world of twenty years ago, confident of his own expertise and the judgements he was able to make on potential recruits to the staff. 'I put the deal to Julie because she wasn't stupid and I thought she'd be careful.'

'And did she accept?'

Michael licked his lips, realizing that he was getting in deeper, becoming more reliant on their clemency, with each of these successive admissions. 'She neither accepted nor refused. I made her the offer. She disappeared the next day. Went out and never came back.' He looked hard at Hook and at the relentless Lambert, desperately wanting to be believed.

Hook's voice softened persuasively. 'Think hard about your answer to these next two questions, Mike. Much better to tell us now and get marks for cooperation, if the answers should be yes. Did Julie refuse your offer to become your dealer? And did you or other people who were directing you decide to eliminate her because of that refusal?'

'No! It was exactly as I just told you it was. She went out and never came back. I thought she'd just moved on, probably to some other squat. And she knew nothing about the people higher up the drugs chain, so they wouldn't have harmed her. I knew precious little about them myself, and Julie knew nothing.' He was wide-eyed with fear now, desperately anxious to convince them.

'Did you simply accept her disappearance? Didn't you ask around the other people in the squat and attempt to find out what had happened to her?'

He was quiet for a moment, wondering what he should say to this. 'I asked Kathy what had happened to Julie – well, I think she asked me, actually. We were each a little suspicious of the other. It's like that in squats: no one really trusts anyone else. It doesn't pay to ask too many questions about anything.'

That at any rate rang true, whatever they made of the rest of his answers. Hook glanced at Lambert, who immediately resumed the questioning. 'When did you decide to change your name, Mr Wallington?'

He glanced apprehensively at the door he had shut so firmly upon his family, and they knew in that moment that his wife knew nothing of this, probably nothing of his time in the squat. 'Two years after I'd left the squat. It was when I began my first teaching job. You don't want people to know you've lived like that when you're going to be shaping the lives of young people. I'd been Mick Warner in the squat, but I wanted to put all that and everything it meant behind me.'

'Especially as you'd been dealing in drugs. I can't see that being a big attraction when head teachers were considering your applications.'

'I said I'd been working abroad for a year, broadening my experience. I'd certainly been doing that, hadn't I?'

'Yes. You'd also been breaking the laws of the land. Not only selling drugs but recruiting others to do the same. I don't suppose Julie Grimshaw was the only one you approached.'

He didn't trouble to deny that. Anything was preferable to the accusation of murder they'd been dangling before him minutes earlier. 'I'm not proud of what I did in those months. It could ruin my career if it came out now – you can imagine what the tabloids would make of it.' He paused for a moment, but Lambert offered him no reassurance. 'I got rid of Mick Warner, became Michael Wallington.'

Just as the Kathy of the squat had become Kate Clark, board member of a great national utility company, thought Lambert. There were skeletons in the cupboard from that squat, as well as the one very real skeleton which had started all this and brought them here on this bright Sunday morning. 'Did you make the change official?'

'Yes. It was all done by deed poll. I became Michael Wallington. I buried Mick Warner and everything that went with him for ever.'

'Or at least until the discovery of the remains of a woman who had lived with Warner at Fairfax Street brought him back into your life.'

'Until this, yes.' He glanced again at the door. 'Please don't bring Mick Warner back into my family life. Debbie and the children don't deserve this.'

'Secrets don't usually help marriages, Mr Wallington. But it's your business how much you tell your wife of this. It will remain your secret, unless the happenings at Fairfax Street become the background for a murder trial. Have you anything further to offer to us?'

'No. I don't know how Julie died. It wasn't in the squat.'

The children came out to see the detectives depart. The boy and the girl beside him waved hard as the car drove away, dancing a little with the excitement, too small and too innocent to have any understanding of a world which dealt in drugs and violent death.

'I hope I'm not intruding, Mrs Dutton.' Steve Williams stood awkwardly at the doorstep of the small semi-detached house.

The widow looked at him suspiciously for a moment. Then her face cleared as she recognized him. 'It's Mr Williams, isn't it? Come in, please. Jack said I was to listen to whatever you had to say to me.'

She was a small woman with grey hair and a slight limp. He wasn't sure as she led him into a living room with slightly old-fashioned and well-worn furniture whether the limp was permanent or temporary. She offered him the best armchair and he sat down carefully on its lumpy and lopsided seat. 'I was very sorry to hear that Jack had gone.'

'It was the best thing for him. Best thing for all of us, really. None of us wanted him to go on suffering, once there was no hope.' Jack Dutton had not been dead for long, but she had got used to saying these words to people who offered their condolences. It was a formula she recited to get her and her well-wishers through the awkward early moments of sympathy. 'I've had quite a few letters. Some from family, some from friends. I didn't know Jack was so highly thought of.'

'That must be a consolation for you, at a sad time like this.' Steve wasn't good at sympathy. He'd danced on a few graves in his time, told plenty of people that they'd had it coming. But he hadn't felt the need to offer consolation very often. He found now that he wasn't comfortable with it. 'I visited him in hospital, you know, not long before he went.'

'The day before he died. He told me you'd been. Said I was to contact you, if I needed anything. Said you'd look after me.'

'Yes. I'm glad he did that. That's why I'm here. Disturbing your Sunday morning when you want to be quiet with your grief.' He gave a laugh which was a little too loud, then stopped it abruptly, realizing that laughter was not appropriate in this house of mourning.

'That's all right. Jack worked for you, didn't he?'

'Yes. He worked for me for a long time.' Dutton obviously hadn't spoken about his work at home, any more than Steve had spoken about his businesses to Hazel. 'We got on well. He was a reliable man, your Jack.'

'Yes. He was a good husband. Do you want tea? I can soon—'

'No. Please don't bother. You've got quite enough to do at the moment, Mrs Dutton.'

'Beth, they call me. Funeral's Wednesday. Church at ten o'clock, then the cemetery.'

'I'll do my very best to be there, Beth. But I came here because I want to offer you real help, not just sympathy.' He looked round at the room and its shabby furniture, stopped himself just in time from offering what he realized would be taken as an insult. 'I'd like to provide you with some financial help, Beth.'

The lined grey face looked at him suspiciously. 'That's good of you, Mr Williams. But we're all right. The house is paid for and I have the pension. And there's money coming in from insurance: I think you told Jack to take the policy out, to supplement our pensions. The funeral's going to cost more than I thought, but the insurance money will see to that, when it comes in.'

'I'd like to pay for Jack's funeral, Beth. It would be my last gesture to a man who was a good worker and a good friend.' Dutton had never been a friend. Williams didn't have friends, certainly not among the people who'd worked for him.

But he was relying on the fact that this woman wouldn't know that, and he was right. Beth Dutton said uncertainly, 'Well, if you're sure, it would certainly be a help – I don't know how long it will be until the insurance pays out. But do you realize how much funerals cost nowadays, Mr Williams?'

'I do and it's all right, Beth. Just make sure all the bills are sent to me at this address.' Steve didn't have cards. You didn't commit things to print, in the businesses he'd operated. He scribbled his address on the back of an envelope and put it by the clock on the mantelpiece. 'Now you'll make sure you do that, won't you?'

He picked up a picture of a young woman which was a few inches to the right of the clock. 'Is this your daughter, Beth?'

'Yes. That's Ros. She's ten years younger than the youngest of the boys. Bit of an afterthought, Jack used to say she was.' Beth looked embarrassed, wondering if she should have said that to the man who had been Jack's boss for twenty years and more.

Steve was relieved that he'd said 'daughter' and not the 'granddaughter' he'd almost used. He put the picture down and said, 'Very pretty girl, isn't she, Beth? Takes after her mother, not her father, for looks.' He was rather pleased with that, as a man not used to delivering compliments or making jokes.

'She's twenty-four now. She's giving up her job and going off to university. Bristol, she's going to. Going to cost her a packet in student loans, but she's very determined, is Ros, when she gets an idea into her head.'

'I'd like to help her with that, Beth. I'll pay her fees. It will be my final gift to Jack, my remembrance of him. Better than a slab of marble.'

'And a lot more expensive. Do you realize how many thousands are involved?'

Steve took a deep breath. 'I do realize, Beth, but I'd like to do it. It would be a kind of memorial to my own son, Liam, you see. He never went to university.'

Beth found herself crying again. She'd wept a lot over the last few days, so that she hardly noticed it now. There was something frightening about this big man with the bald head, even though he had employed Jack and paid him well and was now offering her wonderful things. She dabbed at her face with her handkerchief and said, 'You lost your son, didn't you? It's coming back to me now.'

'Yes. He died in a road accident. His mum can't let go of him, even though he's been gone for eight years now.' He hadn't meant to say that. He didn't know why he'd mentioned Hazel. And he hadn't meant to bring Liam into this, to sully his memory by involving him in this squalid manoeuvre, this attempt to make sure that the dark things Jack Dutton had done on his behalf went to the grave with him.

Grief loosened Beth Dutton's tongue. She said suddenly, 'Why are you doing this, Mr Williams? There's no need, you know. No one here is going to talk to the police.'

Steve was shocked by that. But it was good really, he told himself. This woman he had believed knew nothing was sharper than he had thought. She knew the score – knew that it was essential that she said nothing if the filth came sniffing around. He said firmly, 'I'll see to Ros's fees at Bristol. I owe that to Jack.'

She looked hard at him. Her eyes still brimmed with tears and her cheeks were wet with them. She said only, 'Aye. Maybe you do.'

This was over the top, Steve thought as he drove away. He was offering too much for it to be just a favour to an old friend who was dead. No one would believe it was merely that. Throwing thousands of pounds away wasn't the sort of thing Steve Williams did. But he felt a kind of cleansing in his offer. He was finished now with all the bad things he had done when he was operating his business empire. Sponsoring the studies of this innocent girl would purge him of some of the sins he had committed in the past.

And it would ensure that the evil things Jack Dutton had done on his behalf were buried with him.

SIXTEEN

Andrew Burrell decided that the flat was a good investment after all. He'd wondered at the time of his purchase, because of the price. He'd paid a considerable sum for it, putting down his deposit long before the new block was completed. He'd got what he considered the prime site by doing that.

This flat was on the top floor and had been sold as a 'penthouse apartment'. It had two luxurious bedrooms, a splendidly fitted bathroom and kitchen and a sitting room with views over the Severn. The rooms were unusually spacious for a modern development and this was now one of the most fashionable areas of Gloucester. It was just below the old docks, where in medieval days sailing ships had delivered precious cargoes into the ancient cathedral city.

On this warm June evening, the balcony which had figured large in the estate agent's literature was proving a splendid appendage. It looked west over the river, towards May Hill, that modest Gloucestershire height from which you could view many counties. Andrew had a young woman with him to enjoy this splendid setting. She was delighted with the balcony, and he was hoping she would explore other features of his new residence in due course.

Andrew was almost sure that Clare Sutton would be appointed as a research assistant in the Faculty of Arts at his university in the next few days. In the meantime, it was surely his duty to discover as much as he could about the qualities of the woman who was to become a junior colleague. If that research could extend to the joys of her body, so much the better. You couldn't be too thorough when you were assessing new appointments.

Clare had been a bright student who had worked hard and deserved the distinction she had been awarded in her MA degree. She had declared an hour earlier that she hadn't much of a head for drink, which Andrew had ticked off as another point in her favour. She was now on her third gin and tonic and finding the view from the balcony even more splendid than when he had first introduced her to it. Andrew had complied with her request for plenty of tonic and a generous slice of lemon. But he had been generous with the gin too: you surely shouldn't be stingy when you were serving a prospective colleague.

His conversation had become more racy as the sun had sunk in the west and the gin had loosened their tongues. Clare for her part had been determined when she came here that she wouldn't mention her prospects of appointment to the post she wanted so much. It wouldn't be seemly, and she was a seemly girl – well, for most of the time she was a seemly girl. But Andrew had been very friendly and she felt quite close to him now. He was an older man and an experienced academic, and he surely wouldn't tell her anything about the job which it was not fitting for her to know. He was an attractive mature man, and he hadn't got commitments to any other woman, as far as she knew – but that was surely irrelevant to the question of the new research assistant post.

Her thoughts were abruptly interrupted by his sitting down next to her and throwing his arm casually round her shoulders. His hand seemed quite large and his fingers were lean and strong. It was rather pleasant, really. She lifted her drink carefully from the glass-topped table in front of her, then took a sip which turned out to be almost a swig. 'So what do you think of my chances of becoming the new research assistant?' she said soberly. She thought it was soberly, but the excited little laugh shouldn't really have followed the question.

'I think you have the most splendid tits I've seen on any research assistant,' said Andrew confidently. He shifted his hand to make a more tactile assessment of the right-hand one. 'Yes, quite the most splendid and intellectually satisfying tits I've seen. No other candidate can rival them.'

'That's sexist!' said Clare. But the impact of her reaction was diminished by the giggle which accompanied it and by the fact that she was quite enjoying being stroked.

'It is, isn't it?' said Andrew shamelessly. 'But it's a fact of life. You can't remove attractive tits just by ignoring them. And it seems to me only right that I should pay them due attention. It wouldn't be right not to show my appreciation, on a private and intimate occasion like this.'

She shifted a little, but didn't move his hand. 'We seem to be moving on rather quickly. Perhaps we should—'

'"Had we but world enough, and time, This coyness, lady, were no crime . . ."' Andrew stroked a little more, then turned his blond head to beam at her. 'He knew a thing or two, old Andrew Marvell, don't you think?'

She knew the poem well, knew that there was no real answer to 'Time's wingèd chariot hurrying near'. She wondered for a moment how many other girls he had used that poem with, how many others had been seduced by its arguments. In the warmth of the summer evening, with the curve of the great river running dark and tranquil beneath them and the greenery stretching away towards the hills beyond it, it didn't seem to matter to Clare that she might be one of several, even one of many. Through a pleasant alcoholic filter the world seemed a benign place and all things seemed possible.

Clare Sutton was a very attractive girl, Andrew thought. Bright, too, though he was aware by now that his assessment of female capabilities was radically affected by a pretty face and prominent curves. He sipped his gin and tonic and sighed appreciatively, which encouraged his companion to follow suit. He felt less anxious now than he had been all week about those bones back at the farm and the police who were nosing into his affairs. With a scene like this in front of you and a girl like this beside you, the world was a much less threatening place. He shifted himself a little closer to his companion and let his hand stray a little down her side. 'There isn't much beneath this top,' he said speculatively into her ear.

In her slightly confused state, Clare thought this a rather splendid chat-up line. 'You never know, you might find out just how much later,' she said. She considered that such brilliant repartee that she dissolved into laughter on it.

Andrew hoped that he hadn't overdone the drink. There was no real fun with a drunken woman: they lost control of their movements and couldn't respond properly. Not much better than paying for it really, if you had to make a woman blind drunk before she climbed into bed with you. But Clare wasn't anything like as bad as that. He was glad to hear her returning to the theme of her possible employment in the university. She wasn't entirely coherent, but she conveyed her anxiety, ending with the slightly maudlin assurance, 'It's very important to me, you see. I want to go on working with you all. And 'specially you, Andrew, 'specially you.' She finished her drink, started a little as the slice of lemon rested against her nose, set her glass down on the table and stared at it with a dazed smile.

'You'll get the job all right,' said Andrew. 'They only pay peanuts.'

He realized too late that this was rather insulting, but Clare didn't seem to notice. 'Pay peanuts, get monkeys.' She giggled at what seemed to her a notable witticism. Then she turned to Andrew and kissed him enthusiastically and without warning full on the lips. He put his arms round her and let his tongue savour the delightful taste of gin, tonic and eager young woman. Eventually she broke away and belatedly resumed the conversation with a gentle whisper. 'So long as I get it, Andrew.'

'You'll get it all right, my dear.' He kissed her extensively again, running his hands daringly down her back to the cleft of her delicious backside. 'And it won't be the only thing you get tonight!'

With which robust assurance he proffered his hand and led her gently indoors towards the intimacies of the bedroom. She was not wildly drunk, but she tottered a little on her elegant legs. 'Must have a pee,' she told him unromantically, waving her hand dramatically above her head as she disappeared towards the bathroom. Two minutes later she made no resistance as he led her into his bedroom, showed no false modesty as she removed her clothes. There wasn't much underneath the top and the trousers, as he'd remarked earlier. She slid beneath his silk sheets and breathed a contented sigh. 'I'm not pissed, you know,' she assured him seriously. 'I'm just tight enough to be pleasantly randy.'

Andrew's need was urgent by this time. He gave no reply

but hastened to give her an opportunity to prove her claim. Their coupling was vigorous, rather noisy and entirely satisfactory. 'You'll be a great addition to the academic staff,' he assured her rather breathlessly. It seemed to have gone dark outside very quickly. He lay on his back and stared dreamily at the ceiling. 'Do you want another drink?'

'No. Well, perhaps coffee, eventually. What I do want is another fuck!' She giggled delightedly at the sharpness of her wit. The line was certainly enough to amuse and arouse Andrew Burrell, who hastened to comply energetically with the lady's request.

Clare left early on Monday morning, explaining that she must go home for a change of clothes before appearing demurely at the university. That suited Andrew, who had been planning to explain that there was no way they could arrive together on the campus. He took a leisurely breakfast and checked his phone messages before he left.

The important one had been there for fifteen hours now. It told him that Chief Superintendent Lambert and Detective Sergeant Hook would like to speak with him again on Monday about the murder of Julie Grimshaw.

It was a long time since Steve Williams had been in a police station interview room. He was surprised how ill at ease he felt. He told himself firmly that he'd outsmarted the pigs in the past and he'd do it again. It had been his choice, not theirs, that he should come here. He'd taken the initiative and he could retain it.

It didn't feel like that as he stared at the blank green windowless walls and glanced up at the single strong light above him. The place smelt of disinfectant; he wondered what squalor had been enacted here by the weekend yobbos. Maybe this was just the normal treatment for interview rooms on a Monday morning? Probably they were swabbed out with disinfectant as a routine precaution. It felt like a blow to his status as a major player to be waiting for the attention of the filth in a place like this.

They left him on his own for a good five minutes; he felt now that they'd always planned to do that. People get nervous while they sit and wait to be interrogated in interview rooms, even people as experienced as Steve Williams. He was determined that he would not allow that to happen. Yet he didn't succeed. He felt very much on edge by the time Lambert and Hook appeared and sat down unhurriedly on the steel and canvas chairs on the other side of the small square table.

Hook looked a question at Lambert, who shook his head. 'No need for us to record this, Bert. This is just an informal chat to further our enquiries. Mr Williams is acting as a good citizen in coming here to help us. That may seem strange to you, but no doubt it feels much stranger to him. Probably unique, if he does actually plan to help us rather than obstruct us.'

'You won't rile me, Lambert! If I choose to meet the pigs in their own sty, that's my business.'

'Indeed it is, Mr Williams. Let's hope you continue to control your own destiny, shall we?'

'I've come here because I don't want your kind of shit polluting my house. So get on with it and let me get back there.'

Lambert showed no inclination to do that. 'Why didn't you want us to come to your house again, Steve? Afraid that Hazel might speak to us and reveal things you wish to conceal, were you?'

The mention of his wife pierced the carapace of indifference Williams had been trying to develop around himself to deflect police questioning. He reacted immediately, whereas he'd been merely conventionally hostile to Lambert's opening barbs. 'Leave Hazel out of this! You upset her on Wednesday when you came round to the house with your ignorant questions.'

'Really? Well, I'm sorry about that. You might care to tell her when you return home that we're less ignorant now than we were on Wednesday.'

Williams glanced around the bare, cell-like room. 'I haven't come here because I like these places. What is it you want of me, Lambert? The sooner this is over, the better for all of us.'

He wasn't comfortable, despite his attempted truculence. Last time they had met he had insisted on calling his old enemy 'John', to the great man's ill-concealed irritation. Now he was on edge, despite the contempt he was trying to summon for these two old adversaries. Lambert seemed to know this as he said earnestly, 'We really do know a lot more about the part you and your family played in this business than when we spoke on Wednesday.'

Williams was immediately defensive. 'Well, you must leave Hazel out of this. She has nothing to tell you. You'll only upset her if you come bothering her. She's not a well woman. That's why I've chosen to come to this place today: I don't want Hazel disturbed by your great pigs' trotters tramping round our place.'

Lambert smiled, relishing the advantage which had come to him with Williams's discomfort. 'We shall speak to Mrs Williams if we feel that we need to do so. This is a murder inquiry and sometimes we need to upset people. Sometimes upsetting people can be a positive advantage, when they're trying to hide the truth.'

'Well, it won't be in this case. You just keep away from Hazel.' Williams's single eye stared hard into Lambert's impassive face and he looked abruptly vulnerable. 'Common charity should keep you away from a woman who isn't fit to face your questions and can only be upset by them.'

Lambert knew all about Hazel Williams and the way she had been shattered by her son's unexpected death. Her husband was probably right when he claimed that a visit from them would seriously upset her, and he would not undertake it lightly. But Steve Williams was a villain, a serious one, who had got away with breaking the law and with various violent crimes over a lengthy period. If there was a chance of putting him away, consideration for Hazel wasn't going to stop the law taking its course.

Lambert was first and foremost a taker of villains; he was human enough to hope that there might here be a belated chance of revenge on this man who had thwarted his efforts and escaped justice for the best part of thirty years. He said tersely, 'We'll do what we have to do, Williams. If you've any connection with this death, you won't be allowed to shelter behind Hazel. We shall do whatever we have to do to lock you away for life, if that's what's appropriate.'

Steve forced a sneer, baring his teeth briefly but emitting no sound. This room was getting to him, despite his determination to ignore it. This was playing Lambert on his own ground at his own game, and he didn't like it. 'You don't scare me, pigs. I've nothing to hide, see? When the pigs can't touch you, you feel like spitting in the sty.' He looked at the floor as if contemplating suiting the action to the word, but did nothing. The truth was, he didn't feel the confidence he was trying hard to project.

Perhaps because Williams was glaring so hard at Lambert, it was Bert Hook who offered him the next thought. 'You were elusive about Liam when we last spoke. Other people have now suggested to us that he was much closer to our murder victim than you indicated on Wednesday.'

'You leave Liam out of this. The lad's dead.'

'Yes. Believe it or not, I'm sorry about that. But he was a husky thirty-three-year-old, not a lad, when he died. At the time when Julie Grimshaw was killed he was a highly active twenty-year-old with a history of violence, who we now think had a much closer relationship with our murder victim than you have previously allowed. Lying always gets our attention, Steve. You should remember that.'

'I haven't bloody lied, Hook, and just you bloody—'

'Economical with the truth, are we calling it? You certainly concealed things, Steve. That's equivalent to lying, in our book.'

'I concealed bugger all. And if you know what's good for you . . .' His tongue was suddenly dry. He couldn't conclude his threat, because he no longer commanded the muscle which had once brought swift retribution to his enemies. Retirement had its compensations, when you'd millions in the bank, but you didn't have the swift, immediate power you'd once had. It wasn't politic to threaten the police, not nowadays. But this calm, stolid man called Hook, who looked as if he should have been pedalling an old-fashioned bike round a village in a black-and-white film, was getting to him. He said limply, 'Liam was my only son. His death half-killed his mother as well. Lay off him, Hook.'

But this most considerate of coppers felt little compassion

for a man who had caused untold misery to others in his criminal career. 'How close was Liam to Julie Grimshaw, Steve?'

'Scarcely knew her, I think. It's a long time ago. I can't even picture the girl.'

'Not that long. I'm sure you can remember lots of things about Julie, if you put your mind to it. She was a pretty girl, everyone says – we've only seen her skull. I expect you sized her up as a candidate for one of your knocking-shops. She scrubbed up well, everyone says. And she lived in a squat and was anxious to get hold of drugs. Sitting duck for you and one of your paid pimps, I'd have said.'

He was being deliberately provocative and offensive in search of a reaction, and he got one. 'Just shut your fucking filthy mouth, Hook! It wasn't like that and I wasn't interested in the girl. And neither was Liam.'

'All coming back to you now, is it? All this stuff from long ago that you couldn't remember a scrap of, just a minute ago? Well, that's what we all wished for, isn't it? Tell us about Liam and Julie, now that your amnesia's departed. Two dead people who were once close to you, Steve. Tell us all about them and how they felt about each other.'

Williams glowered at Hook's studiously inoffensive countenance. 'I've said all I'm going to say, copper. They knew each other, that's all. They weren't close.'

It had been easier in the old days, when people on both sides had known you were a villain, Steve Williams thought. When he was being questioned by the filth then, his principle had been to say as little as possible. You grunted at them, gave them at most a grudging yes or no. If there was any real danger you had a brief at your side and you gave them a steady 'No comment', grinned at them and watched them get more frustrated. This was different. It was they who were taunting him. And he was supposed to be genuinely trying to help them, not obstruct them. He'd come here intending to be in and out in two minutes. This was not only taking much longer but it was being played by their rules, not his.

There was a pause in which they studied him before Hook said, 'Our information is that Julie and Liam were very close.

Did she perhaps try to give him the push and get her comeuppance for doing that, Steve?'

'No she didn't. Liam had nothing to do with her death. Don't you soil his memory by trying to pin this on him, or you'll regret it.'

'Sounds almost like a threat to a police officer, that, Steve. We'll overlook it, because you seem to be getting quite overwrought. But we need to ask these things, because we know that Liam was quite a violent lad when he was twenty, don't we? Given to outbursts of violence – fact, that is, not an attempt to sully his memory. Several brushes with the police at that time, hadn't he? Several episodes of violence with other young men of his age and persuasion. The police in Gloucester and surrounding areas have them well documented.'

'It wasn't Liam who killed the girl.' Steve forced himself to keep his lips tight and offer them no more than a simple denial.

Hook smiled at him, as if he knew the processes of his mind and was amused by them. 'There were two lads of the same age at the neighbouring farm, weren't there, Steve? And we know that at least one and possibly both of them were rather keen on Julie Grimshaw. Source of conflict with Liam, that would be. Young, red-blooded men with pricks ruling their brains, and a predilection to solve things with fists or bottles or knives. Recipe for disaster, that can be. Certainly was, in Julie's case.'

'Julie Grimshaw wasn't killed with a knife.'

Hook raised his eyebrows elaborately. 'Know that, do you, Steve? Well, it's most interesting for us to discover that you're aware of the killer's modus operandi.' The police press release hadn't detailed the method by which the victim had died. There'd been speculation in the popular press about blows to the head with a blunt instrument, but Bert wasn't going to concede that.

Williams remained tight-lipped while they studied his reaction in detail. Eventually he repeated his mantra doggedly. 'Liam didn't do this.'

Hook glanced at Lambert. 'I suppose that if we stretch our credulity to its outer limits, sir, we could consider it possible that Liam killed the girl without his dear old dad knowing anything about it. Perhaps the girl gave him his marching orders and he didn't take kindly to it. Perhaps he reacted violently to something not going his way, as we know from several other incidents he could do. Perhaps his dad and his mum knew nothing about it at the time.'

Lambert weighed the possibility and pursed his lips. 'Doesn't seem likely though, DS Hook, does it? It's very possible that Liam killed the girl as you suggest, but hardly likely that his criminal father wouldn't have known about it.'

Williams could stand the taunting speculation no longer. 'Liam didn't kill the fucking girl! And neither did I, you fucking bastards!'

'This man's losing his head a little now, wouldn't you say, DS Hook? Deterioration in language usually means that a guilty man is losing it, in my experience.'

'I've had enough of this!' The big man levered himself clumsily to his feet. 'You can fucking well—'

'Sit down, Williams!' Lambert's command was like the crack of a whip in the quiet, claustrophobic room. 'We haven't finished with you yet. You walk out of here and we'll record the exact circumstances in which you left. With your record, it won't look good. It might almost be a confession of guilt. We'd like that.'

Williams lowered himself back on to the seat in slow motion, his look of steady hatred fixed on Lambert. 'You're going to force me to bring in my brief.'

An empty threat, and all three of them knew it. He hadn't been charged with any offence, and he was experienced enough to keep quiet if he felt threatened without the need for a lawyer to tell him. Lambert positively beamed at him, genuinely enjoying the discomfort of a man who had given him much grief over the years. 'You're free to bring in your brief when-ever you feel you need him, Williams. I'm no legal expert, but it strikes me that you might need legal advice very soon now.' His expression changed to hostility in a single second. 'You visited your old heavy Jack Dutton last week.'

Williams was shaken, despite his knowledge of the police machine. Had they put a tail on him? He didn't think so, but it was disconcerting to find that they knew so much about his movements. 'The poor bugger was dying. Are you saying I'm not allowed to visit an old mate on his deathbed?'

'You are allowed to move freely, at the moment. Hospice visiting and charitable impulses haven't been your things in the past, though, have they? Any change of habit at your time of life is likely to excite police interest. That's one of the penalties of being a criminal celebrity, Steve.'

'Jack's dead now. Let him rest in peace.'

'Yes. Died the day after you saw him, didn't he? Before he could be questioned about the reason for your visit.'

'I like to look after my employees, when they've given good service. Jack had done that for many years.'

'Yes. He'd beaten up a lot of people in his time, hadn't he? And supervised the beatings of many more, when you put him in charge of your muscle. One or two deaths over those years, which we never managed to pin on him. Loan sharks like you rely a lot on muscle, don't you, Steve?'

'Piss off, Lambert.'

'But you're not well known as a visitor of the sick. Acts of mercy aren't part of your repertoire. It makes curious CID men wonder, when you break your normal routine. When we find you racing to offer financial support to Steve's widow, it makes us even more curious. Suspicious, in fact.'

'None of your bloody business what I do with my bloody money.' Williams snarled a token defiance.

'There's a lot of blood smearing your money, Steve. But you don't normally throw it at former employees and their families. That makes us wonder whether you're trying to ensure that mouths remain shut. And our particular concern is whether mouths are remaining shut when they might be telling us things about the death and burial of Julie Grimshaw.'

'I look after the people who work for me.'

'But you don't, you see, Steve. This is a very notable exception to your usual practice. As such, it merits our full and diligent attention.'

'I come in here to offer you my full and voluntary cooperation and this is the thanks I get! This is the last—'

'No! You came here to prevent us visiting you at home,

Williams! But be assured, if you have any connection with this death, we're going to find the evidence which will convince any court in the land. You've got away with murder in the past – literally. You won't get away with this one.'

Bert Hook thought that he had never seen John Lambert breathing quite so heavily.

SEVENTEEN

'I think I could get quite interested in churches, if I had the time to study them.'

It wasn't a line Kate Clark had ever envisaged uttering to Harry Purcell. She had breathed all sorts of passionate things into his ears, revealed all sorts of intimate secrets about herself, when they had held each other hard during the long nights of sex. But she had never thought that she would reveal to him this conventional, middle-class interest of hers in churches and cathedrals.

His reply was just as unforeseen. He smiled at her and said, 'I could probably teach you a little, if you promise not to be over-critical. I'm not too hot on dates, but I know a little about the development of church architecture. My dad was a vicar, you know.'

'No, I didn't know. You have hidden depths, Harry Purcell.' She reached up and took his arm, giving it an affectionate squeeze as they walked round the back of the fourteenth-century church and through its ancient graveyard. 'There are all sorts of things I don't know about you – and you about me, I suppose. We neither of us reveal much about ourselves, except when we're . . .'

'Except when we're rogering each other like there's no tomorrow, you mean?' said Harry. He gave her a small, affectionate peck on top of her well-groomed head as they moved among the moss-covered gravestones.

Kate was a little shocked by his language, out here in broad daylight and in this innocent setting. But she liked his affectionate little peck and she liked the strange softness and innocence of the day they were enjoying together. Without considering the implications she found herself saying, 'We should get to know each other much better.'

'I'd like that,' said Harry. It was equally spontaneous. He'd been content to hold much of himself back until now and also to leave much of this interesting and powerful woman unexplored. It was part of modern life, he supposed: you knew the intimate recesses of each other's bodies before you'd troubled to explore the recesses of the minds which operated them. It had been exactly the opposite for the dead father he had just mentioned and the mother who was now stricken with Alzheimer's and did not recognize him. He hadn't been born until they were forty-one and his parents had always seemed to him to inhabit an earlier and very different world.

He and Kate had agreed a month earlier that they'd take this Monday off work and have a day together. It had seemed a good idea when they were snatching a hurried breakfast after a night together. It had been an unspoken recognition that there should be more than sex in their relationship, a mutual agreement that they wanted to know more of each other. In the weeks which followed that hasty early-morning decision each of them had had second thoughts about the arrangement to spend this day together. But how did you call it off, without implying that you had doubts about the relationship?

Now both were glad that they'd carried it through. For two workaholics, they were making quite a fair shot at a day of leisure. They'd forbidden the word 'unwinding' after both of them had used it during the first hour of this strange day. The church had been a good idea. They'd just seen it as they were driving past and Harry had swung the Audi into the deserted parking area. They'd been able to get in and look round, because a woman had been cleaning the altar brasses. She'd told them a little about the history of church and village, becoming shyly proud of her knowledge as Kate asked her a couple of intelligent questions about Reformation priests and Victorian architectural alterations. She turned to look back at the weathered stones above them as they reached the wicket gate. She looked up at Harry and said, 'I'm glad we stopped here.'

'It wasn't planned. It was just an impulse as we were driving past.'

It sounded almost like an apology, she thought. It was as if he was diffident about involving a woman of her stature and influence in anything as petty as an unscheduled visit to a quiet country church. Was that how he thought of her, she wondered? As some kind of empress who should not have to suffer the distractions of ordinary life? As a woman who dropped her inhibitions and became a mating animal in bed, but must otherwise be respected, not loved?

Kate Clark felt suddenly very lonely. The isolation she normally cherished and preserved for herself seemed now not a claim to privacy but a sort of imprisonment. She wanted someone to talk to about the trials of work, the petty day-to-day conflicts, the small triumphs and the occasional defeats. Above all, she wanted to have someone to confide in about the events of the last week; about the police and the way they were pressing her; about those half-forgotten days in the squat; about the girl who had slept beside her and was now dead.

Kate glanced at Harry Purcell. He was looking at her speculatively as he fastened his seat belt. He was probably wondering what she was thinking. If he only knew, he might be looking to dump her at the first opportunity! She said, 'I know a nice pub by the river for lunch, if I can still find it.'

The country lanes gave her a little difficulty, but she managed to direct him to it. It was a few miles above Ross-on-Wye, beside a secluded stretch of one of Britain's loveliest rivers. It was warm enough to sit outside and look over this wide, quiet reach of the Wye. They had soup and home-made rolls and continued the unwinding they weren't allowed to mention. She'd asked for bitter beer and he'd ordered her a pint, like his, and then said she looked very small behind it.

'I don't think I've ever had a pint before!' Kate said. She took a large pull at it and tried to belch like a man, but couldn't quite manage it. They both dissolved into laughter and as that subsided she found that he'd stretched his arm across the table and taken her hand in his. She looked into the deep brown of his pupils and said, 'You have nice eyes, Harry. I've never really studied them before.'

He looked at her but didn't say anything. He was searching for words which would not come to him. He looked down at the river beneath them, feeling privileged to have this spot to themselves at this quiet Monday lunchtime. Save for a tiny eddy near a bend a hundred yards above them you could hardly detect movement on the surface. Eventually he said, 'There's something reassuring about water, don't you think? This stretch of river we can see was here long before we came, and will be here long after we have gone. That puts our petty concerns into proportion.'

'We need to talk, Harry.'

'That sounds ominous. Are you telling me you're going to ditch me?' But he didn't sound threatened.

She smiled, looking, like him, at the river and thinking of his words. 'No. I don't want to ditch you. And I hope you don't want to ditch me. Rather the reverse, if anything.' She was grateful for the reassuring squeeze from his hand. 'When I say we should talk, I suppose I really mean I should talk. There are a lot of things you don't know about me, Harry.'

'And a lot you don't know about me. Is this going to be confession time?'

He was joking, but confession time was exactly what she'd been thinking about. She felt the need for someone to talk to about her and Julie and what had happened to them, even more desperately than she had earlier. Before it was too late. She'd never thought of it like that before. She might need the help and support and love of someone as the police closed in upon her. And Harry was not just the only person available, but the one she now knew she wanted as her confidant. She said, with a tremor she could hear in her voice, 'I did things a long time ago which will shock you, Harry. I think I'm ready to talk about them, if you can endure hearing what I have to say.'

'Is this where we get the bit about the shoplifting? Was it lollipops or lipsticks or meat pies?' He was trying hard to make a joke of this, because it was the only reaction he could think of. But he knew even as he spoke that it was the wrong reaction. 'Sorry! If this is about other men, I shan't be shocked. And I'll tell you all about my other women, if you really want to hear about them.'

'This isn't about previous partners, Harry. We're neither of us angels, but those kinds of things won't shock us. This will.'

He felt a small dark cloud descending upon his bright day. 'How long ago was this?'

'Twenty years ago.' She was glad of the question, leading her into what she needed to say. There was no going back now.

He said very quietly, 'That's when that girl died. The skeleton that they discovered last weekend.'

'Yes. It's about that. Julie, she was called. We were in a squat together. In Gloucester. We were friends. We were as close as it gets, in squats.'

She spat out the phrases, each one a fact which she had previously suppressed, each sibilant hissing the squalor she had previously concealed. She felt curiously detached, as if she was hearing someone else say these things. She was going to tell Harry everything now. They would know each other much better, after she had told him. She wondered quite how shocked he was going to be.

Andrew Burrell had chosen to meet the CID men in his flat. He didn't want them coming to see him again at the university. That would invite gossip at best, and speculation and suspicion among colleagues and students at worst. 'I'm free from three o'clock on Monday. I'd prefer to see you at home rather than at my place of work.' He gave them the address and cursed himself for sounding defensive as he did so.

He arrived home with just ten minutes to spare before they were due to arrive. He raced round the place trying to remove all traces of Clare Sutton and the fact that she had spent the night here. Even as he did so he told himself that he was being ridiculously defensive. His private life was no concern of theirs and they wouldn't and shouldn't be interested in it. Yet he felt that when they'd seen him six days ago they'd been interested in everything about him, and every extra fact they'd discovered about him had seemed to weaken his position in their eyes. He put the picture of the two children he scarcely saw since his divorce prominently on top of the television as his badge of respectability.

In 1995 he'd been the close friend and would-be partner of a girl who'd lived in a squat and who'd been the subject of dispute between him and his parents, between him and Jim Simmons, between him and others of whom he hoped they still knew nothing. And all that was left of Julie Grimshaw, that girl whom twenty years ago he had thought he loved, were the bones they had dug up last week. The girl he had thought was out of his life for ever had re-entered it forcefully. He tried not to picture what her head must have looked like when it had come out of the earth at what had once been Lower Valley Farm.

It was Lambert and Hook again, the senior men. He must be a leading suspect. Of course he must, he told himself firmly. It was only natural that they should consider him such when he had been so close to Julie at the time of her death. Nothing to wonder at in that. He wondered who else they had in the frame for this. Who and how many? But they wouldn't tell him that. They'd let him think he was their only suspect, the bastards.

Police had always been bastards, in those days twenty years ago. They'd always been the opposition when he was a young man, the enemy who regarded everything you did with suspicion. But they hadn't discovered that Julie had been murdered, had they? Not until some gardener turned the evidence up and set it before them. The bastards weren't as clever as they'd always pretended they were. Andrew Burrell determined to keep that idea in his head when he talked to them today.

His resolution didn't hold for very long. It ebbed away from the moment when Lambert stood in his doorway, almost touching the top of it, and said, 'We know a lot more now than when we spoke to you last Tuesday, Mr Burrell.' It was voiced like an accusation, Andrew thought.

He said as briskly as he could, 'I'm glad to hear it. Perhaps our local police service is more efficient than the city ones about which we hear so much scandal. They seem to be characterized by inefficiency and corruption.'

'I see. If you know of any corrupt officers in this area, it is your duty to apprise us of the facts.'

'I'm sorry. That was a mistaken attempt at humour, or at least levity. I realize that neither is appropriate in the context of a murder hunt. It is gratifying to know that you have been making progress as you look for justice for poor Julie Grimshaw.'

Andrew had thought that he could easily outwit them in this verbal fencing, but he realized now that they were better equipped for it than he was. Facts gave you the advantage, and they probably had lots of facts by now, whereas he knew no more than he had known when they first spoke with him. As if to emphasize who held the cards Lambert said quietly, 'You withheld many things from us when we spoke on Tuesday. I advise you strongly to be more frank with us today.'

'I can't think what you mean! I was as honest as I could be when we spoke on Tuesday. It was the first time that I knew that Julie had been killed and my mind was still reeling from that knowledge.'

'Then perhaps you can attempt to put things right by answering our questions more fully now. Tell us everything you can about your relationship with this woman we have now established is a murder victim.'

It was a command, not a request, but he was in no position to take exception to that. 'I was close to her. I wanted to marry her, at one point.'

'But that didn't last.'

'I'm not sure that I could say that my wish to marry her didn't last. It had gone wrong between us for a variety of reasons, but we were lovers and I still wanted something more permanent in the summer of 1995. Then she disappeared and it was all off anyway.'

'We now know that she didn't simply disappear, as most people thought she had done at the time. She—'

'As we all thought at the time. It wasn't just me.'

'As everyone affected to think at the time. We now know that she disappeared because she was murdered. One person at least, and perhaps more than one, knew that she'd been murdered. Almost certainly this person or persons killed and buried Julie. It's our belief that her killer is someone whom we have interviewed during the last seven days.'

'You're saying that you suspect me of killing Julie.'

Lambert gave him a very tiny smile. 'Unless we have an obvious killer, we work by elimination. That is particularly so in the case of a crime committed twenty years ago, where every scent has long since gone cold. We should like to eliminate

you: that would make our task easier as well as being a relief
to you. So far we have not been able to do that. Tell us again
why you broke up with her. Give us the most complete picture
possible.'

Andrew Burrell seemed to have aged even during the few
minutes they had spent with him. Like many fair-skinned
people, he showed strain more visibly than he would have
wished. He looked pale and drawn and his lank fair hair seemed
to insist on falling over the right side of his face. He brushed
it away suddenly and said, 'Julie said she wasn't ready for
marriage. I don't think I was that keen on it myself. I wanted
us to be an item and see how it went from there. Also, I'd got
this place on a history degree course in Liverpool and I was
determined to take it up – I think I wanted to show my dad
that I was finished with farming and there was no turning back
to it. Julie was living in a squat and in danger of becoming
addicted to drugs and for half the time didn't know her own
mind. I think all of these things were involved in our relationship, so it was complicated. But nothing was set in stone at
the time of her disappearance – at the time of her death, as
you now insist.'

'Thank you. That is a fuller account of the situation between
the two of you than you gave us on Tuesday. We're policemen,
not lawyers, but it's my opinion that there are still areas where
you are not telling us the whole truth and nothing but the
truth.'

'I've told you what I can remember. I can't do more than
that.' He was sitting in his favourite leather armchair, with his
interrogators opposite him on the sofa. He saw now that his
fingers were white with tension as they grasped the ends of
the arms. He felt very exposed. 'I can't do more than that to
convince you of my innocence.' He looked suddenly at Hook,
hoping for a more sympathetic hearing from that less threatening presence.

It was not forthcoming. Instead, Hook said, 'We're talking
about a girl who was probably murdered and certainly buried
on the land of Lower Valley Farm, which was your home at
the time. On Tuesday you told us very little about the other
people who were involved with you and Julie during this

period. You haven't added anything so far today. What can you tell us about Jim Simmons?'

Andrew wondered if they knew that he had been in contact with Jim. He didn't see how they could know about his phone call to Jim on Friday, unless Jim had told them of it. But they seemed to know all sorts of things which he hadn't thought they would know. You couldn't rely on their ignorance of anything. Yet this was one of the areas where he could talk safely. He couldn't see how in talking about Simmons he could possibly incriminate himself, so he might enlarge a little on how things had been between the two of them.

'Jim and I were rivals, in a way. But we weren't competing for Julie. I think Jim liked her, but he didn't want her in the way I wanted her. We were wary of each other because he had designs on the farm, which had been intended as my inheritance. That suited me, really, because I'd decided farming wasn't for me and I was going off to Liverpool University to pursue an entirely different career and lifestyle. But it put him in a difficult position, and I think I was still rather jealous of him when I saw how Dad was relying on him and favouring him. It's illogical, I suppose, but you still feel a little jealous when you see someone else taking on the role intended for you – especially when they're demonstrably much better fitted than you for the role.'

'Mr Simmons felt that your mother was also helpful to him as he found his feet in farming.'

Hook was watching him carefully, Andrew felt, probing for a weakness, seeking an unguarded reaction. But he could surely baffle this pedestrian plod in any battle of words. He smiled patronizingly. 'If you're looking for an Oedipus complex, DS Hook, you're much mistaken. I maintained an excellent and perfectly normal relationship with my mother until the day she died. I'm no Hamlet, with my whole conduct dictated by a fractured attitude towards women.'

'I do hope not, Mr Burrell. The Danish prince concluded that play as you know with multiple killings, an outcome we should prefer to avoid in your case.'

Andrew remembered too late Lambert's warning during their previous meeting that Hook had a rather better degree than he had himself. He said sullenly, 'As far as I know, Jim Simmons didn't kill Julie. I can't see what motive he could have had. But I'm sure you've already questioned him about the matter.'

'Indeed we have. He was quite frank about the fact that he saw an opportunity at Lower Valley Farm when he realized that you were no longer interested in taking over from your father. He told us in fact that both your father and your mother were not only friendly and supportive but actively helpful to him as he took over the running of the farm and eventually secured the ownership of it for himself. They seem to have been extraordinarily well-disposed towards Mr Simmons – some might even say abnormally so. Do you think that their support for him might in fact be a recognition of something he had done for them?'

'A quid pro quo? I can't think of anything a man as young and inexperienced as Jim would have been able to offer Mum and Dad.'

But Andrew could. He was stalling for time, wondering how he might play this to his advantage. It wasn't helpful to him that Hook seemed to be able to follow his every thought process. The DS now pointed out, 'Obviously we cannot speak with your dead mother on this. But we know that both she and your father were bitterly opposed to your proposed long-term association with Julie Grimshaw. She disappeared at a very convenient time, from their point of view. We now know that she was murdered. You will be relieved to know that we are satisfied that neither of your parents was directly involved in her death. There remains the possibility that someone else chose to remove her in order to accommodate them. In view of his subsequent career and his present ownership of Lower Valley Farm, Mr Simmons is the obvious candidate.'

Andrew's mind raced with alternative reactions to this. As a suspect himself, it could only help him to incriminate someone else, and Hook was offering him Simmons on a plate. But the right tactic must be to seem reluctant to accept the plate. He said, 'I can see exactly what you mean. I'm shaken, because it's a possibility I hadn't entertained. To be frank, I wasn't surprised when Dad turned to Jim to run the farm as he looked towards retirement: Jim was the only obvious candidate, once Dad accepted that I'd ruled myself out. But I confess I was rather surprised when he told me a year or two later that he was selling the farm to Jim Simmons. Lower Valley Farm has been worked by our family for centuries. I thought Dad would have wished to retain ownership of it, even though it wasn't me who was taking over from him.'

He'd done that well, he thought. Voiced a doubt about Simmons with apparent reluctance. Drawn attention to the key factor in any suspicion of Simmons, the mysterious and surprising way in which he'd acquired Lower Valley Farm. Andrew had no compunction about what he was doing to Simmons: it was dog eat dog, when it came to saving your own skin in a murder inquiry.

Andrew rather hoped Hook would pursue this further. He was on strong ground here. He would show more reluctance as he dropped Jim deeper into the mire. Instead, it was the sterner Lambert who now resumed the questioning. 'Julie Grimshaw was an attractive girl and a vulnerable one, as you and others have told us. That often causes problems, when such a woman is amidst a group of red-blooded young men in their early twenties, as you and Simmons and others were at that time.'

Andrew Burrell didn't like the mention of 'others'. He managed to summon a small sneer as he strove to reassert himself. 'If by "red-blooded" you mean heterosexual, I can confirm that as far as I am aware none of the men in our set at that time was gay.'

'Thank you for the information. We are very interested in the men and women who were in what you call your set. Tell us about this woman Kate, who at that time was calling herself Kathy. She was physically very close to Julie throughout those months in the summer of 1995: they shared the first floor of the squat in Gloucester, whilst others came and went around them. Because of that, she had a clearer opportunity to kill Julie than anyone else we've spoken to. Do you think that might be what happened?'

Andrew tried not to leap in here. He sensed that they would find it easier to believe him if he once again appeared loth to incriminate others. 'I hadn't thought of that. It's a possibility. They were together in the squat, as you say. All kinds of things happen in squats. The desperate, sometimes unbalanced people who live there are more disposed to violence than people living in more settled conditions. Julie was into drugs in a big way – she wasn't an addict, but one of my fears for her was that she was on the way to becoming one. Drugs make people unpredictable; they make people behave abnormally and sometimes violently. I had some experience of this myself with Julie. I suppose it's possible that the two of them had some sort of violent row and that Kathy killed her during that. Have you considered the possibility that Kathy might not actually have intended to kill her?'

'We have indeed, Mr Burrell. We have to include it as a possibility for almost everyone who was close to our victim at the time, including you. You could confess to the lesser charge of manslaughter right now, if you thought that was appropriate.'

Andrew looked to see a smile on Lambert's long gaunt face, but he didn't find one. 'I don't think that's either appropriate or funny, Chief Superintendent Lambert. I didn't kill Julie Grimshaw and I don't know who did.'

'I see. Well, it seems to us significant that despite numerous opportunities you have not named one other male who was in contact with both you and Julie at that time. Omissions can be more informative to us than inclusions, on occasion. They suggest to us that someone may have important things to hide.'

Lambert was picking his words as carefully as Burrell, showing the academic that he could confront him on his own terms and outwit him, because he held all the important cards in this particular hand. Andrew said with an assumed weariness, 'This is all a long time ago, as we've agreed. I didn't think you would be interested in people who were only peripheral or occasional members of our set.'

'A man who was a rival of yours for the favours of Julie is hardly peripheral to our investigation, Mr Burrell. I'm sure that anyone striving to be as objective as you are will recognize that.'

This was sarcasm with a deadpan delivery. Andrew recognized defeat and said dully, 'I suppose you mean Liam Williams.'

'It's taken you a long time to get there, Mr Burrell. Now that you have, please don't omit anything significant.'

How much did they already know, having grilled others as effectively as they were now grilling him? Everything, perhaps? Were they hoping that he'd enmesh himself even more hopelessly in the net they prepared for him? Andrew said carefully, 'I suppose Liam was exactly what you described him as just now: a rival for Julie's favours. He lived in the house adjoining our farmland. He was good-looking, I suppose, though I wouldn't have admitted that at the time. He had long hair and an earring, and he had money. Plenty of money.'

An old animosity flashed briefly into Burrell's blue eyes and pale face, then was equally swiftly banished. 'I'd known Liam since he was at school with me. He was a year or two behind me and not as bright.' He smiled over that small barb, then moved swiftly on. 'He didn't go around with our set all the time in 1995, but joined us on occasions when it suited him. Mostly when we went to pop concerts or wanted to listen to particular bands. Liam always had money and he could always get tickets.'

'Thank you. That gives us the background to this. Now tell us about Liam and Julie Grimshaw.'

'He fancied her from when he first saw her, I think. But it was towards the end of the summer when he took up with her. Julie and I were finished by then. In retrospect I don't think Liam and I were ever rivals for Julie's favours. And I don't think she played one of us off against the other, in case you're setting that up.'

'We're not setting anything up, Mr Burrell. But we need to know exactly what happened. And we cannot question Liam Williams on the matter, as you are no doubt aware.'

Andrew nodded. 'Poor bugger killed himself in a car smash, didn't he? I don't suppose you'll believe this, but I was sorry about that.'

'Do you think Liam killed Julie?'

'He might have done, I suppose. He was much given to

violence, when things didn't go his way. That was why he wasn't one of the regular members of our set.'

'Why did you conceal his presence alongside you during the summer of 1995 for so long?'

Andrew contrived a shrug, his brain working desperately on the phrases he would give them now. 'For obvious reasons, Mr Lambert. At the time of her death, Julie Grimshaw seemed to have opted for Liam. Hell might have no fury like a woman scorned, but young men can be pretty furious as well, when the hormones are raging and their pride is wounded. Revenge on Julie, if you could call it that, gives me an obvious motive. As a man completely innocent of this crime, I didn't want to provide you with that.'

'But you've just claimed that your close relationship with Julie was over by the time Liam's began. And we've had to find out about Liam Williams's connection with Julie from others, when you could have given us all these details on Tuesday. Concealing things makes the motive you've just outlined seem much stronger. The body was buried hurriedly in land which was then part of Lower Valley Farm. I now ask you again whether you had any connection with either the death or the burial of Julie Grimshaw.'

'No. I didn't kill her and I don't know who did. I hope you discover who murdered her and put him or her away. I'd almost forgotten Julie, but this has brought back my affection for her. I want her death to be avenged.'

Andrew gave himself a stiff whisky when they'd gone, then tried to review their meeting dispassionately. There'd been some sticky moments and they'd had him mentally squirming for most of the time. But he hadn't done badly, overall, he decided. He certainly hadn't incriminated himself. He didn't think they'd anything more definite on him than when they'd arrived.

EIGHTEEN

L ate on Monday afternoon the clouds dropped in heavy and low over Gloucestershire and it became very humid. The sun would not be seen for the rest of the day and it seemed that the warm spell might end with thunder.

Lambert had the window wide open in his office, but it still felt airless when DI Rushton and DS Hook came in to compare notes on the Julie Grimshaw case. Rushton reported first on the results of routine house-to-house enquiries around the spot where the skeleton had been found, then on the evidence provided by those Gloucester police, both active and retired, who had patrolled seventeen Fairfax Street and the surrounding area in 1995.

'Most of the people in that squat were passing through rather than occupying it for any length of time. But we've managed to identify and subsequently interview a surprising number of people who were there for periods during that summer. We've eliminated anyone who wasn't using the house at the time when Julie disappeared. Kate Clark is almost certain that Julie was around until late August and what other people have told us confirms that. That means that the two people in the squat who have to be suspects are the ones you and Bert have spoken with twice already: Kate Clark and Michael Wallington.'

Lambert nodded. If DI Rushton said there were no other realistic suspects from the squat, he trusted him absolutely. No one was more thorough than Chris in recording every snippet of information and in seizing upon facts which others might have missed or overlooked. Lambert said, 'To those two we can add three men who had close associations with the murder victim and who lived near the spot where she was hastily interred after she'd been killed: Jim Simmons, Andrew Burrell and Liam Williams. We've interrogated the first two of these pretty thoroughly. Liam Williams was killed in an

RTI in 2007, but we've twice spoken to his father. Steve Williams as you know is an old enemy of ours, and thus well aware of his rights and exactly what we can and can't do to him.'

Hook smiled grimly at the mention of Williams. He knew that Lambert, whilst being far too professional to be anything other than objective, would love to be able to implicate Steve Williams in a murder inquiry. He said, 'If this murder was committed by a dead man, there will obviously be a swift closure. But we need to establish the facts, if only in the interests of our other suspects, who have a lot to lose if the media get hold of the information that they've been involved in our investigation.'

Rushton said almost proprietorially, 'The two who were with the victim in the squat at the time of her death are the ones with the easiest opportunities. On his own admission, Michael Wallington was selling drugs and Julie was a user. We think he tried to recruit her as a seller. If she refused to become a dealer in his network or threatened to expose him, he'd want rid of her. And if he didn't wish to kill her himself there'd be plenty of muscle available to him if he gave the word to the people higher up the drug hierarchy.'

Lambert nodded. 'He says that he didn't get to that point with Julie, and that he wasn't high enough in the drugs empire to implement that kind of killing. But in the immortal words of a young lady in another context, he would, wouldn't he? Wallington is a bright man who's made the most of his subsequent opportunities and now has a senior local authority job in education. But I wouldn't trust anything he says when he's fighting to preserve his own skin.'

Rushton said almost diffidently, 'I saw Kate Clark myself briefly, but you two have interviewed her twice since then. What do you make of her?'

Lambert smiled ruefully. 'Ms Clark's a tough cookie, as no doubt she's had to be to reach the board of one of our great national utility companies. She's very anxious that her position and aspirations at Severn Trent aren't compromised by her involvement in a murder inquiry. But she can't alter certain facts. She was by her own admission – and this tallies with

other accounts we've heard – the female who was closest to
Julie Grimshaw, both spiritually and physically, during those
crucial months in the summer of 1995. Much of what we know
of Julie comes from her; we have to remember constantly that
she has her own interests to protect. She'll fight like a cornered
tiger to protect herself, though that doesn't mean that she's
committed murder or manslaughter.'

Bert Hook had been impressed by the woman who in 1995
had been Kathy Clark. He was striving to be objective as he
said, 'Ms Clark was by her own admission a fairly desperate
and disturbed young woman when she was in that squat twenty
years ago. Violence is part of the way of life for people living
on the edge of society, as the people at seventeen Fairfax Street
were. She's a woman who would no doubt be quite capable
of violence if she thought it was necessary. My guess is that
she also keeps in check a fierce temper beneath a calm exterior.
I don't see her committing cold-blooded murder, but I could
see her committing manslaughter – perhaps by striking a blow
to the head with some sort of implement in the course of a
violent disagreement with a friend who everyone says was
unstable.'

Lambert nodded. 'That's speculation, but it's an example
of why we're meeting here as an experienced trio. I wouldn't
want speculation among twenty people when I conduct a team
meeting, but in the privacy of this office we three should be
prepared to say exactly how things strike us. So what do you
make of Jim Simmons? He was working his way into a senior
position at Lower Valley Farm in 1995, favoured by the owner
and his wife and anxious to do whatever he could to please
them. We know that the older Burrells wanted to be rid of
Julie because they fiercely disapproved of her liaison with
their son. Did Simmons see an opportunity for himself there?
Did he dispose of Julie one night and bury her hurriedly near
the edge of the ground he knew so well and worked every
day?

'Andrew Burrell made the point that he was quite happy
for Simmons to assume the running of the farm, but was
surprised when his parents actually transferred ownership to
him at a bargain price. Andrew has his own agenda, of course,

but it seems a valid point. Was Daniel Burrell fulfilling some sort of unwritten understanding when he transferred the farm?'

Rushton said unexpectedly, 'But what is a fair price for a small mixed farm nowadays? I had no idea, but I've made certain enquiries among local agricultural agents. It's difficult to make a small farm pay and you work damned hard to do it. Lower Valley Farm is in a secluded pocket of land near the Wye. Because of its isolation it doesn't interest the big concerns who operate factory farms in areas like the Salisbury Plain: they want to consolidate farms into much bigger units. Simmons got a good deal, but not an outlandish one. The sort which might be acceptable to both sides when the seller had a soft spot for his purchaser. Favourable to Jim Simmons, but not necessarily suspiciously so.'

Lambert was once again grateful to his DI for his thoroughness. 'Thank you, Chris. That's a relevant fact, when facts are thin upon the ground. I suppose we should expect them to be so after an interval of twenty years. I found Simmons rather irritating in the way he seemed to wish to parade his charming wife and his equally charming children in front of us. I wondered if his eagerness to show himself as a sound and reliable family man meant that he had something to hide from that earlier era. But I'm probably just a cynical old copper who's seen too many villains parading attractive wives as shields against us.'

Hook, who'd spent most of his boyhood and adolescence after the Barnardo's home working on farms, couldn't withhold a certain respect from his judgement on Simmons. 'For what it's worth – and I'm well aware that it doesn't mean he's incapable of murder – Jim Simmons is a good farmer and he works damned hard for whatever success he enjoys. No one has claimed that he had a close relationship with Julie Grimshaw, though they all seem to think she liked him. I suppose it's possible that he had some sort of secret association with her, but that seems unlikely. His one plausible motive seems to be his ambition to own and run his own farm.' He paused, then in the interests of balance added reluctantly, 'But that can be a powerful one, for a countryman.'

Lambert said briskly, 'Andrew Burrell. I didn't much like

him, but that's totally irrelevant to our inquiry. He tried to deceive us when we first saw him last Tuesday, and every fact we've elicited from him we've had to wring out of him. A leading candidate for this crime, because he was heavily involved with Julie. So much so that his parents were very anxious to send the girl away and end the affair. By his own account, he wanted to marry the girl or at least to live with her. He claims that it was all over between them by the time of her death, but the others who were close to the pair seem less certain about that. Fact: Andrew Burrell had secured a place at Liverpool University, which he was determined to take up at the end of September. Did he want to be rid of Julie for that reason? Was she clinging to him and refusing to be simply shrugged off? On the other hand, did the affair end acrimoniously and was it Burrell who was bitter about that? Did jealousy drive him to violence when he saw her taking up with someone else? Those are all questions we could explore much more easily if this death had occurred last week. Answers are much more difficult to find in the case of a crime which was committed twenty years ago. Andrew Burrell has exploited that: he's given us nothing. We've had to work hard for everything we now know about him and Julie.'

Hook, like his chief, was on new ground with a death which had occurred so long ago. 'The worst thing about this is that there are people we can no longer question. There are still people who were in that squat who haven't come forward. We don't even know their names and unless they answer our appeals we'll never find them. And there are people who are dead who could have given us valuable insights. Emily Burrell died three years ago; she could have given us information and opinions on her son Andrew, on Jim Simmons and even on Kate Clark. And we can't even question a man who has to be one of our leading suspects, Liam Williams, because he's been dead for eight years.'

Lambert nodded, noting that Rushton looked a little surprised by this description of the dead Williams. 'It's taken us some time to establish Liam Williams as a suspect, because people have been reluctant to acknowledge how close he was to Julie at the time of her death. It's another difficulty when following up a crime twenty years after it's happened. Andrew Burrell in particular was very reluctant to acknowledge the part Liam had played in this. It seems that Liam was a rival for Julie's affections. Andrew says that he'd dropped out of contention in order to pursue his studies in Liverpool and that there was no serious dispute between him and Liam. It's possible of course that Burrell was much more bitter than he admits and took out Julie as a result. Or even that Liam killed her after some lover's tiff if she threatened to desert him or go back to Andrew. We need to know exactly what part Liam played in this, but he isn't around to question. His mother seems to be emotionally crippled by her son's death. As for Steve Williams, he wouldn't give us the time of day if he could avoid it.'

John Lambert shook his head at the hopelessness of the case, at the obfuscations introduced by an interim of twenty years and the absence of key witnesses. Yet the phone call which would provide him with the key was but a couple of hours away.

Michael Wallington spent two hours playing the happy family man. He wanted to be entirely conventional. He became almost a walking caricature of normal fatherhood.

He ate with the family and asked Tom and Jane how they had fared in the first day of their school week. He congratulated eight-year-old Tom on his arithmetic and his football; he echoed his wife's enthusiasm for five-year-old Jane's gold star for her collage work. He loaded the dishwasher and then read bedtime stories, first for a very tired Jane and then for a more ebullient Tom. The boy wanted another chapter, but his father looked at his watch and was firm. 'You need your sleep if you're to race down the wing and leave Darren Wilson behind you tomorrow, son,' Michael said firmly.

The boy lay back and looked at the ceiling. 'Who was Doubting Thomas, Dad?'

Michael's theology was sketchy, but he could cope with this. 'He was the one of Christ's apostles who was doubtful about Him having risen from the dead. He said he would actually need to see his Lord before him before he was prepared to believe that He was back with them.' Michael had no wish

to go into the business of Thomas touching the holes in his
master's hands before he would believe: that was far too
ghoulish for a lad who needed his sleep.

'John Pooley said Thomas put his fingers into the holes
where they'd nailed Christ to the cross, and wriggled them
around. That was a bit creepy, don't you think? But Pooley's
dad's a vicar, so it must be right.' Tom settled down beneath
the sheets with a contented smile.

Michael went downstairs and said to his wife, 'I have a
meeting, I'm afraid, dear. I'm hoping it won't take very long.'

Debbie was tidying away toys and making the sitting room
habitable for adults. 'Do you have to? There's nothing on the
calendar for tonight.'

'No, there wouldn't be. It's not a formal meeting, it's just
a one-off. Two people who want to confer with me off the
record about the possibilities of getting specialist help for slow
readers.' It was always easier if you claimed you were helping
the disadvantaged; no one questioned your motives if you cited
the disabled or the mentally handicapped or slow learners.

His wife sighed resignedly. 'You're too conscientious for
your own good at times, Mike. Don't let these people keep
you out any longer than they need to.'

'I won't, but I have to give them my time when it's needed.
Think how desperate you would be for help, if our two were
suffering. You look tired, darling. I'll be back as quickly as I
can, but don't bother to wait up if I should be delayed.'

These were the longest days of the year. He was impatient
for the night to arrive. Michael didn't know quite why, but
darkness seemed appropriate for the confrontation he was
planning. Dusk had arrived and cars had their lights on by the
time he drove into the suburb of Tewkesbury and sought out
the residence he wanted. It was a pleasant place, as he would
have expected, with a view of the Severn to the rear. He could
see the glint of the last light on a stretch of the great river as
he parked the car. The flats were a conversion of a spacious
Georgian house about a mile above Tewkesbury Abbey and
the centre, safe from the flooding which was one of the perennial hazards in some areas of the ancient town.

He hesitated for a moment before he rang the bell, wondering how he was going to introduce himself at this late hour and after all this time. It was very quiet here. He thought he could hear the distant sound of the river, running low at the end of the drought; the forecast said there would be rain before morning. She opened the door more quickly than he'd anticipated, throwing the full blaze of the light behind her on to his face, catching his moment of surprise and apprehension as he fought to produce words.

'I'm sorry to call so late. My name is Michael Wallington. I don't suppose that means anything to you, but we were—'

'I know who you are. I recognized you. I can guess why you're here. I feel I was almost expecting you, somehow. You'd better come in.'

Kate Clark turned and led the way into a spacious, pleasant lounge. The developer had preserved the long Georgian windows and one of them was open six inches at the bottom. She switched off the television and he could definitely hear the sound of the Severn now, a soft surge over stones, sounding surprisingly close through the gathering darkness. She looked out and then drew the curtains, though no one could observe them here.

Then she turned to him, motioned him to sit in an armchair. She studied his face for a moment before she sat down opposite him. She said, 'You haven't changed much, you know. The stubble's gone and you've filled out a bit, but I'd still recognize you.'

He felt that he should offer her the routine compliment, tell her that she too hadn't changed much, that he'd have recognized her immediately although twenty years had passed. That was the sort of thing people said, even though women didn't believe it. He sensed this woman wouldn't want it, might despise him for it if he voiced it. He said, 'I expect the police have been in touch with you.'

Kate gave him her first smile, but it was impersonal rather than friendly, an acknowledgement that they had suffered similar embarrassments. 'They have indeed. Three times, if you count the initial contact from a rather handsome Detective Inspector. That was on Wednesday. Then the man in charge and what I think they call his bagman visited me on Thursday afternoon and again on Saturday afternoon.' She enjoyed the precision. She always went for accuracy in her working life; it often seemed to give her an advantage. 'They wanted to hear all about me and Julie Grimshaw. They wanted to know everything I could tell them about you, as well.'

She hadn't offered him a drink or any kind of hospitality and she'd come straight to the point. She'd worn well, he thought. She must be around forty-three years old now, he reckoned. But she looked less than that. Not having children probably helped, he thought, making automatic allowances for his Debbie and her very different way of life. This woman had short dark hair which framed her broad, strong face very pleasingly. He'd never found grey eyes very attractive but these ones were, wide and bright on either side of a rather sharp nose.

He knew now that she would be irritated rather than pleased by any physical compliments. He said, 'You've come a long way since we were together at seventeen Fairfax Street.'

'Is that the address? I couldn't even remember it.'

He doubted whether that was true. She was too meticulous a woman for her recall to be patchy. But he said, 'I suppose we've both spent twenty years trying to forget about the events of 1995.'

'Not the events. I've tried to forget about my lifestyle then and the way we lived from hand to mouth in that house in Gloucester. But I've no reason to erase the events from my mind. I've nothing to be ashamed of in 1995.'

Michael smiled, trying to lighten the tension, to establish some sort of bond between them. 'I've nothing to be ashamed of either. Both of us need to convince the police of that.'

Kate Clark folded her arms, well aware that her body language was shutting him out. She was refusing or at least delaying the kind of agreement he wanted. 'You've more to hide than I have. I wasn't dealing drugs, or even using them. I didn't try to induce a girl who we now know became a murder victim to become a drug seller. I'd say you have a lot more to hide than I have, Mick.'

She used the diminutive almost like an obscenity, recalling to him that world he was trying to obscure. Her own recall was vivid enough. She'd been frightened of this man in the squat, where he'd dealt drugs and had money and seemed to control everyone who lived in that house. She'd been careful not to annoy him then, even though she'd maintained her independence. The boot was on the other foot now: he'd made a journey on the edge of darkness to meet her in secret and ask for her support. The man who'd issued orders and treated her with a surly truculence at Fairfax Street had now come here begging for favours.

Kate said, 'The police asked me a series of questions about Mick, who dealt in drugs. I told them what I remembered of those months in 1995. We're involved in a murder case, Michael, and the fuzz don't take kindly to attempts to deceive them.' She wouldn't tell him that she'd held back as much as she could at her first meeting with Lambert and Hook, that they'd treated her almost as a hostile witness when they'd come here for the second time on Saturday.

Wallington said, 'They think it's possible that I killed Julie Grimshaw when she disappeared so suddenly. Presumably they think the same about you. I should have thought it was in our interests to compare notes and present a united front to them.'

Kate looked at him coolly. 'And what happens if they're right and one of us is in fact guilty? If we do as you suggest, the other one would become an accessory after the fact.'

Michael found her spiky attitude very persuasive, as he had all those years ago in Fairfax Street. And she looked to him much more attractive in her maturity than she had in her youth. He ordered his loins to cease stirring and reminded himself sternly that he was a happily married man, with two lively children and a splendid wife. He said brusquely, 'I'm not guilty. I didn't kill your friend Julie. Did you?'

'Would I tell you if I had done? And do you expect me to accept your bald assurance that you didn't commit murder? You've just told me that you haven't managed to convince the police of that.'

Michael grinned at her, trying desperately to lighten the tension. 'You're very attractive when you're serious and intense. But I expect you know that.'

'And maybe you look more handsome when you're trying

hard to be persuasive.' Her lips curled suddenly into a smile. 'But we're not about to leap into bed, Michael. Is that why you came here tonight?'

'No, of course it isn't!' He felt like a gauche boy being checked by a girl prefect. 'I suppose I wanted us to compare notes on our experiences with the police, that's all. I find it very disconcerting when they know all sorts of things from their other interviews which they aren't communicating to me.'

'That's something at least that we can agree upon. I find that disconcerting too. Or to be more accurate, downright annoying. But I don't see that putting our heads together is going to do much to relieve our frustration.'

'They gave me the impression that I was their prime suspect, that their net was closing in around me.'

Kate looked at him very seriously, with her head a little on one side. 'Did they really? Well, I have to tell you that they didn't make me feel like that at all. I can only assume that they think they've got you bang to rights for this one, Michael.'

She was teasing him, wasn't she? Having a bit of fun at his expense, even in this most inappropriate of contexts? He was almost sure that she was teasing him. He said rather forlornly, 'I thought they made everyone feel as I do.'

She could sustain her gravity no longer; she dissolved into mirth. 'Of course they do, Michael. It's part of their technique. They tell you nothing about what they've discovered about anyone else. And then they make you feel that they've got you cornered, that every bit of evidence they've got to hand points to you as their culprit.'

Michael Wallington felt very foolish. 'I thought we could compare notes on what the CID had on us. I can tell you that they know about my drug dealing in 1995 but don't propose to take it any further. They know that I was at seventeen Fairfax Street throughout the summer and they say they haven't so far been able to clear me of this killing.'

Kate Clark smiled at him almost fondly, as if he was a simpleton in need of her help. 'Turn that the other way round, Michael. They haven't yet any solid evidence that you committed murder. They're keeping you in the frame, but they can't pin anything on you.'

He brightened a little. 'And no doubt they know that you were Julie's constant and closest companion throughout the summer, but can't unearth any evidence to show that you killed her.'

'I'm not sure about that "closest". At least two men slept with Julie Grimshaw during those months. I'd say both of them are still in the frame, and perhaps stronger candidates than either of us. And now I think you should journey back to the bosom of your anxious family.' She kissed him full on the lips at her door, but it was an embrace dictated by a common understanding rather than passion.

An outside observer, or even a trained police presence, would have learned even less than they had about each other. Either or both of them might still be involved in this murder from a previous generation. They were very different people in 2015. Only the Severn flowed exactly as it had in 1995.

NINETEEN

John Lambert was trying hard to concentrate on the ten o'clock television news. Not much of it was good, as usual. He retreated from life into sport. It seemed that England might be able to put out a full-strength team for the forthcoming Ashes test against Australia. Bert Hook had reservations about the spin attack. But neither of them would see much of the match on television, if the skeleton from 1995 continued to occupy them.

Christine brought him a beaker of tea and decided against offering him fruitless advice about not overdoing it at work. 'Don't you go dozing off in the chair: you need proper sleep at your age.' That was one of the phrases she used as an in-joke between them. 'I've had a long day, so I'm going up now.' She still used those words when she was tired, though they'd lived in a bungalow for ten years and more now.

It was ten minutes later when the phone shrilled beside him. He snatched it up immediately, anxious that his wife should not be disturbed. This was no family crisis – that was the usual fear when a call came in at this time of night. It was the police station at Oldford, apologizing too fully for contacting him at ten forty in the evening. Perhaps the station sergeant also thought that he shouldn't disturb a Chief Superintendent of his age. Lambert brushed away the man's contrition; he knew that an experienced officer wouldn't ring him at this time unless he considered the matter urgent – or unless this was something which needed a decision he wasn't senior enough to take.

'Anonymous phone call, sir. Asking for whoever was in charge of the Lower Valley Farm skeleton case. I had it traced immediately. Public phone box; the caller was long gone when our car got there, as you'd expect.'

'Content?' The officer must think it wasn't just another of the score or so of loony phone calls which they'd had in the last week – dramatic findings like bodies buried twenty years ago always brought out the over-imaginative and the downright crackpots.

'There's a name in the call, sir. One of the ones we haven't revealed to the press. I thought you should hear it for yourself and see what you thought of it. It's probably nothing, but only you can decide on that.' The usual disclaimer, and a fair enough one. Rank carried responsibility. The old watchword of the junior copper was that he – or increasingly she – wasn't paid to make decisions. That still held true.

Lambert heard the sergeant fiddling with the machinery and then a distorted and muffled voice came through his earpiece. Part of the distortion was because this was recorded, but most of it came from the original call. A handkerchief or some similar fabric over the mouthpiece, probably: an old but still effective method of disguising the identity of the speaker. The voice was female, he thought, but he couldn't even be completely sure of that. He listened hard, then asked the station sergeant to play the call back to him again.

The voice asked to speak to the man in charge of the case, then said, 'You should speak to Stephen Williams. He knows more than he's telling you. Don't let him get away with this.'

Stark and simple. Advocating an action he had already been planning to take the next day. There was nothing in the call beyond that simple message. The only odd thing was the choice of forename. In extensive dealings with that wily villain he'd never heard Williams called anything but Steve before. Stephen was the kind of formal name which might have been used by a mother of her son, perhaps. But Williams was sixty-six and his mother had been dead these many years. A wife, possibly? Even a vastly experienced detective felt his pulses quicken at that thought.

The thunder came during the night, never directly overhead but rumbling in the distance for hours, disturbing Lambert and fostering in him the speculation which was already fracturing his night. He rang Bert Hook at seven forty. An hour later he was waving a greeting to his sergeant's cheerful teenagers as they departed for school. He picked up Bert at his gate at twenty to nine.

It was the worst time for schools traffic. Lambert was planning what he would say to Williams, as well as briefing Hook on last night's phone call. He felt in no hurry now, very calm. It was a mood that he could not have analysed or explained.

It took them longer than he would have expected to reach the big detached house which was the nearest residence to Lower Valley Farm, but that did not matter to him now. The house had been isolated at the time of Julie Grimshaw's death, so that the spot where she had been buried must then have seemed remote. The new housing estate reared like a harsh modern intrusion at the edge of the farmland. But if these raw brick houses and bungalows had not been erected, poor Julie Grimshaw's remains might have lain undisturbed for another century.

Lambert looked across towards the back garden of pensioner Joe Jackson's bungalow, where those bones had been turned up only ten days earlier. He had the sense of a wheel turning full circle.

Steve Williams looked at them with open distaste, then dropped immediately into ritual abuse. 'This is harassment, Lambert. I've had enough of the stink of pigs around my house. The two of you can piss off.'

'If we go, you go with us, Williams. We can do this here or at the station. You can have your brief present, if you wish.'

'I've done bugger all and you know it. This is harassment!'

'Here or at the station. Your choice.'

He stood looking down at them with undisguised malevolence for a moment, then turned without a word and stalked into the front room of his house. It was set out as a dining room, with table and chairs in the centre. He slumped into the chair at the head of the table, watched without further comment as his two adversaries disposed themselves on each side of him. He was still in shirt sleeves, with a pair of red braces stretched over his wide shoulders, perhaps as a statement that this was his house and it was still early in his morning. His single eye focused maximum hostility upon John Lambert.

'Say what you've got to say, then fuck off and don't come back.'

Lambert said quietly, 'We need to talk to you much more about Liam, Steve.'

It was at this point that the door which Williams had carefully shut behind them opened silently and a woman stood motionless in its frame, standing stark as a sleepwalking Lady Macbeth, staring wide-eyed at the scene before her. But this figure was not in night attire. Hazel Williams was perfectly dressed and fully made up, as if she wished to provide a deliberate contrast to her husband's morning scruffiness. She looked at each of the three men in turn, then apparently decided to focus her attention upon the last of the trio, DS Hook.

Williams, who had been stilled by this dramatic entry, found his voice. 'There's no need for you to be involved in this, my love. I'll tell you all about it when these men have left our home.'

'I'm staying. You're going to talk about Liam.' It was almost as if she was issuing orders to him.

'They really shouldn't be here harassing us like this.' Williams gave Hook a brief basilisk glare, perhaps because it was upon him that his wife had chosen to focus. 'It's bad enough them coming here giving me grief and disturbing my life, but I'm not having them upsetting you, Hazel. If you go into the kitchen and make yourself a cup of tea, I'll tell you what's happened when these pigs have gone. That will be very shortly.'

'I'm staying.'

'That really isn't necessary. And it probably isn't a very good idea.' Williams's voice was uncharacteristically tender. He shuffled awkwardly to his feet and moved around the table towards his wife.

'It is very necessary. We're going to talk about Liam. All of us.' Hazel moved in slow motion to sit beside Hook at the table, rejecting her husband's touch and seeming perfectly composed. Once seated she sat still as a statue, staring straight ahead of her. She waited as if listening for her cue in some pre-ordained ceremony, one with which she was familiar and they were as yet faltering. She was at that moment the calmest person in the room, though none of the men there knew how brittle her composure might prove.

The moment of silence caused by her words seemed to stretch for a long time before Lambert said to Williams, 'You've been very cagey about your son and the part he played in the last weeks of Julie Grimshaw's life.'

'That's because Liam had nothing to do with this. You should let the dead rest in peace.'

Steve Williams had lost his truculence and his obscenities now. He was seeking to direct his words at his nemesis, Lambert, but the glance of his single eye kept straying towards his wife, separated from him at the table by Hook's sturdy frame. He desperately wanted her to look at him, to acknowledge some kind of bond between them, but she stared straight ahead, cocooned in her own concerns, waiting for her moment to speak in this tense ritual of her own devising.

Lambert said coldly, 'We need to take action before the dead can rest in peace, Steve. Julie Grimshaw was murdered and buried without concern or goodbyes. We can let her rest in peace only when her killer has been brought to justice.'

'Liam didn't kill Julie. He had nothing to do with her death. So let him rest in peace.'

His eyes were on his wife and the other two men glanced quickly at her as he repeated his claim. But she continued to hold her stillness, smooth as monumental alabaster. Hook wondered whence that phrase had sprung into his head.

'You'll need to convince us of that, Steve. Liam was very close to Julie in her last days. We know that now, from what others have told us. You concealed it from us, which now makes it seem more significant.'

'Liam didn't kill her. You lot will never be able to prove that he did. It's time you left this house. You'll upset Hazel if you stay, and I can't have that.' He reached a hand automatically towards her, but she held her pose as if he had spoken not a word.

Lambert said calmly, 'Julie had ended her association with Andrew Burrell and taken up with Liam. We believe that it was a serious relationship. Perhaps it might even have led to marriage in due course, had it not been fractured; other people have indicated that to us.'

'That isn't true. It could never have become serious.'

Lambert continued as if Williams had not spoken. 'We obviously cannot question Liam about this. We cannot take his statement on what happened, though his might well have been the most vital testimony of all. If, as you claim, he had nothing to do with her death, you owe it to him as well as to Julie to answer our questions.'

'No comment.'

Williams would normally have accompanied the denial he had issued so many hundreds of times over the years with a contemptuous sneer, but today he could not muster that. He was intensely conscious of the silent female presence beside Hook, as were all three men in the room. Lambert said coldly, '"No comment" isn't good enough this time, Williams. Your dead son's reputation is at stake here.'

'Liam had nothing to do with that girl's death.'

'Then convince us of that. Tell us what you know of the death and how those bones came to be in the ground so near to this house. We're not going away.'

'Liam had nothing to do with this. He's right in that.' The female voice when it finally sounded was as even and impersonal as a Delphic oracle. It carried the ring of truth because of its calmness and utter conviction.

Bert Hook turned his weather-beaten, outdoor face very slowly to confront the woman at his side, careful as if he was preparing to handle an injured animal. 'It's time now, Hazel. You should tell us now, don't you think?'

She didn't look at him, staring straight ahead whilst she nodded almost imperceptibly. Her firm chin jutted upwards a little with her determination. Her stillness and the grief she carried permanently with her gave her a dignity which was compelling, even in this starkest of contexts. Hazel Williams enunciated her words evenly and very clearly. 'Stephen did it. He didn't approve of Julie. She wasn't good enough for his son.'

Even now she didn't look at her husband, but there was not a scintilla of doubt about her statement. Hook said gently, 'How did he do it, Hazel?'

Williams's single eye flared wide with fear. 'She knows nothing about this. She's feeding you her fantasies. Hazel, please go away and leave this to me. You're only upsetting yourself here.'

But there was despair in his voice and his wife ignored him completely. She did not want him in the room and she now banished him from her presence by sheer force of will. 'He thought Julie wasn't good enough for our son. He said she was a junkie. But she wasn't. Liam and I would have got her off the drugs. She wanted to be rid of them, really. Julie would have been good for Liam. They were good together. He never had another girl after Julie. Not a real girl friend. Not one he could have settled down with.'

Williams looked desperately from Hook to Lambert. 'She's rambling. She doesn't know what she's talking about. We should get her out of here. She's going to upset herself and then lock herself away again. You don't see what I have to put up with. You don't see the trouble you cause when you come here prying into things which have long gone.'

There was a hopelessness about his pleas now. His tone moved from desperation to despair as he spoke. And still the inexorable, oracular female voice continued, without acknowledging his presence, let alone what he had said. 'Stephen told her to be on her way and to get out of our son's life. Liam was going to be his father's heir and take over his empire, Stephen said. He couldn't afford to have a little tramp like Julie holding him back.'

The phrases Williams had thought she had long forgotten came ringing back like a legal sentence. He said hopelessly, 'She doesn't know what she's talking about. This is harassment and my lawyers are going to have you for it. Hazel, it's time for you to shut up and get out now.'

'He hit her over the head with something. A bottle, I think.'

'This is rubbish. I never—'

'I heard him talking to his man about it afterwards. The man he usually got to do his dirty work for him.'

Hook nodded, gave her a small smile of sympathy. 'Jack Dutton, that would be.'

Hazel looked at him as if she had forgotten his presence

beside her. 'That's the man, yes. Jack Dutton. I think he's dead.'

'He is, yes, Hazel. Only last week. But our officers have been able to talk to members of his family.'

Steve Williams said dully, 'That little slut was never going to be good enough for Liam. I was safeguarding our boy's interests.'

It was the first time he had not attempted to deny it. It was his first acknowledgement that this was going to end as his wife had determined it would. Lambert said, 'You can't shut every mouth with gold, Williams. Even dead men can tell tales, when you throw blood money at their families to buy their silence. It was Jack Dutton who buried the body for you, wasn't it?'

The big man was sixty-six. He looked abruptly much older than that. There was a long silence before he said, 'I told that Grimshaw girl to go, but she wouldn't leave. I wanted her out of his life for ever before Liam came home that night. But she refused. She said she was waiting for Liam, that she'd only go if he told her to go, not me. I wasn't used to people saying no to me, in those days.'

Williams sounded suddenly, naively, puzzled. His self-control was seeping away, now that he knew he had lost this game he had thought he never could.

'So you hit her because she would not leave your house.'

'Because she would not leave the house and because she would not leave my Liam. I had to safeguard his interests, didn't I?'

He seemed to have forgotten now that he was speaking to his sworn enemies, that he was asking for sympathy where he could expect none. Lambert said with unusual passion, 'No, you did not, Williams. Not if safeguarding what you saw as his interests meant breaking the law. Not if it meant a murder you have contrived to conceal for twenty years.'

He uttered the formal words of arrest and issued the formal warning to his old enemy that he did not have to say anything but anything that he did say might be used in the court case which was to come. Williams said dully, 'I don't think I meant to kill her. I saw red and I just wanted rid of her.'

'But you concealed her body. You wanted to make sure that no one knew of your crime.'

'Jack Dutton was a good man. He never let me down. He was round in ten minutes when I rang him. We had to get rid of the corpse quickly. Liam drove in through the front gates as Jack took the Grimshaw girl out at the back. Jack found some ground at the edge of the farm which had already been disturbed and he put the body in there.'

They took Williams out to the police vehicle Lambert had arranged should be waiting. Their prisoner stopped for a moment in the doorway of his dining room, looking down at the still motionless figure of his wife at the table. 'I didn't know that you knew, Hazel. I wanted to protect you from it.'

Still she did not look at him. She stared instead at the table as she said evenly, 'You didn't know a lot of things, Stephen. You didn't care what I thought. You behaved as if I did not exist, in those days.'

Lambert went out and saw his quarry handcuffed to a uniformed officer in the back of the police Mondeo. He wasn't taking any chances with Steve Williams, even in this broken state. He radioed for a female officer to come and oversee the next few hours for Hazel Williams. He had given a brief nod to Bert Hook, who had stayed in the room with the stricken woman, offering her a sad smile but no words.

They drove within yards of the place where that skeleton had been discovered ten days earlier. What was left of Julie Grimshaw was to be interred under her mother's direction in a different, more appropriate place, with a headstone to protect her memory.

It was, he supposed, a kind of closure on the life of that troubled, curiously innocent girl.